FLOWERS
OF GRACE

FLOWERS
OF GRACE

a novel inspired by a true story

TERESA HIRST

LITTLE FOREST big spring Press

LITTLE FOREST BIG SPRING PRESS
Flowers of Grace
Teresa Hirst

Cover Design by Kirsten Hirst © 2015 Little Forest Big Spring Press
Front Cover Photograph © John Panatin/Dollar Photo Club

Published by Little Forest Big Spring Press
ISBN 978-1-937059-02-6

This is a work of fiction. The characters, situations, settings,
and dialogue are products of the author's imagination and are
not intended to portray real people, living or deceased, or actual
events, corporations, or circumstances.

For Holly
whose legacy of nurturing inspired me
to love more freely and give more fully,
ultimately leading me to write this novel.

This book is also dedicated
to my mother, sisters, friends, daughters,
and women everywhere.

Prologue

The swinging door on the back dressing room struck Grace's conscience. Her face heated. Her stomach curled. She knew what she would see. But still, she lurched forward and saw something worse than what she feared.

The missing planter lay on its side on the corner bench of the dressing room. Half the soil had spilled atop the cream plush carpet. The other half clung to the exposed roots of the hibiscus plant. Just one brown stalk with several thinner stems protruded from the sideways angle. No leaves defined it as a living plant anymore; any leaves that had filled those stems were now scattered about the floor as crispy brown and gray shriveled paper.

Grace fell against the door. "I didn't do it," she said with fists hiding her eyes. "I didn't kill it."

She fought her way out of the tight alcove into the open store, ready to accuse. But who could she blame? She'd cut the plant and left it there to die. *She'd* killed Lilly's plant.

Section One

Lilly's Plant

Chapter One

Grace pressed quickly past the other upscale boutiques to the mall entrance, hoping to hide her stockpot and her embarrassment until she reached the safety of the parking lot. She presumed carting homemade soup to work, even if it was a gift to take to the ill, would mark her down in the minds of the other store managers—especially because the soup pot was a hand-me-down from her mother's cast-offs and not at all like the ones in the heavy-duty professional collection at the kitchen store next to Honeybee.

By the time she rounded the corner, she saw a clear path to the entrance, swung the pot around in front of her, and gripped both handles firmly to keep from spilling the creamy broth all over the floor. Just as she pushed her back against the door, she felt it give way quicker than she anticipated. She stumbled off-balance, falling backward.

"Hold on to the pot," a man said behind her. She fell against his chest at the same time he spoke. The soup swished over the edge with the words, "I've got you."

She jostled forward to recover and turned toward the voice—a deep one she didn't know, attached to a man just above her height. She blushed at the closeness to his olive eyes, which never left her face. She stepped to the side to let him pass—and to see him from a better angle.

"We could create a new trust fall with that move," he said. His longish brown hair flopped back as he pretended with exaggerated but chivalrous gestures to catch her again.

"Not unless I used a thicker soup," she said, wiping at her wool pea coat with a worn glove. Instead of embarrassment at a chance encounter with a snobby boutique manager, this one seemed surreal enough that she could shrug off how she might appear.

"Can I help you to your car?" he offered, even though red touched his cheeks from the cold air he'd just left. Unconsciously, her eyes followed his cheekbone to the point it met his hairline and traced his jaw line back down to his neck. He wore a leather jacket that accentuated his attractive build. She shook her stare away from his chest, focusing back on his eyes and the question.

"No, I'm okay," she said. "But thank you for the rescue." He held the door open, and she continued into the dark parking lot with her soup. At her car she set the pot on the ground to search for her keys. "Now why did I say that?"

Just as she had become conditioned to tell the grocery clerk that she didn't need help with her cart, she turned down this offer without giving it a thought. Maybe he would have been a big help—or maybe even more.

She turned on the radio to catch the latest traffic report but really to stop fretting over the missed opportunity. Instead of turning out of The Plaza toward home, she drove past the over-priced grocery stores, restaurants, and hotels with their pretentious traditionalism and slid onto the freeway.

Grace had only been to University City, the St. Louis suburb where Lilly lived, a couple of times and only once to her house after taking Lilly's car to a repair shop. From the passenger seat Lilly had guided her past the stately houses in Ladue and Clayton and then the towering campus buildings of Washington University. This time Grace mapped a more direct route to U-City, as it was known, through the established neighborhood of larger homes just north of Delmar and west of the Loop, an eclectic urban strip of shops and nightlife.

The streets she passed were named after colleges and universities—Princeton, Cornell, Radcliffe, and Tulane. Lilly had told her that thirty to forty years ago these had been the homes of the up-and-coming Jewish families. The neighborhood now revealed a diverse mix of neighbors—couples without children, private school parents, African American and Asian families, and older widows like Lilly who still clung to the family home.

On Trinity Street she located Lilly's two-story brick house, which was set back from the street but still close enough to see the television on in the window. Grace rang the doorbell on the dark porch, and the blue television light disappeared for a moment before the bright porch lights cast themselves upon her in an unwelcome gasp.

"Gracie, you've come to me." Lilly reached out and pulled Grace into the foyer.

Grace had to steady her pot of soup again as she held it out with a questioning look toward her sick employee. Lilly wore gray flannel trousers and a soft purple sweater, not the loungewear Grace expected. She had also combed her silver bob, made up her eyes, and lined her lips with a brighter-than-normal pink lipstick.

"I thought you were sick in bed. Not able to get up. Not able to cook."

"I am sick. I'm not up, and I can't cook."

"You look 'up' to me," Grace said, pulling the pot back toward her.

"I couldn't answer the door in my nightgown."

"At least tell me where your kitchen is so I can reheat some of my mom's famous chicken wild rice soup."

"Through the arched doorway and to your right." Lilly pointed down the hall. "The stove's electric—it will take a bit to heat. Bowls are in the hutch."

Lilly had prophesied at the store inventory last month that the St. Louis winter would turn her gray and do her in someday.

"Do you into what? You're already gray. Into quitting and moving somewhere tropical?" Grace had asked Lilly when she made her declaration of death.

"Shh . . . Grace. My time is near. Something will take me back to be with Bob again soon enough. You wait and see."

Grace adored this woman as much as her own grandma, but Lilly imagined her death more often than most people imagined they needed a new outfit. With a smile on her face and a finger on her pulse, Lilly Klein was a paradox—and a hypochondriac. Her current illness, however, was real.

Grace knew Lilly was much worse than she looked or even acted, but despite not knowing how Lilly really felt, the smile that played in her eyes conveyed the connection between them and a promise to open up over hot soup, which they did.

In the front room Lilly tried to sit up at the coffee table to eat but resorted to stretching out on a daybed with a blanket over her slippered feet and the tray on her lap. She only took bites sporadically when Grace reminded her and then coughed afterward for several minutes. Grace left the Queen Anne chair where she was seated to hand Lilly a glass of water. The emotional distance closed when Grace stood beside her.

"I can't come back to Honeybee for awhile," Lilly admitted.

"Come back whenever you've recovered," Grace said. "I'm not going to schedule you until you feel well enough. And maybe you'll want just a day or two a week then."

"I'll be back before the tulips."

"Before the tulips? That's more than six weeks away. The flu won't keep you down that long."

"I hope not, but don't let Sylvia replace me either way."

Lilly's hesitation and weary hands when Grace passed her the soup bowl caused her to wonder if Lilly could return to work at all. Since Lilly was an associate, not a manager, her weekly hours could be filled from the sales staff. Sylvia, the new associate with an aggressive attitude, would gobble up the extra hours if they were offered.

"She can't. No one can. But work can wait," Grace assured her. "Healing comes first. Can I bring you something? Tylenol? Ibuprofen? Antibiotics?"

"I'm good. Had some cough syrup before you came. If the cough gets worse, I'll go to the doctor again and get something else. But enough about that, tell me something cheerful."

"A woman verbally attacked her husband—the most elegant older man—outside the dressing room this morning for giving her honest feedback."

"That's not cheerful," Lilly said.

"No, but our conversation made me smile. After she went back with a larger size, I told him, 'you are so generous to shop with your wife. Not many men do anymore, especially not any as patient and charming as you.'"

"And what did he say?" Lilly asked.

"He flattered me back with compliments about my 'lovely eyes,' and smiled until they left the store with two big bags." Grace cut her story off, lifting her eyes toward the ceiling, and stood in delighted surprise. "*Those* are cheerful."

Vintage hats created a three-dimensional border at the top of the plaster walls where the cornices curved into the high ceilings. Every two feet a unique hat hung like a drop of brilliant color and ornamentation—a small velvet one with rhinestones, a boater with a polka dot ribbon, the white felt cloche from the twenties, a beaded beret, and the colorful sweeping ones in between with multiple feathers.

"Where'd you get them?" Grace asked.

"I wore them. Ladies always had a hat."

"But you don't wear them anymore?" Grace dropped back to her chair. "You could."

Lilly shook her head. "Too conspicuous."

"We should sell hats again."

Lilly leaned back in her day bed and wrapped her arms around herself. "That would fun, but it's a different time. Things are more causal; even where we work."

"You're not casual, even here; that's obvious from everything around you. My mom always said, 'You don't really know a woman until you see her in her home.'"

Another object beneath the window attracted Grace's interest—a luscious green plant of medium height, with tree-like branches and a large red flower.

"What is it? It's beautiful."

Lilly leaned forward with her whole upper body. "A hibiscus," she said, with a voice that trailed off without an end to it.

"It has a story, doesn't it?"

"Of course."

"Tell me," Grace prompted.

"Ten years ago, a woman lived next door to me. Right in that house." Lilly pointed toward the fireplace wall. "I didn't know her very well; in fact, I can't even remember her name."

Lilly pulled the blanket up, tightening it around her shoulders. "After I lost Bob she called and offered me the sincerest sympathies. I went to thank her in person. She was in bed, dying herself. Every day after that I would sit by her bed on a pink stool and listen to her talk."

"Like your three-legged stool in Honeybee's back room?" Grace asked.

Lilly nodded. "The very one. She talked about death—what she thought would happen."

Her eyebrows rose with a flash of emotion and then rested gently back down again. "She imagined her death would be the end of it all. No hope of more. She felt useless, lying in bed. 'An incomplete life,' she said."

"Didn't that depress you, even more?" Grace asked. "With Bob gone?"

"Depress me? No. Perplex me? Yes. I didn't agree with her view of death, but I didn't argue with her. I just asked her about her life. She'd been a nurse for the Red Cross in the war, and she had stories to tell."

Lilly motioned to the hibiscus on the floor. "After a month she told me to go get this plant from the corner of her room. She said she'd given quite a few cuttings from it to her friends.

I feared she would offer to give me a cutting. But instead she pushed the whole plant toward me and said, 'Take it.'"

Lilly sighed, leaning back against her pillow. Grace curled up in her chair.

"I left it on her parlor window when I went," Lilly whispered.

"You didn't!" Grace leaned forward.

"I had to; I wasn't anyone to her, and that plant was too important."

"So how did you get it?" Grace asked.

"The next day she looked much worse. She could barely talk, but when I sat on her stool, she chastised me in a hoarse whisper, 'Lilly, you never came and got your plant.'"

Lilly coughed. She reached for her glass, drank several gulps of water, and wiped her lips. "I said, 'I'll take it today. Thank you.' But, she chastised me, 'You never say thank you for a plant.'"

"Why not?" Grace asked.

"I didn't understand what she meant either, at least not then. I just smiled and kept saying, 'Thank you.'"

"What happened to her?" Grace said, anxious to know the end.

"She died the next day," Lilly said.

"That's terrible."

"Maybe, but the beauty of the plant awakened something in me." Her tone changed, quieting her voice. "I don't know how she knew, but I needed her to acknowledge death—to talk about it—even in a way I didn't agree. No one else did. It was the only way I could cope with Bob's passing. But even as she did that, she had also acknowledged life."

"Why do you think she gave the plant to you? She must have had daughters, sisters, or friends."

"None that I knew, but maybe she did," Lilly said, then paused for a long stretch of silence. Just when Grace wanted to ask more, Lilly spoke again. "For many years I considered what she meant when she said, 'You never say thank you for a plant.' Now I know. She wasn't giving me a gift. She was giving me a stewardship, a responsibility to nurture this plant and make it flower."

Grace left her chair and knelt beside the plant. Up close the red petals opened even wider to reveal the fringed white center with a column of yellow nodes shooting out. She turned and looked at Lilly stretched out in illness and far from the seasoned saleswoman who took her in when Grace was a new manager.

"You did that, Lilly. Not just for the plant but for me."

Lilly didn't say anything, but she smiled and patted the cushion beside her. They chatted a bit more, but when Lilly yawned for the fourth time, Grace left.

As she turned off Trinity Street an object in the road startled her, forcing her to brake hard. Her car jerked to a stop two feet from a tiered black base with a white ball light. She rhythmically sucked in the air to still her pulse.

An old-fashioned streetlight on a concrete pedestal stood right in the middle of the intersection. Around the neck of the ball hung a five-sided lit sign, each with the name of a street and an arrow pointing toward it. It marked the center of a roundabout, directing cars toward multiple choices.

"I suppose I could circle around it all night and get fairly lost," she said. A similar feeling of shock gripped her when she collided with a larger obstacle in life more than a year earlier, leaving her in her own intersection of choices—except this one didn't have a light attached. Not sure whether to go back to school, find a new religion, make a career change, or just move to a new place, she finally chose the job at Honeybee, which was out of state and away from what was familiar, not knowing if it would lead her in a circle or onto a more permanent path. She took the chance that a change of setting would define a new direction for her. The job at Honeybee introduced her to Lilly and a friendship that helped her to heal and gave her the confidence to move forward.

Tonight that destination was easy enough to reach—her two-bedroom rented house in Webster Groves, an inner-ring suburb southwest of St. Louis with an old-fashioned main street and side streets lined with elms and oaks, old Victorians, and smaller turn-of-the-century bungalows. Her own unlit porch was not a dramatic destination for a single woman on a Friday night, but her work clothes were as tight and tired as her muscles. She only wanted a little television humor, not more conversation.

In the morning Grace traded her covers for naked skin in a hot shower, then jeans and a sweater for her ritual Saturday walk. Just as she opened the front door, the mailman was climbing her steps with his heavy mailbag slapping against his bare legs.

"I doubt it feels like shorts weather." Grace pointed to his bare skin.

"I don't wear them for the weather. I wear them to show off my legs," he teased, reaching into his bag for her stack.

She snickered, not at his attempts at humor but at his knees sticking out of the uniform above his knee-hi socks. With her pile of advertising circulars and the utility bill set behind her green door, she threw her own bag over her shoulder for her walk to the miniature, over-priced grocery store on Lockwood—two blocks up and three blocks over.

The bank anchored one end of the main section of Lockwood. A new salon and the grocery store held up the other. If these were the only businesses on Webster's main street, it would appear as showy as The Plaza, but the pet store with birds fluttering in the window and the fabric shop kept it all genuine, not a marketed mirage for trendy shoppers. Some of the replicated or restored store fronts seemed contrived for that purpose, but most were real businesses for real necessities—a dry cleaner, a hardware store, a drugstore, a dentist, and a floral shop.

Two children burst out of Tasty Pastry with éclairs in hand and chocolate smiles. The glazed doughnut smell followed them out. Tempted to indulge but motivated to escape, she promised herself a treat at the enticing bookstore.

Webster felt homier than her own childhood home in Minnesota, where she'd grown up in a suburban subdivision of ranch houses that were frozen not only in climate but in a decade of bad design. She longed to escape the mediocrity and predictable life patterns that stifled her throughout the long winters. The pull to get out and see something else—something she couldn't even name—pushed her toward art, then fashion, and eventually fashion merchandising and a business degree. She craved character and personality wherever she lived and worked.

She opened the door to Darlene's Bookstore and some of her favorite time of the week. The back corner housed Darlene's picks—the books any woman might choose to curl up with to escape for a few hours or all day, a few books that you knew you should have read in college but never got around to, and a sampling of nonfiction books on decorating, cooking, gardening, watercolor. She slipped onto the purple suede chair with two: a copy of *Woman in White*, which was a fun but intelligent literary mystery that she might take to Lilly, and a container garden book to inspire her own spring project.

She flipped through the color photographs of flowers, vegetables, and assorted containers before pausing at a photograph of a city apartment balcony covered in pots of trees, bushes, and low planters of red flowers in the front.

Red flowers. That's what she would choose. Red flowers like the one on Lilly's hibiscus.

Last night she'd verbalized something she'd never recognized. Even though she was Lilly's boss, Lilly had mentored her. Her encouragement had allowed her to grow, not only as a store manager but also as a woman.

Grace valued Lilly's age and experience from the start of their relationship, often pressing her for knowledge of the store's history, the mall, the surrounding communities, and the dynamics between different employees and customers. Lilly's coworkers trusted her, and her customers remained loyal.

Grace, herself, felt more confident in her own interactions with customers and employees, as well as in her management decisions. Until she heard Lilly's story about the hibiscus, she'd never known why.

"What will you plant when spring comes?"

Grace looked up from the garden photograph still open on her lap. Darlene stood a head below the shelf with an armload of books and a questioning look on her face. Her glasses seemed like the epitome of a bookseller, but her spiky head of short black hair didn't fit that image. They'd never officially met but often nodded to each other when she entered the bookstore for her weekly browse or occasional purchase.

"What would you recommend?" Grace asked.

Darlene questioned her about space and light and dipped toward another shelf for a title, holding it out for Grace. "Make sure you don't buy too many at once. Plants—not books—that is. Give yourself a few to start, inside and out, before you tear up all your existing beds to plant it all."

Grace thanked her and gathered her gear, choosing to buy the more practical of the garden books and the Wilkie Collins book for Lilly.

****

Lilly didn't return to Honeybee in February as expected, or more clearly, as Grace expected. Others had different expectations, and all felt the void.

"Grace," Chanel, her assistant manager, called out as she snaked through the walkway of the backroom overflowing with clothes on racks overhead and UPS boxes underfoot. "Mrs. Foster is out front requesting Lilly's help to find the perfect jacket to wear this Saturday. Can you help?"

"Not likely," Grace said. "I'd show her straight to the Cynthia Archer pink number to boost the store numbers for the month's end. That would be perfect for *me*, but certainly not for her figure."

Chanel retreated with a laugh. They both knew she would choose whatever would look best on this matronly mother of the bride who planned to host her daughter's soon-to-be in-laws for the first time.

"Where is Lilly?" whined Roberta when Grace appeared. She scoured the sale racks and fitted her with a lilac cardigan and black trousers, then tied her all up with a stylish print scarf, and encouraged her to stop at the front to sign a card for Lilly. She sold the jacket later that day to a perky customer who couldn't be over a size six.

That type of personal attention satisfied most customers like Roberta who missed their favorite sales associate, but the employees still pestered Grace about Lilly's condition.

"When's she coming back?" they asked.

In an attempt to not magnify the situation to the staff, who were unaccustomed to long absences from the most consistent employee, Grace reported upbeat instances of Lilly's happenings.

"She watched Martha Stewart on three cable channels yesterday," she told them Tuesday.

"She walked to the mailbox and back two times," she said Wednesday.

"She chewed out her newspaper carrier for not throwing the paper up on the porch because she had to retrieve it in her robe," she relayed Thursday.

When Grace called her for Friday's report, Lilly said, "It's not like I'm dying."

"You're not? That surprises me. Has the death sentence you've given yourself faded now that you are truly ill?"

"People have much more serious ailments. This is just the flu."

"But complicated a bit?" Grace said, seriously. They talked over her needs, planning to get together that Saturday. "It's March first; we can celebrate the beginning of the end of winter's gloom."

Grace often visited at the end of the workday and liked to bring something with her—a book, some cards from the customers, or a clearance bracelet. But for this Saturday's visit, the morning sun brought its own gift. Instead of her usual stroll to the grocery store in her Webster neighborhood, she thought they might go to the farmer's market in the Loop. Lilly had mentioned it as a place she frequented, and since Grace had never been there, it seemed the perfect day to drive them the couple of blocks to get out in the fresh air. She hoped Lilly would agree.

But Lilly hesitated at the door. "I'm not sure there will be anything at the farmer's market this time of year. Nothing is growing, and it's still too early to even sell plants," she said.

"We'll drive over so you can show me where it is for later," Grace responded, not anticipating Lilly's reluctance, hoping her plan would lift Lilly's spirits and bring better health. "Where's your sweater? You'll still want that."

Lilly pulled on a heavy red cardigan sweater. They arrived at the cross streets behind city hall, and as Lilly had assumed, only a few vendors had set up pre-spring stalls with hand-made crafts.

"The majority of the vendors won't be around until the last week in March," the woman in front of a stall with baskets said. "That's when the daffodils and tulips, asparagus and perennial bedding plants come out."

Grace's heart sagged. "I'm sorry for dragging you out."

"Let's walk a bit instead," Lilly suggested.

She led Grace down the street, stopping after a block or so to point out the rectangular columns with lions on top that divided the public spaces of the Loop from the residential areas beyond.

"The Lion's Gate," she said.

They found a bench beneath the lions to watch college students jogging, a mother carrying her baby in a sling, and two preteen youth unlocking their bikes outside the library. The street bustled with a wider variety of individuals than her usual place for Saturday people watching.

"When did you let your children ride to the library on their own?" Grace asked.

"When they were ten, earlier if they took an older friend."

"How did you know they would be safe?"

"I didn't. I just trusted that they needed to make good decisions, giving them more and more responsibility as they did."

They watched the tweens ride past and sat for a few minutes without speaking.

"I'm going to Florida," Lilly said, abruptly.

"You're going to go visit Clare?"

"No, I'm going to move in with her."

"Move?" Grace raised her voice in concern and twisted on the bench toward Lilly. "Are you able to do that right now? Do you have the strength?"

"Not really. I'm still so tired, but my doctor is sure it's not pneumonia or bronchitis. I guess I'm just tired from the stress of the illness. He said it would help to live with someone."

"I can take care of you. I can bring dinners over three times a week and do your laundry on Saturday," she offered.

"Grace, I want to go. I miss Clare and my grandsons. I want to spend time with her and see her children. I've worked for thirty years—since she was out of elementary school. Now I want to rest."

"When will you leave?" Grace asked.

"In a couple of weeks. Clare and the kids will come on spring break. She can help me sort what I don't want to keep and pack the rest. Her husband is going to bring his brother, load a truck, and then drive back at the end of the week. Clare and I will fly down with the kids."

"Do you think you can get it all done in a week?" Grace wanted to prolong the questions, as if that would prolong the days before the move.

"I'm not sure," Lilly said. "I might start going through things now."

She couldn't remember what else to ask. Having directed all her concern toward Lilly's immediate needs, she hadn't even considered that her family might have made plans of their own.

"That's soon," she said. It was hard to not consider the repercussions—losing an employee and a friend. The void at work would expand.

"Gracie, I've been trapped in my house for nearly two months," Lilly sighed. "I'm dragging myself out of bed to just sit on the couch, watch television, and read. I don't interact with anyone but you, the cleaning lady, and the delivery guy. I'm lonely, but I can't come to the store. I just can't come back."

"What about staying and doing something else with yourself?"

"Like what?" Lilly questioned. "Join a bridge club? Volunteer at the senior center?"

"Well, yes," Grace said matter-of-factly and stood up from the bench, anxious that she couldn't convince her.

"Honestly, I'm not looking to develop new relationships in some other group; it wouldn't replace contributing to the store," Lilly emphasized with her tone. She searched Grace's face for the connection they shared. "But even if I could, I need the enthusiasm of youth in my life. You brought me vitality and reminded me that life is still growing, even while I'm fading.

That's why I want to be with my grandchildren, my daughter, and her family."

Grace stared up at the lions to avoid Lilly's look. She wanted to strengthen Lilly—to take care of her—in return for all she'd done for her. Happiness for Lilly should be her priority, but any expression she considered sounded hollow in her head. The words wouldn't form.

Grace turned back to Lilly. "What can I do to help?"

"Take my plant," Lilly said. Her voice communicated the importance of that task. "And take care of it."

Grace dropped back down to the edge of the bench beside Lilly, startled that she would trust her with such a significant symbol from her life. She hesitated. The weight of responsibility felt more akin to raising someone's child than just meeting physical needs.

"I'm not sure I can do that," she finally said.

"You can. I'm sure of it." Lilly clasped Grace's hand.

Chapter Two

Sometime during Lilly's absence and Grace's distraction, the store's sales had slowed. Lilly's full-time position at Honeybee could remain empty, but Grace needed to at least find a part-time replacement. Within days of putting up the "Help Wanted" sign in the front window, Roberta, of all people, came right up to the counter and requested an application.

Sylvia screwed her face into a tight contortion trying to not laugh at this manicured Ladue woman. Grace shooed Sylvia away from the sales counter.

"For you?" Grace asked.

"Of course not," Roberta scoffed. "Trenna graduated from college last year but hasn't applied for any jobs, yet. We've been too busy planning her wedding."

She barely glanced at the application when it showed up in her in box. Grace didn't expect much from someone who would send her mom out to do her job search, but she flipped through it and others before reaching for the phone to set up some interviews.

"I've applied to a couple of out-of-state schools, but I might stay in town," said the high school senior she interviewed first. The girl wanted an after school and evening position. Grace needed more than a transient teen. Besides, Audrey, their stock girl, could always be trained for sales if necessary.

"I'm ready to do something for myself," said the mom of two school-age children who wanted weekday hours only, "now that I'm thirty."

"Who isn't?" Grace, who had celebrated her own thirtieth birthday the month before, wanted to say, but she literally bit her tongue. She'd worked in retail six years before she had a choice about working nights and weekends.

"Now what?" Chanel asked.

"I guess I'll make an appointment with Roberta's daughter," Grace said about the last applicant.

Almost every evening, she took black plastic trash bags and Honeybee boxes to Lilly's house, asking, "Which room today?"

Lilly directed traffic from her padded folding chair in whatever room they chose. While Grace sorted, they uncovered decades of surprises that invited conversation. Some items landed in the trash bag. Others she carefully packed to preserve.

Grace gleaned all she could from the stories Lilly told, knowing none of the applicants could replace Lilly's years of experience in style and service.

The interview with the third applicant surprised Grace. Trenna Foster, a petite brunette with a trendy haircut, arrived overdressed and overqualified but eager for the interview. She held a marketing degree and years of summer retail experience.

After the typical questions Grace asked, "Honestly, would you or your friends shop at Honeybee?"

"I do, but The Plaza feels like our moms' place to shop. They've come here with their girlfriends a couple days a week as long as we can remember. We want our own place that fits our own style. Not necessarily a different style of clothes from what Honeybee sells, or even another mall, but a new way of shopping right here."

The answer interested Grace, but she didn't press her for specifics. She simply shook her hand. "I'll let you know after the weekend."

Trenna had the right personality and background to do well with the customers, the majority of whom were just like her mother, but she also had something Grace wanted—youthful inspiration. She'd be an interesting choice.

She batted over her thoughts, discussing the alternatives with Chanel. At the end of the day, she called Lilly. A jumble of voices sounded in the background.

"Would you like me to come help today?" Grace asked.

"What did you say? I can't hear you," Lilly repeated several times. "Shush, everyone . . . The kids are here, Gracie."

"Never mind. I'm just checking on you," Grace lied. She feared the packing sessions would prompt family memories, leaving Grace to sort in silence or laugh ignorantly at private jokes. Her fears kept her outside the work she had so recently shared with Lilly and diminished the memory of the care she'd given for the past months.

"I'll stop by later in the week," she said quietly and hung up. Even though it had been only a few hours since the interview, Grace called Trenna's number. "Can you start a week from Monday?"

After work Thursday Grace detoured home where she changed into jeans and ate a burrito at the kitchen counter. She contemplated calling Lilly's house before she popped over but worried she would lose her resolve to give a hand with the final packing and cleaning. Maybe she'd waited long enough to just pick up the plant and say goodbye.

A woman wearing a busy ponytail of dark brown hair opened Lilly's door with as much graciousness as her mother. The smile told her this was Lilly's daughter but the voice spoke with a question, "Yes?"

Grace backed up slightly from the door, shifted her weight, and brushed back the blond strands in her eyes.

"I'm Grace," she floundered, feeling the impermanence of her relationship with Lilly beside someone who shared Lily's past, present, and future.

"Oh, yes, and I'm Clare." She pulled Grace in by the shoulders and pressed her cheek against Grace's own end-of-the-day hair. "Mom's told me how you've helped. Thank you."

Grace looked beyond her, expecting to see the house emptied and the contents boxed into the corners, but all appeared similar to the way it was when she left last week. Clare followed her gaze.

"We're packing," she explained, "but mostly upstairs. We're not even close to ready for my husband to get here with the truck."

"I'll stay and help," Grace volunteered. Over the next hours she barely saw Lilly, who fed and entertained the two grandchildren while Clare and Grace packed the dining room hutch, the kitchen cabinets, and the linen closet in the hall.

Clare turned out to be a little like her mother—witty and wordy, but not as wise. Working alongside her reassured Grace that Lilly would be cared for and content with her daughter in the years ahead.

"We'll wrap it up here before the men arrive tomorrow afternoon," Clare said.

Grace looked at her with a question.

"No, you're right. We won't finish by then," she said. "But Greg will help us when he gets here. We hope to leave Sunday. Why don't you come for pizza Saturday evening?"

"Okay. Let me know if you need more help before then. I'm working tomorrow, but I can come in the morning on Saturday."

Neither Clare nor Lilly called so Grace didn't return until late Saturday afternoon. The house was still even after she rang the doorbell. She stood on the porch for a few minutes and peered in the windows. The inside looked empty of the furniture and boxes. A moving truck blocked the alley, but she slipped by the side of the house and tried the back door. Locked.

Grace leaned over to pluck a dry oak leaf from under a pebble on the porch steps and tore little bits from the stem. The crackling paper pieces fell to the ground, leaving her holding only the stem with its crooked corners. Lilly had premeditated her demise so often, but now to Grace the departure felt like a death. She shifted her weight and sank to the top of the cracked concrete stairs to wait.

Grace had few close female friendships, and Lilly made this rare one easy. She listened but actively added insights as well—sharing her experiences without advising. She was a friend who accepted Grace's small successes without competition or envy, gave praise without flattery, and showed acceptance without Grace seeking her approval. Grace felt ageless beside her and free to grow. Whether that was only her perception or if this was the way Lilly really acted, it didn't matter. She'd been a mother, a sister, an aunt, and a friend—all in one.

"Boys, come on, we're almost there," Lilly called from down the street. From her voice, Lilly sounded healthier than she had in months, but when Grace slipped back around the front of the house, she saw that Clare, not Lilly, was the one calling.

Lilly was walking alongside her daughter who was turned backwards, waving toward the two boys goofing around a half block behind them. Two men in sweatshirts and jeans completed the picture. It could be any family returning home together from a weekend walk at a multi-generational gathering.

They reached the porch with noisy greetings, and Grace tripped back into the overgrown shrubbery, separated from their cheerfulness. Lilly sent them all to the bathrooms to clean up for pizza while she took Grace to the front room for the plant. Although the hibiscus spread out its leaves from the pot on the wood floor, the plant wasn't blooming with the beautiful flower Grace had seen a month ago.

"It will bloom again," Lilly reassured her. "Just give it the right spot with plenty of sunshine. Don't over water it; wait until it is dry, then give it about this much." She held Grace's hands together to form an invisible cup. "And, feed it."

Lilly handed Grace a box of fertilizer that had been sitting on the ground behind the pot. "A teaspoon of this dissolved in a gallon of water, every other week. Feed it until July and then back off again until spring. If you want it to grow bushier and not so tree-like, you can also cut it way back. Don't worry—it's been hearty for me, and it will be for you."

"Should I write this down?" Grace said.

"You'll remember." Lilly leaned down to pick up the plant off the floor.

"I'll do it," Grace said, but she was too late. Lilly had already lifted the pot half way. She swayed, placing her feet further apart to manage the weight. Grace knelt down with outstretched arms, placing her arms underneath it. They stood up together, both holding the plant.

"What else do I need to know?" Grace asked as they stood eye to eye.

"You can take cuttings from it and give them to friends. Get to know it for a while first; then, you'll know when and who to give one to. I've given lots of them. But the plant—it's for you."

"I hope I don't kill it."

"Gracie, you won't kill anything unless you let it die."

Lilly handed Grace the whole plant, and Grace hugged it to her body, as if that would protect it. Lilly put her hands on top of Grace's hands.

"I'll miss our backroom chats," Lilly said. "But you need to keep growing, too. Space and new relationships will help you do that. Then, not only will *you* grow, but everything around you will, too."

Lilly reached up and wiped Grace's cheek with her sleeve. "Salt water's okay, but not too much, all right? Now, let's go get some pizza."

Grace shook her head. "I'm just going to go. Is that okay?"

Lilly nodded, and they walked back to the front door.

"Goodbye," Grace said, as she walked onto the front porch.

Lilly followed her to the stairs. "Take care of yourself, Gracie."

"You, too." Grace wasn't sure what to say, nothing came to mind that didn't sound trite. "And Lilly, thank you."

"Never say thank you for a plant," Lilly teased.

"I know."

****

"Where do I put it?" Grace asked herself that question over and over. The hot afternoon sun in a corner of her living room floor looked promising. "Here?"

She opened the shutters in her bathroom and sat on the toilet seat looking at the shelf above her head. "Or maybe here?"

She moved her kitchen table to mop and found sunlight stretched from the ceiling, past the chair rail to the thick baseboards. "What about here?"

Grace even called her mom and asked her advice. Her mom couldn't tell her where to put it, but asked, "Where is it now?"

"It's in my car," she told her.

"Go get it right now," her mom insisted. "It will die. It's winter."

"Technically that's only for one more day. The car has windows, and it needs lots of light anyway."

"It will freeze in there at night," her mom said, exasperated.

"This isn't Minnesota, Mom. It may be cold there, but it's actually warm as spring here. We even have tulips. But tell me, where should I put the hibiscus?"

"Well, at least bring it inside until you decide."

But she didn't. The plant stayed in Grace's car for almost a week—the week of indecision, the week of mourning the loss of Lilly, the week of straining to understand what Lilly wanted her to do with the plant.

On Monday Grace rushed through her morning routine. She wanted to arrive at work two hours early to train Trenna, the newly hired salesperson. On the way, Grace turned a sharp left in the U-turn lane. The potted hibiscus fell over in the back of her car, spilling potting soil onto the floor mats.

She walked in just a minute or two after eight, with her dirty hands held out from her side. Trenna stood at the gate where Lilly had always waited. Grace smirked to herself at the memory of Lilly standing in that same place, every weekday. No matter how early Grace had left home, Lilly had always arrived ahead of her and was waiting at the store gate.

Trenna wore an enviable outfit in bright spring green. Grace wore black.

"Love the color," Grace said, hiding her hands behind her back.

"Oh, I never wear black. Basic and boring . . ." Trenna responded before she caught herself midsentence. "I didn't mean you look basic and boring."

"Of course you didn't." Grace knelt, inserting her key card into the gate. When she withdrew it they could both see her soil-covered hand.

All pretenses left. Grace turned the other hand over and held them both up. "I replanted a hibiscus out in the parking lot without my gardening gloves."

"What?" Trenna laughed. The honesty lightened the tension of the awkward newness between strangers and smoothed away the ache that Trenna was not Lilly.

For the next two hours she gave Trenna a tour of the store, trained her on the computer system, and completed the payroll paperwork. She assessed Trenna's skills and identified her strengths. Trenna learned the organizational systems but ironically didn't catch on as quickly with monotonous tasks like folding sweaters or resizing the sale racks. Their comfort level increased, allowing them to converse easily on a break.

"How are the wedding plans coming?" Grace asked.

"Oh, my mom's doing it all since I'm her only girl," Trenna

said. "She asks me all day long what I think about this or that. 'Do you prefer polished peach or lemon yellow?' Then she chooses what she wants anyway."

"Don't you care?" Grace said, surprised to find a bride who wasn't fighting to have it just the way she wanted.

"I guess I do, but I wonder if isn't just easier to let her do it the way she wants," Trenna said, resigned to the situation. "She'll only have this one wedding."

"And so will you. Or do you plan to do the same thing to your daughter?"

"I thought I'd just escape and leave it in her hands, like I'm doing with my mom, I guess."

Trenna glanced at Grace, who acknowledged the confession with a little nod and a knowing smile. Smart and opinionated but she doesn't want to rock the boat.

Tuesday and Wednesday brought the new summer line to replace the spring merchandise, even with more than a week left in March. Audrey unloaded ten UPS boxes with new items. With the merchandise scattered all over the back room, Grace needed Faye, the company's window designer and merchandiser who shifted from store-to-store throughout the metro area.

Trenna helped Audrey count, hang, and steam the new but wrinkled clothes while Sylvia waited on the stray customer or two that wasn't out enjoying the weather on the golf course or a spring cruise.

Faye came from the Clayton store at lunchtime on Wednesday to move the old inventory into three round sales racks at the back of the store and hang several new displays across the left wall. She and Grace worked together until midday Thursday rearranging the store to fit the summer styles. This forty-something single mom of twin ten-year-old boys never tired, but Grace did.

Grace wanted to perch on Lilly's stool and absorb her wisdom. She rustled between mannequins and boxes of hangers to find it beneath the clothing racks. A pink wooden leg poked out from behind a stack of shoeboxes and a pile of bubble wrap.

"There." Grace flipped the three-legged stool upright from where it rested seat-side down and settled on the low top. With her knees pulled almost to her chest she waited for her favorite employee's encouragement to fill the backroom, but she wouldn't hear Lilly's voice in the store again.

By Thursday evening, she couldn't even appreciate the fresh feel of the store. Her distracted stupor of sadness returned as the wave of activity wound down. Still, she stayed until closing to help Faye, who wanted to clear the old window display to be ready for a new one in the morning. Then she went to Tasty Pastry to eat a chocolate chip cookie sundae for a late dinner.

Despite the sugar rush, Grace slept as if it was a weekend and faced the store on Friday morning with a new outlook. The light from the mall atrium court seemed brighter in the empty window, waiting for Faye's touch. After lunch, when Faye had dressed the window with colorful summer outfits, Grace approached her with an idea. She often tested them out with Faye, even though Chanel was the assistant manager. Her natural instincts seemed closest to Grace's.

"I never gave Lilly a going away party," Grace confessed while they stood in the mall hallway viewing Faye's display in the front window. "What do you think about a post party?"

"Honestly? It's awkward, especially without the guest of honor."

"Yeah, I thought so, too," Grace admitted. "It's just that I have this plant she gave me. I have to get it out of my car. It keeps tipping over. It looks dry and needs water, but I can't water it in my back seat. I'm afraid it will die if I don't give it away."

"So what are you thinking? That you're going to auction it off to the person with the greenest thumb?"

"Or just ask if someone else wants it. I wasn't the only one who loved Lilly."

"Okay. If you invite them, I'll come and drag anyone else I can with me."

The employees met on Saturday at The Landing, a restaurant at the mall entrance. Faye and Trenna arrived in the east parking lot within minutes of each other and found Grace a few cars down dragging the plant out of her back seat. Once inside The Plaza, they peered down the interior hallway and saw Beth, another part-time sales associate, riding down the escalator.

"They'll be here in a few minutes," Beth called. "Chanel's showing Sylvia how to close."

When everyone arrived, Grace set the plant in the middle of the table without a word about where she got it or why she'd brought it. Even though the hibiscus wasn't blooming, the atmosphere felt like the hushed conversation of guests at a funeral.

"Lilly always thought she was going to die," Sylvia said dramatically as she pushed her auburn hair off her face.

"She convinced me to take a million vitamins, and she still got sick," Beth said.

"Did you know she never took a sick day until this year?" Chanel said. "But, she did magnify any little symptom, didn't she?"

Faye fingered the scarf tied at her neck. "I would have never owned a scarf if Lilly didn't wear one nearly every day."

Trenna, who had been standing around the backroom when Grace invited everyone, had decided to come, too. "I didn't know her, but my mom thinks Lilly has great taste," she said. "She'd bring home her Lilly outfits and wear them just like Lilly put them together."

"She could accessorize anything," Audrey, the stock girl, said. "Whenever we received a new belt or purse or necklace, she would suggest ten things on the floor it would go with."

The awkwardness of the eulogizing sounded as lame as it was. "Lilly's not dead," Grace finally said. "I've missed her all week, but she's not dead. She's just moved to Florida."

"But she's been a fixture at the store since the beginning," Beth said.

"Even fixtures need changing," Faye said.

They sat silently, not looking at each other. The waitress brought the food, and everyone arranged themselves with napkins, condiments, and drinks. After everyone started eating, Grace held her onion ring in midair and said what she never expected to say to her coworkers.

"When I walk in the back room, I keep expecting to see Lilly, but she's not there," she began. Her voice quieted, and she set down her onion ring. "I'm empty when I come to work, and I'm empty when I go home. I don't understand it. You're all still here. My work is here. But a space still exists that's hollow yet heavy."

Grace looked around. Some caught her eye and smiled, but most just stared at their food or the other side of the restaurant. All of them recognized the intimate and rare emotion clinging to Grace's words.

"I just said she's not dead. But it feels like that, doesn't it?"

She turned to Chanel beside her, who nodded. "She's gone to Florida, but she really won't ever be back. People come and go from the store, but that relationship we have with them, it just stops. With most I just let it go. What was there to miss? Hearing their love woes? We can all manage without that."

Audrey visibly cringed across the table. "Sorry, Audrey," Grace caught herself, knowing she had moved too far away from her role as manager. "I like to hear about Nick. I shouldn't have said that."

But she still felt compelled to open her heart, knowing that she needed to throw off her manager hat altogether. "What do you do when it just stops? That relationship just stops."

"Is that a rhetorical question?" Sylvia whispered to Beth.

"I never expected it to just stop with Lilly," Grace continued. "Even if I called her every week, it won't restart. It's not current."

"She gave you the plant. She gave it to *you*. Doesn't that mean something?" Faye said, motioning to the plant in the center of the table.

"It's a plant. Not a person. It doesn't talk back," Grace said. "Besides, I can't even decide where to put it. That's why I brought it. That's why we're here. I want to give it to one of you. Who wants it?"

No one spoke. The awkward silence pressed into Grace's lungs, like she couldn't breathe without their feedback. Should she ask again or just hand it off to someone?

"Grace," Faye said, gently.

"What?" she asked.

"She's the only one who called you Gracie," Faye reminded. "I can't take it."

"Me either," Chanel said, grabbing her drink, probably to prevent any further explanation.

"But I don't know how to take care of it."

"You can learn," Trenna offered.

She closed her eyes, knowing she needed help, but fearing she would lose their respect. They waited in silence until she opened her eyes. They weren't just employees but women she wanted as friends. They could only be that if she trusted them.

"The front corner window fills with light around ten from the atrium," Grace said. "It stays bright until almost three-thirty. What if we put Lilly's plant in the front window on permanent display?"

Grace looked at Faye first, who looked surprised, then quizzical.

"With a permanent item to work into the design," Faye finally said, "it would define what we can do there. We'll always have a plant. I'm not sure we want to do that."

"Can you even make a decision like that? What would Sue say if she saw it?" Chanel said. Sue managed the Missouri region of Honeybee's St. Louis and Kansas City stores for the parent company.

"We don't have to point it out to her. It can be natural looking," Faye suggested.

"Why here? In the store?" Sylvia said with a confused and belligerent attitude.

Grace didn't answer, and the question weaved into their thoughts.

"Could we help?" Trenna said. "If it's here, we can help, couldn't we?"

"Yes, I would need your help. I do need your help. I don't think I'm going to kill it. I'm just afraid it will never bloom again."

She paused, knowing she was in a vulnerable position, but

grateful to be in colorful and noisy surroundings to ask what she really needed.

"Will you help me?"

She looked to Chanel first. Grace was worried, not knowing how her open admission and request would be accepted. Chanel reached up to smooth her black hair, brought her polished dark fingers along the side of her face, and nodded.

Grace then turned to Faye, who'd been so vocal about the place she'd proposed. The windows were her territory. Faye flashed passionate approval with her eyes, whipped the scarf from her neck, and wrapped it around the plant.

"I can bring in new pots to mix and match it with other plants. I'll accessorize it. Lilly would love it."

Each woman at the table, one-by-one, agreed to Grace's proposal to bring the plant into the store. Some even suggested ways they wanted to help—to research, water, fertilize, or prune. No one but Grace, though, really knew this wasn't just any plant. If they had, they might be as nervous as she was at the prospect of its care.

Chapter Three

Before Grace took Lilly's plant to Honeybee, she took it out of her car and brought it inside her house. Except for picking it up from the spills in the back seat and a week of worry over where to put it, she'd left it alone. Now that she'd answered that worry, she attended to its other needs. She watered the hibiscus, gave it some fertilizer, and picked off some dry and crispy leaves.

Then she searched the web for care instructions. Most of the basic reference sites were too general or described how to bring hibiscus inside over the winter, but then she found a site that gave specifics on how to care for tropical hibiscus as houseplants. Her main objective was to help it bloom again. One website promised that if the plant could receive some direct sunlight every day, you would see flowers. That advice and other information about watering and nutrition validated her choice of location. They could provide all that in Honeybee's front window.

One of the garden books at Darlene's suggested keeping a garden journal. With the plant watered and fed, and a care plan in place, she left it on her living room coffee table to search old boxes of books in her second bedroom. She knew she had a blank journal in them that she'd purchased a few years before on a weekend trip to Wisconsin. She'd never written in it because she loved the red leather cover and pages of handmade paper too much to mar them with her scribbles.

She found it at the bottom of the third box of old college textbooks, junior high diaries, and the paperback romances she read the summer after she'd graduated from high school. The red cover on it matched the blooms she wanted to bring back, and now it would be Lilly's plant journal. Back in the living room, Grace kneeled on the area rug beside the coffee table and wrote her first entry in the journal: March 28. Watered. Fed. Taking you to Honeybee tomorrow.

With the busy tasks done, she leaned back against the couch in the sunlight of the front window. The warmth reminded her of lying in front of the sliding glass doors in the family room of her adolescent home. She would lie on one side of the door, and her brother's dog would lie on the other side of the glass, soaking in the sun. That connection was as close as she wanted to get to him. She liked the idea of a dog as a companion, but she didn't care for the mess of a dog. Thankfully, Brett took care of the rest.

Now, she curled up in the patch of the sun on her area rug and stared through the glass from the underside of her coffee table at the hibiscus plant until her sleepy eyes lost focus. Although warm and comforted, she didn't sleep. The glass between her and the plant felt like the transparent barrier in her heart that kept her from real connections with other people.

She didn't search her mind for the cause. She recognized the ache of loneliness since she'd analyzed that feeling many times before—when her best friend in junior high moved away just before high school, when her grandpa died from cancer, when her older sister left for college, when her mom returned to work, and when she sat by herself in her college dorm a month into her freshman year and nothing seemed familiar.

And when she broke up with Jeff and moved here.

All were normal life changes; yet, each pierced her with a surprising feeling of loss—a feeling she not only wanted to identify but to understand. Maybe then she could fill it.

She'd learned some hard lessons from overreacting to that feeling.

That's how she ended up with Jeff. He was the opposite of what she knew, what she thought she wanted. But he had energy and was an activist for his cause of the month. His attentiveness to everyone attracted her. And when he turned that attention on her, she left behind the vague notions of the future family she thought she wanted for the man in front of her.

Now with some time behind her, she could see that her overeager effort to jump into new relationships or pursuits had always created more complexity, not less, and taught her that filling a loss would only come in time.

But she still waited for the opportunities she gave up with Jeff to appear in her life again—albeit this time with someone who wanted children. Lilly's friendship, a relationship that for once helped her understand and grow a little past that experience, had also disappeared.

In the quiet Sunday afternoon of that spring day, rather than being motivated by a penchant to solve the problem, she felt the contrasting reactions to her loss—passivity. As she succumbed to her sorrow at the impermanence of her important relationships, sleep came, and she napped for several hours. She awoke to a dimmer room, the sun having shifted toward the other side of the house. The spot that had warmed her now left her chilled.

The rest renewed her enough to walk for an hour along the residential streets of Webster. She admired the landscaping and the extra care that some gave to their exteriors. She wondered how many tended to their homes and yards themselves or paid someone to do it. One or two homes were neglected, especially around the sidewalks. When she returned and looked at her own yard, which she maintained as part of her agreement with the landlord, she made a mental list of the spring projects she would need to complete.

Even though she knew this wasn't her permanent place, she took care of it like it was. She knew when she did eventually move, whatever she added to the property would carry on for the good, no matter who lived there.

Back inside, she prepared Lilly's hibiscus for the trip to Honeybee the next day. She had worried at first that she was avoiding the responsibility of keeping it alive at home, but her feelings on the walk cleared her second-guessing. Lilly created a nurturing environment for the customers and employees at Honeybee. Even as manager, Grace could have envied this, but she embraced it, thriving from the mentoring conversations they'd shared.

Maybe bringing Lilly's plant into the store would cultivate that same quality in the staff as they cared not only for her plant but also for the customers. Grace wrapped the plant in brown paper so it wouldn't spill in her car again and carried it to the entry table. She felt the weight of Lilly's legacy in her arms and was glad she could share that with the women at work.

****

The hibiscus received an abundance of attention on its first day and first few weeks in its new location in Honeybee's front window. Faye dressed it in a bright yellow pot and set it on the forgotten pink stool as an accent to the display of spring print dresses. Grace passed the journal around for them to all sign their names in the front cover as caretakers of Lilly's plant and then placed it on the top shelf behind the counter, just above the tissue wrap and shopping bags, for everyone to record what they did.

Sylvia in her usual busybody role tried hard to impress everyone by making a feeding and watering schedule, but Chanel vetoed her charts for individual assignments that rotated monthly. Sylvia settled on the first month's assignment for watering, and Beth took on the feeding. Both agreed to coordinate their efforts with notes in the journal. Grace shared the material she printed from the American Hibiscus Society website. Audrey volunteered to condense the instructions on water, nutrition, sun, and hygiene (washing the plant's leaves periodically to reduce the dust and spider mites) onto a smaller card they could tape into the back flap of the journal. They each created a pattern of walking by the window on the way to or from work to check on it.

During those weeks, Grace worked the closing shift with Trenna several times. Often the last hour of this shift consisted of straightening the clothes on the sales floor for the next day and watching out for the few customers who might stop by on their way to see a foreign film at the cinema. She'd folded the last of the sweaters when Trenna stepped out of the door to the window display with the watering can in her hand.

"You're already helping?" Grace gestured at the watering can.

"I took Beth's hours this week. Her daughter is home sick, and she asked if I would cover her plant duty as well," Trenna explained. "Have you had a turn?"

"Not yet. I actually feel like I've neglected it with everyone else helping out."

"But it still feels like your plant, doesn't it?"

"I did bring it here so everyone would tend it together, not so that it would be mine. Sometimes when I first come in I feel like I'm part of making that happen, but when the rush of the day starts, I forget a little. I think I have to consciously do something with it every day."

"You want to stay in touch with it, though, don't you? Make a connection, right?" Trenna asked.

"Of course," Grace said.

"My mom plants all kinds of annual flowers ever year—in pots, in symmetrical garden beds, in free form plantings." Trenna set the watering can by the back room. "Even though the landscape crew mostly takes care of them, she calls them her babies and talks to them."

"What does she say?" Grace laughed at the image of a well-dressed but plump Roberta bowing over her plants with a pep talk.

"I'm not sure. She's outside muttering to them all the time, and I assume she's talking to the flowers." Trenna gathered empty hangers from the dressing room and came back to where Grace shuffled size four pants out of the size twelve spots. "Maybe she's just talking to herself; I should ask her."

"Oh, no—please don't. Then my image of her will either be completely warped or utterly true." Grace checked her watch. "It's time."

She walked to the front to pull down the gate and shut the front doors. Trenna laid the hangers in the bin behind the front counter.

"Do you want to go get something to eat? Or maybe go see a movie?" Grace asked.

Trenna hesitated. "Well, I . . ."

"Oh, some other time, then."

"It's not that I don't want to. I do. My mom just expects me."

"Really?" This response seemed more like one she'd get from Audrey but never would. Even though Audrey was still in high school, she had a fair amount of freedom. "Aren't you living on your own?"

"Mom's remodeling the carriage house for Max and me to live in after the wedding. She wanted me to be close to supervise it, so I moved back home after graduation. But, really, I haven't done anything. After Max drew up the plans, she took control."

Why would she insist Trenna come straight home after work? She didn't know Roberta beyond her regular shopping interactions, but the picture of who she was became more defined with each of these conversations with her daughter.

"When Max comes back on the weekends—beyond mobbing him for architectural advice—she gives us our space," Trenna said. "So, I don't mind that I don't have my own place. No worries about rent or food. I can just focus on work and getting ready."

"Sure, that's always the nice part of it," Grace said, but she was really thinking of the other side of those apron strings. She finished closing out the cash register while Trenna disappeared to the back room and then appeared a few minutes later with her purse and a shopping bag from another store in the mall.

"I'm picking out my flowers for the centerpieces tomorrow," Trenna said. "Mom has another appointment at the same time. Do you want to go with me?"

"If timing works out . . . sure," Grace said.

"I'm meeting with the florist at seven. I don't work tomorrow, but you could meet me there."

"Yeah, that might be nice."

"How about I text you in the morning with the address?"

****

The address for The Floral Shop happened to be in Grace's Webster neighborhood, between Tasty Pastry and Darlene's Bookstore. Even though Grace knew where it was, she'd never been inside. She drove straight home after work, ate leftovers at her kitchen sink, and walked there from her house. The black-trimmed windows on the white storefront looked more elegant than country cute, and the arrangements in the window were similar in style. But what caught Grace's eye was the tropical plant backdrop behind the arrangements.

"Is that a hibiscus?" a female voice said from over her shoulder.

Grace turned to find Trenna on the sidewalk beside her. "You see it, too?"

Finding "their" plant in the florist's window was like buying a red coat and then seeing red coats on every woman on the street. But unlike seeing a burst of similar coats, which usually caused regret, the hibiscus in the storefront window reminded them of their shared project and bound them in a secret. They walked into the store with a little more togetherness of friendship.

Liz, the florist, showed them tulips, roses, lilies, and orchids—all in pastels. "Your mom has picked some wonderful arrangements for you to approve, hasn't she?"

Trenna turned away from those and returned to the colorful hibiscus plant in the window.

"What about these? Tropical blooms on the tables would be so colorful."

"But we don't do hibiscus arrangements."

"I guess we can just go with the peach roses. What do you think, Grace?"

"That's a nice formal choice."

"But which would you choose?" Trenna pressed.

"I have to see it before I can create a picture in my mind," Grace said. "Besides, you have to decide. Not me. Not your mother. You."

Trenna scanned the centerpiece arrangements on the table. "Each of these looks like my mother. Soft texture. Soft color."

"So what looks like you?" Grace asked.

Trenna walked silently around the store for five or ten minutes, bending down to look at floor arrangements, peering into the refrigerators, and flipping through books on the desk.

"Liz, could you research these flowers a bit more?" Trenna said, pointing to the hibiscus again. "I'm good with silk if we can't get live hibiscus blooms, but I'd like to see what you can get. Will you do a sample for me for next week?"

Despite Trenna's initial indecision, once she decided what she wanted, she insisted on it. The disparity amused Grace—but not Liz.

"That will mean changing the bouquet and other flowers to match. And that's already been settled," she complained.

"So we will change those, too," Trenna said. "There's time, isn't there?"

Liz nodded reluctantly and made some notes. "I won't call Roberta with the final numbers until you come back next week."

"Perfect."

Grace and Trenna finished the evening with ginger scones at Tasty Pastry. Trenna told her the story of meeting Max in Kansas City between her junior and senior year of college and his proposal on her graduation day.

"His firm's transferring him, but since last year, it's just been weekends and short vacations. Sometimes he comes here. Sometimes I go there."

"You must miss him."

"Without a doubt," Trenna said, rubbing the crystal sugar from the scone around on her napkin. "In the beginning, when I still doubted that I was really getting married, I was anxious about him not being here. Now it feels real and secure, but I'm lonely. Even with work and wedding plans, I still have a lot of time to myself. Not very typical of a bride, is it?"

Grace shrugged at the thought that there was a stereotypical bride but said nothing.

"Even though we talk all the time—or text—the physical proximity isn't there. I want to see his eyes. And when we're on video, I want to feel his touch."

Grace missed that—the strength of companionship that comes as a couple. Holding hands with Jeff had felt so secure. Her heart hurt wanting that again but knowing she couldn't turn back.

"I'm not Max, but I can listen," Grace offered.

"Thanks."

"Do you run or walk? Maybe getting outside would help."

"I used to run, but I stopped a couple of years ago. Besides, I'm not very good."

"Me either," Grace said. "Want to start? The sun stays up much later in the evenings now. How about tomorrow? We could meet at Tilles Park around seven?"

"Sure," Trenna said, finishing the last of her scone. "Maybe it's more than missing him; maybe I just feel the anticipation of the wedding. Not so much the wedding itself, but the marriage. The 'hand off' is what my dad calls it. Handing me off to Max. That sounds so possessive, doesn't it?"

"A little."

"They are. Or my mom is. But Max isn't. That's what I love about him. He's patient—that's what he is—with me and with her." Trenna looked at her cell phone. "It's nearly nine. Tomorrow, then? Tilles Park. By the duck pond."

"Yes. I'll need it," Grace said, gesturing at the empty plate of crumbs before her. After Trenna left, she watched the people out the window. Darlene, the bookstore owner came by the window, waved, and came in. Grace met her at the door.

"What did you decide to plant this year?" Darlene said.

"Oh, impatiens on the front porch in pots. It's shaded. Then I'll start an herb garden outside my kitchen door and maybe a tomato plant. Just a little at the beginning."

"Beginnings are best. The hardware store puts out their plants on the sidewalk in a couple of weeks, the first week or so of May," Darlene volunteered as they stepped outside.

"Thanks, and have a good night." Grace turned toward home.

"Good luck," Darlene called as they headed in opposite directions on Lockwood.

The black lampposts lit the street until Grace passed the second block south of Lockwood. Only the neighborhood homes were lit beyond the edges of the dark, uneven sidewalks, casting shadows in her path. Her toe caught on the lip of one, pushed up by a tree root underneath, and she stumbled forward, catching her balance midway through a forward fall. She recovered herself and walked slower with her arms extended a bit, in case she fell again, looking behind her and then down the sidewalk to her house—seeing only the darkness ahead. The people she might come across didn't scare her as much as those obstacles she couldn't see under her feet.

With that longing and uncertainty rising in her heart again, she could feel how her anxiety of being alone herself created the stumbling block in her heart. That's why she couldn't feel the joy of Lilly's farewell with her family or embrace her plant immediately. It certainly needed her to nurture it to stay alive and bloom, but how would that happen for her?

She stepped into the light of her own front porch and walked around to the back door, past the place where she had told Darlene she would plant her herb garden and tomatoes. The garden bed on the corner still held a tangle of weeds and worn out yews. She bent over it, sitting on the backs of her heels and pulled a few weeds.

Beginnings are best. All these weeks her growth seemed stifled, as if she were at the end of something. Could this season really be her beginning?

****

On Monday and Wednesday evenings Grace and Trenna met by the duck pond at Tilles Park. They laced up their running shoes and struggled together around the perimeter of the park for the weeks leading up to the wedding. The first time they only made it one-quarter of the way around before Grace needed a rest walk. On subsequent days she watched her feet when she ran and focused on the weeds and grass growing along the trail. Trenna always looked ahead but often tripped over these overgrown weed clumps.

By the end of the second week, Grace pushed her longer legs ahead whenever the trail narrowed with overgrowth; Trenna picked up her pace to match. The weeds grew bigger until the day they made it two laps around without stopping. The day the mowers came out, fresh grass clippings flew under their feet on the trail. By the time the dandelions scattered their seeds, they had worked up to three laps.

Spring shifted between wet days and sun-filled ones, but when the weather settled into a more predictable pattern of warmth, so did their new running routine. Monday runs broke Trenna's downcast moods that came from Max's return to Kansas City. Wednesday runs lightened the conversation.

"I haven't even met Max." Grace slowed her pace at the sight of the cars ahead. "What if you two came to dinner this weekend?"

"We'll both be in Kansas City. A bridal shower with my college friends."

"Oh. Some other time."

They were just finishing up and were slowing to a walk beside their cars.

"Grace, I want you to meet him. But I have a favor. I know this is weird and all, but I haven't chosen a maid of honor. Would you . . ."

"Throw you a shower here? Of course I would. We could invite the women at work. And do it at my house." Grace grabbed her sweatshirt from around her waist and sopped the sweat off her forehead.

Trenna paused by her car, not answering and bent forward for a long minute. Was she irritated at the offer? Trenna lifted her head up, and her face was pale white, not red from perspiration.

"Are you okay?" Grace asked, wondering if her idea was that bad.

"Yeah, a little lightheaded, I guess."

"You're probably just dehydrated." She pulled two bottles of vitamin water from her car and handed one to Trenna.

They drank in silence before Trenna answered, "I'd love a bridal shower at your house. And thanks for saving me." She held up the water bottle; the color had returned to her face.

They agreed on Memorial Day so she could host it outside in the backyard. Grace proposed a guest list of women from work, and Trenna thought it would be nice to invite Roberta and a few of her other friends that hadn't been included in the more lavish shower for relatives and old family friends that her aunt was planning for another May weekend. Grace agreed but began to regret that decision when she evaluated her backyard through Roberta's manicured eyes.

A row of lilac bushes on one side screened Mr. Reynolds' yard next door from view and an evergreen-lined privacy fence against the back and along the driveway enclosed the 15 by 30 foot grassy yard. The grass wasn't cushy barefoot grass. Dandelions and other weeds grew in uneven color. It did look good, though, right after being mowed and trimmed. The patio, where she would serve a buffet had several large cracks across it. She didn't even have any large table to distract from those. Maybe she could rent a couple.

Her first priority needed to be a spring cleanup, then planting of her herb garden and annual flowers. A wild gray perennial weaved through the side bed that received the most light. She yanked it out along with the tired yews, scooped fall's dead leaves from where the existing hostas poked through and trimmed the low bushes around the front porch and back patio.

At the store Grace took on the plant feeding assignment and marked her arrival each morning with a stop in the storefront window to greet Lilly's plant and check her progress.

"These chats will stretch me—just like running," she said the first time. "Are you happy here?" Why feelings? A plant doesn't have feelings. She almost backed out of the window display, feeling sheepish talking to a plant.

She tried another approach. "Trenna and I just ran last night, and I'm very sore this morning." Well, that was incidental information, but it wasn't bad or too stupid.

She continued with short little phrases of things going on at the store or happenings at home. "This prickly concrete-colored perennial keeps sending up shoots in my garden. I yank it out, roots and all. In a few days, it's back. Would it help to set it on fire?"

Obviously she didn't expect the plant to answer her back, but it appeared to listen, perched on that pink stool. She gave it even more care and attention on those morning talks when she fed her from Lilly's special mix. She even put a little in a bottle of water and spritzed the leaves once a week.

The week before Mother's Day, her new routine fell behind schedule. Trenna mentioned the gift she planned to buy for her mom, which reminded Grace that she hadn't done anything for her own mother. She stopped at the grocery store in the morning, bought a card to mail at lunch and hurried in to open the store, twenty minutes later than usual.

Although she didn't expect any employees until after 9:30, she knew she would only have a few minutes to check on the plant. She filled her spritz bottle with a fertilizer mixture and let herself into the display.

"Good morning. Just got a minute before everyone's here." She bent low, examining each stem. Tidbits of green growth poked from spots along each stem. "Look at you this morning. How beautiful."

She turned the plant on the stool and found new growth on the opposite side. "How did you warm up to this place so fast? It's taken me years to adjust."

Grace stood on display with the plant in the storefront window admiring it. The front glass shook with a knock.

Sylvia smirked at Grace from the other side of the front window. The mall was awakening, and people filled in the background. Sylvia rolled her eyes and turned toward the store entrance.

Grace fumbled the spritz bottle and the few yellow leaves she'd plucked and exited the window display just as Sylvia walked in the doors, already talking.

"You looked like you're smiling at your baby," Sylvia said with sarcasm. "Did it smile back at you for the first time?"

"It has some new growth. You'd have been happy to find that, too, wouldn't you?"

"Sure. If I cared like you do."

"Don't you? You were the one who wanted to be first on the schedule last month."

"Oh, I did, and I found out, like you will, that it's just a plant. There's nothing special about it."

"Well, of course . . ." Grace started, confused by Sylvia's tone. "What you add to it is what you receive from it."

"What does that mean? That I'm not giving enough around here?"

"No, I just meant with the plant, it takes time to recognize . . ."

"Don't tell me what I need to learn from that stupid plant," Sylvia blurted. "I do my job well."

The urge to defend herself heated Grace's tongue until she saw herself reflected in a mirror on the dressing room door. You're the manager. You're the manager. You're the manager, she repeated to herself.

"Hello," Trenna said as she walked through the front doors.

Sylvia stalked to the backroom with her overflowing tote, and Trenna followed with her purse and umbrella. Grace cautiously entered to return the spritz bottle to the shelf, but Sylvia immediately turned her shoulder away from Grace and huffed out to the sales floor.

"Did you find a card?" Trenna said.

The introduction of a tension-free topic didn't alleviate the pressure headache and the clenching in her neck, but Grace related her twenty-minute search through the sentimental and funny cards.

"I'm still not quite sure after 30 years which kind my mom would prefer," she confessed.

When they came out of the back room a few minutes later laughing, Sylvia turned away from them. The intentional silence she gave Grace that day felt like weighted air pressing against her.

Grace smiled outwardly, but it was only a visual barricade of the emotion that covered her inside.

After work Grace shopped the sidewalk garden sales. Besides the salmon-colored begonias for her front porch, she chose marigold and alyssum transplants to line the vegetable beds. For the vegetables, she picked a traditional Big Boy tomato plant and an abundant cherry one, as well as a cucumber and a zucchini plant. Finally, she bought seeds for rosemary, basil, thyme, and cilantro. She splurged on three pre-planted pots of mixed petunias rather than more transplants to speed up the color for some décor in the backyard for Trenna's shower.

She pulled into her driveway with a trunk full of plants and too little experience as she eyed her side garden. The tips of something curled up from the soil. She stepped out of her car and toward it. New sprigs of the dreaded gray plant creeped along the brick of the house.

Without changing from her navy pinstripe trousers and matching sweater with white piping, she grabbed a shovel from the shed and ripped into the dirt. Instead of gently transplanting new plants like she'd planned, she fought those same roots that crawled through the soil with a hoe. When that didn't work, she used a hand rake, then her fingers and nails until the blank soil, uninterrupted by weeds, looked ready for the plants. In this conflict of dirt and weed, suspicions about Sylvia stirred in Grace while she dug at the soil.

Section Two

Trenna's Bouquet

Chapter Four

Rain poured all over town from morning until evening on Memorial Day in a typical St. Louis spring burst. No one walked down Grace's driveway to admire the freshly planted garden because they all dashed inside the front door dripping wet as if they'd stepped out of a shower, not as if they were stepping into one. They left their shoes piled on towels in the hallway, and Grace carted wet jackets and umbrellas to the bathroom.

Ten guests crowded the small front room by the time Grace opened the door for the guest of honor and her mother. Audrey and Beth sat in one love seat and two of Trenna's school friends had the other. Faye and Chanel were sitting in folding chairs behind. And several others stood talking in the doorframe between the kitchen and living room.

Trenna wore a floral print dress and poppy-colored hat as if the garden party were going forward as planned. She hugged Grace, waved a hello over her shoulder to her friends in the room and then leaned in to whisper in Grace's ear, "She won't let up over the centerpieces."

She—Roberta—crossed over the threshold behind Trenna and stood in place, not quite far enough in the room to allow the door to close behind her, as if she feared joining the party.

Her plastic grin betrayed her impressions of the guests or the house—or both. Trenna pulled her mom toward the shoe pile and slipped off her own red sandals while Grace closed the door.

Grace gulped. "Roberta, Trenna, come sit here."

She guided Roberta, who hadn't removed her black sling backs, to a striped armchair by the fireplace, and Trenna followed in her bare, damp feet.

The women squashed in her tiny kitchen and the cramped front room with Chinet balanced on their laps felt informal—Roberta may even call it tacky—but her only other choice would have been to cancel the shower completely. With the planned buffet salad supper in the yard moved into this tighter setting, her humble position showed. At work she had all the resources to dote on Roberta, but here, with the rain trapping them into her tiny rented bungalow, she couldn't even pretend.

Grace slipped away from her guests into the bathroom, stepping over trench coats to the blue toilet seat. She wanted a private spot to pull herself together, but the cramped bathroom with its mismatched fixtures only increased the reality. Colorful umbrella tents popped out of the tub. Weather and hygiene had to be the greatest equalizers of humanity.

"Get a grip," she told herself. How could her need for approval not look silly? No one—not really even Roberta—had treated her with any less respect than usual. She checked the mirror, wiped the mascara from under her eyes, and returned to the party with a renewed sense of humor and clearer sense of self.

"We were married on a Thursday and flew to Atlanta that very night," Beth said in a voice loud enough to carry out into the hallway as Grace opened the bathroom door.

"Why didn't you just get a room here and go the next day?" said the friend in a lime green sweater.

"I wanted to get to Florida and wake up together the next day—New Year's Day—in the cottage we rented," Beth answered, glad to have an audience listening to her. "Never mind that we would have gotten there at 2 a.m. We stopped in Atlanta with a delayed connecting flight. A winter storm somewhere. Then John got sick."

"Oh, I can see where this is going . . ." Faye said behind her hand to Grace who stood in the doorway.

"Beth's wedding night horror story?" Grace wondered under her breath. Faye nodded.

"I spent the rest of the night reading a magazine while he kept running to the bathroom," Beth continued, louder and shriller than before. "I felt fine and never got it, but he was panicked that he would have to get on a flight feeling like that."

A few girls in the corner broke into a story about their own sicknesses on airplanes. But Beth had the rest of their attention.

"They canceled the flight, anyway—on our wedding night. We took a shuttle to a hotel across from the airport. John was still sick the next day, so we turned around and headed back home on the afternoon flight."

"So he flew sick, after all?" the lime green girl asked, pressing for the end.

"Well, he wasn't vomiting, he just felt gross," Beth explained. She saw she'd lost interest without a horrific punch line and tried to rescue the story, "But we've still never been to Florida. I pulled out the brochure six months ago for our next wedding anniversary. Thought maybe we'd go to the cottage that we paid for but never used. It's been demolished for a planned community."

"I'm glad we're not leaving for New York the same day," Trenna said. "How miserable if we got sick."

"Being stranded was probably worse," Beth said, not willing to relinquish the spotlight before she made her point. "I had all these expectations. Unfulfilled expectations. And that took longer to get over than the sickness."

They opened gifts, and Grace only cringed a little when Beth added the bows to a paper plate until it was decorated like a bride's bouquet. This looked a lot more like the bridal showers she remembered her mom hosting than she imagined that Trenna and Roberta attended in their social circles. Maybe the rain had broken the ice of false formality, but nearly every woman there, some of whom she least anticipated to participate, contributed additional pieces to the bride's gift-wrapped ensemble—a string of curling ribbon pearls around her wrist, a choker of pink ribbon on her neck, and a fist-sized faux diamond made from the plastic packaging from the iron that Faye had given her. Roberta, most unexpected of all, slipped on the final touch—bunches of smoothed purple tissue paper that she tucked into Trenna's belted dress as if it were a train. Trenna even took her walk down the hallway "aisle" for the digital cameras.

Only Sylvia, who had arrived late during the gift giving from the store's early holiday close, didn't join the paparazzi session. She sat stiffly in a folding chair pressed tight against the wall and far from conversation. But when Chanel fell back from the pictures to chat with Roberta, Sylvia left her position and joined their group. Sylvia's voice dripped with a sales person's affectation toward the mother of the bride.

"You look beautiful in those pants, Roberta," she cooed. "So springy to wear white pants with a black jacket. So crisp. What did you wear to the other shower at the club?"

Grace turned toward Faye, who'd also overheard from where she stood poised, and they smiled grimly. Sylvia had changed her tactics and wasn't playing to win Grace's good favor anymore but was going right to the customers themselves.

Faye intervened with a compliment of her own. "Sylvia, I'm sure I didn't see that scarf look better on anyone in the store than you. It must be your red hair. Can you come into the guest bedroom and show me how you tie it up like that?"

Roberta actually looked relieved for the escape. When Chanel and Sylvia and Faye left her, she sat back down in her striped zone and closed her eyes with a sigh. Trenna returned to strip off the gift wrap while the other guests took plates and glasses to the kitchen.

"You can't let them dress you for the actual day," Grace said, grateful for a little down time as hostess.

"Never," Trenna said. "But would you?"

"Me? I thought that was the mother of the bride's job."

"Oh, I'll be there," Roberta said, with her eyes still closed.

"But I want you, too," Trenna told her. "Be my maid of honor?"

"Me? Really?" Grace said. "I don't know what one would even do."

"Mostly keep me calm the next few weeks, make sure I look irresistible for Max, and then walk ahead of me down the aisle."

"It's so soon, but of course, yes. What do I wear?"

"Really, Grace," Roberta eyes were open now. "This is not about you."

Grace slipped back in the kitchen chair, hands on the edges, bracing for more assaults. Roberta wasn't even paying attention, more interested in the cake Audrey was cutting.

Trenna grabbed hold of Grace's hand. "She says that, but then it feels like it's all about her."

"How do you cope?"

"Like any bride does. Counting the hours till I'm free."

Grace laughed. The anticipation on Trenna's face shined with hope, but from the impressions Grace had and the planned living arrangements in the carriage house, that freedom from Roberta's ever-present meddling only meant Trenna wouldn't have to hear it every hour of the day.

****

Even though Grace stood beside the bride in nearly every decision-making moment during the weeks after the shower, she'd still not met Max. One week before the big day he completed work in Kansas City and joined Trenna in St. Louis. He even moved into the newly renovated carriage house—alone.

Wedding week for the couple was still a busy workweek for Grace, so she had to bow out of the remaining pre-wedding events in favor of the rehearsal dinner and the main event the following day.

"Chanel's here," Sylvia called to Grace who was pulling the cast-off clothes from the hooks in the dressing room. "Now you can get ready."

Good, no big drama from Sylvia before she left. Grace arranged the clothes into their spots on the sale racks.

"Flowers are blooming," Chanel said as she came into the store.

"Don't you love spring? Those overflowing pots of ivy geraniums would look great on my porch. Should we steal them from the south entrance or the west?"

"Not the geraniums, Grace—the flowers on Lily's plant."

"Really?" Grace and Sylvia, ironically, answered together like gleeful little girls who'd been offered a ride on a Ferris wheel. They rushed out of the store and around the corner to look in the front window where they saw a small bud opened slightly along the front of the hibiscus. Toward the back and on the left side one big red blossom formed a starburst bloom.

"We did it," Sylvia said.

"Yes, *we* did, didn't we?" Grace said, puzzled with Sylvia's rebounding interest in the plant.

"I'll record it in the journal since you have to go," Sylvia said. Grace looked at her watch. Ten minutes to change. Ten minutes to get there.

She scooted into the back restroom and pulled on the print skirt and blue top—Trenna had converted her to color—that she bought earlier at Ann Taylor. They held it for her until that morning when she also picked up the guest book from the luggage and leather goods store next door. She tried to hide the Ann Taylor bag under the other one, but in her rush to the backroom, she ran straight into Sylvia, dropped the book, and revealed the traitorous merchandise.

"Oh, I love Ann Taylor, too. We won't tell anyone, will we?" Sylvia said.

Grace retouched her makeup in the mirror. Today she would get the details right—look good, arrive on time, and mingle comfortably. If she could find that comfort level tonight, tomorrow would be a lot less intimidating with even more guests. She assessed herself in the mirror with a minute to spare and mentally checked off appearance and promptness.

Since she'd been to the Foster's before, she could now follow the curves and hills of Litzinger Road without getting lost. Right after the bridal shower, Trenna had invited her to assemble invitations at her parent's home. Then she'd driven down two long but wrong driveways before she found the right address posted on a brick entrance leading to the Foster's circle driveway. Two weeks later, the bridal photographer shot pictures in Roberta's garden—the wedding location. Trenna invited Grace to style her gown during the shoot. Roberta just fawned over the flowers like *they* were the babies who'd grown up and were leaving home—strange, given Roberta's controlling hand in Trenna's life.

Grace drove into that same circle drive now and admired the colorful display of spring blooms that lead to the solid but weathered, sprawling stone house. Over-control or not, she envied this house and knew that Roberta's influence, in addition to a whole lot of money, created its elegance.

She stopped her car behind a more expensive one and a uniformed young man came toward her. A valet service? Really?

Grace grabbed the gum wrappers and sticky notes off the center console and stuffed them in her purse and stashed an empty water bottle under the seat. She hesitated to exit her car, looking one last time behind her at the crumbs that littered the seat cushions before she handed her keys reluctantly to the dark-haired college boy.

""Have a good evening," he said to her.

"You, too." That sounded dumb. A good evening parking cars?

The arriving guests had already grouped up or coupled off on their way toward the back patio. Heat rose from her chest to her neck, a blush of embarrassment creeping upward to her face. Nausea welled in her stomach, but she felt it in her head. Breathe deeply. Look like you belong. Focus on someone you know. Walk toward a place you are comfortable.

Grace coached herself all the way to the front door, where she hoped to slip inside and escape to a powder room she knew was right past the entrance. She straightened her shoulders as if she opened stranger's doors every day, pretended she was on assignment from the mother of the bride, and looked toward both sides of the sculpted evergreens that flanked the heavy arched wood doors. The knob turned in her hand. Inside, the empty air-conditioned hallway cooled her anxiety as she relaxed against the back of the door for a minute, allowing her pinched toes the chance to restore themselves in the cushiness of the rug.

"I know you."

Startled by someone catching her, she gasped in too much air and coughed. She turned toward the voice in the front room.

"Are you okay?" A man with dark brown hair, about her age, sank into the cushions of the yellow couch as deeply as his familiar voice sank into her. Although he looked like someone she should know, she couldn't place him or his voice. He stood—tall, even for her—and answered the confused look on her face.

"We shared your soup a few months ago at the mall."

She pursed her lips, concentrating on making the connection. Soup. Ah, falling backward with the soup. The man who'd caught her. The heat in her face returned.

"I'm Max," he said, holding out his hand.

"Max," she squeaked, but her voice didn't even make any discernible noise. Grace stepped off the rug onto the wood floor to steady herself on a hard surface but sidestepped his extended hand in the process. Gone went any charm she'd shown at that accidental encounter and all the poise she hoped to have for this first introduction with Trenna's fiancé. Her face had to be as red as her shoes.

He lowered his hand. "Are you Grace?"

"Apparently today I'm not."

He laughed. The spontaneity of her remark initiated a calm reassurance that she could be herself, even in this awkward moment. She laughed, too, and extended her hand to him.

"Max. It's nice to know you finally. I *am* Grace, but it seems that I've lost that both times we've met."

The sound of feet on the stairs and Trenna's voice moved Grace involuntarily back a foot or two. "Max and Grace. You've already met. You're both ahead of me." She hopped down the stairs and grabbed the top of each of their arms. "When did you get here? Did you get a nametag? I know it's like the first day of school, but we're all going to have to wear one. Mom says."

"Hi." Max leaned over and kissed Trenna. "I think they're laid out on the table by the garden gate. Do you want me to get yours, too?" He turned to Grace.

She nodded, hoping her cheeks had cooled. "Sure."

Trenna watched him walk out the patio doors, and when they slid shut behind him, she said, "Isn't he hot? Is he what you expected?"

"No, not what I expected," Grace gulped.

"Let's go meet my dad." Trenna grabbed Grace and pulled her through the kitchen to a man with his right hand in an ice bucket and his left reaching to sample the shrimp from the caterer's tray.

He nodded an apology toward his hand. "I thought I'd help out the kitchen crew, but I burned it just opening the oven."

Roberta motioned to Trenna and Grace from outside, where a crowd of friends and family mingled on the patio. A man and woman walked on the lawn from the carriage house and stopped to chat with Max at the table with the nametags.

Trenna pulled Grace over to get a nametag and punched Max playfully on the upper arm and introduced Grace to the couple. "This is Grace, my maid of honor; she's also my boss."

The woman stretched her hand out first, without reservation, "Michelle Oliver," She said and then motioned to the man, "and my husband."

"David," he said as he shook her hand.

After some small talk, the bride and groom and parents lapsed into their own world, talking about people she didn't know. The couple and parents chatted, and Grace backed away from the conversation without another one to enter. A lot of painted smiles and forced laughter came from amongst the other gathering groups. Apparently she wasn't alone in the social awkwardness.

She approached an older teen ladling dip on her plate. "Hi, I'm Grace. And I'm trying to introduce myself to as many people as I can before we eat. What's your name?"

The girl turned, pulling her eyebrows into a confused expression. "Elyse."

"How do you know the bride or the groom?" Grace asked.

"I'm Trenna's cousin," she said and shoved a chip in her mouth.

Over Elyse's shoulder, Max and Trenna circulated among their friends and family. He stood almost a foot taller than Trenna but her head tucked right under his arm in a protective embrace. He welcomed the guests into their circle with his ever-present outstretched hand, but his soft tone of voice and more passive conversation hinted that he reserved his true nature for less public places. She admired that confident approach, as if he didn't have to prove himself to them.

At dinner Grace sat with three bridesmaids—two with dates and the other engaged to the best man—and Trenna's younger brother, Ryan, and another cousin. All of them, except the best man, were at least a few years younger than her. The youngest ones were the loudest, so she felt like she was sitting at the kid's table.

After dinner Roberta directed them all in their assignments for the next day as if she was directing traffic, not people.

"Come, come," she waved to Grace.

Grace hobbled to her place on the lawn as quickly as she could in heels but apparently not fast enough. Roberta grabbed her arm and pulled her into place beside Trenna about a foot away from the fishpond, where the ceremony would be. Grace's heel struck a tree root, and she wobbled toward the edge. Max lunged forward and pulled her back against his chest. They'd been here before.

"Maybe we should rethink the location, Roberta," he said. She felt the warmth of his breath on her ear. Flushed, being so close to him yet again, but this time with Trenna right there, she edged into her place.

"Or we could just be more careful," Roberta said directly at Grace, and pulled Trenna and Max aside to talk with the minister. She inched behind the tall hedges until she was hidden and then snuck away on the fine-mulched bark down the garden path.

Roberta's untamed tongue wasn't the only thing she wanted to escape but also the tingle she felt from this third physical encounter with Max. The natural attraction she had to him on their first meeting complicated what she felt now as she tried to interact with him as Trenna's fiancé. The physical distance from Roberta and Max cooled her irritation and her guilt.

About four yards behind the hedge, Grace stood beneath a canopy of wisteria. Her mother had grown wisteria in their backyard, climbing along the outside of a gazebo rather than a wrought iron archway. Roberta's version seemed more peaceful than the suburban attempt at tranquility alongside the family trampoline. She stepped through that archway and into the grassy enclosure and found Max's mom on a bench by herself.

Grace stepped back. "I'm sorry to interrupt. I'll find another place."

"I didn't come here to be alone, just to rest my feet. I couldn't take off my shoes in front of everyone out there, could I?" Michelle said.

"Well then, can I do the same?" She slipped off her red heels and walked across the grass before Michelle could even answer.

"Of course. Nice, huh? Grass is one of life's luxuries."

"For real?" Grace asked. "There are all these beautiful, intricate and glorious flowers, and you think grass is a luxury?"

"Well, not so much a luxury as a comfort—like nature's outdoor carpet. Max adored the grass when he was little; we stayed in the grass for hours, just the two of us for the first few years of life."

"That sounds like the glory of motherhood, more than the glory of grass."

"Maybe so."

"So, what's it like to see your first born getting married?"

"He's my first born, but not the first one married. We have a younger daughter who was married last summer."

"Were you as uptight about it as Roberta?" Grace said but quickly apologized. "That's pretty rude. I've just left her fawning and need a break so I didn't say something wrong. Looks like I did anyway."

"It's okay. But, yes, the first wedding stressed me. I wouldn't necessarily call Roberta uptight. Overly aware may be more like it. I reached a point in parenting when I had to close my eyes so I could allow my children to choose without me looking on."

"Well, I hope I can be like you and not stifle my daughter," Grace said. "If I ever have one."

"We can hope, Grace. It's Grace, right?" Michelle questioned. "We all love according to the circumstances we've been given."

Grace twirled a piece of grass between her fingers. Then she looked up and said, "Circumstances we've been given? So we just accept what comes and love that. If we don't accept it in the way it's offered, then what?"

"Are we still talking about mother love or something else?"

"I don't know." Grace peeled the grass in half and flipped one to the side and began twisting the thinner half. The pitch of emotion burned her throat. "Excuse me. I need to see about something."

In the gathering dark shadow of the hedge Grace tried to suppress the tears. She wanted to rejoice with the bride, but the conversation with Michelle reintroduced all her fears that she had lost her chance for her own family. The coincidental meeting of Max hadn't helped either. She walked slowly back to the party from the pathway, willing her mouth to turn up and her eyes to reflect a little cheer.

Grace emerged into the open garden with only a trace of a tear streak on each side of her cheek, but no one noticed. The older Fosters, Roberta and Alan, held court in the middle of a circle of laughter on the lawn. The caterers cleared away the party leftovers. The younger crowd had stripped off their shoes and socks, and two of the guys threw one girl's sandal back and forth while she ran screaming between them.

Grace skirted the activity and veered toward the house for a trip to the powder room before she left. She opened the French doors off the patio right on the handholding couple.

"Grace," Trenna said. "Mom's called us all together for a last minute speech. We were just coming out."

"I thought I'd go . . ." Grace pointed to the powder room but really meant something else.

Trenna dropped Max's hand and said to him, "I'll meet you there."

"Be right back," Grace said over her shoulder and stepped inside. After pulling herself together, she wiped at the mascara marks under her lashes and took a few calming breaths. When she opened the door, Trenna stood right in front of it holding a large envelope and a shopping bag.

"Here's the list of things to do tomorrow morning." Trenna pointed to the instructions on the front of the envelope. "It looks like Mom's added something to the list, too. Hope it's not too much to get done before one. The photograph for the front of the book is inside. Did you pick it up today?"

The book! Grace sucked in her breath and closed her eyes.

"How does the embossing look?" Trenna asked with concern.

"The embossing is nice, but I left it at the store, right on the back room table, in my rush to get here."

"Well, maybe you can just stop by in the morning on the

way over here. Or maybe someone can bring it over and you can finish it up once you get here."

The worry brewed in Trenna's crinkled forehead. Loyalty to her friend silenced Grace's internal boxing match. "I'll go now. I'll just leave now and go get it."

She embraced Trenna, hoping to take back the distress she hadn't intended to pass off on to the bride. The hug soothed Trenna, and Grace sent her back to the gleeful wedding party.

On the way back to The Plaza, a luxury sedan crawled along the twisty road in front of her. The sedan turned at the four-way stop, and Grace shot forward, keeping her eyes open for police traps on the side streets. Once in the parking lot, medians of manicured bushes and just a few cars broke the pattern across a field of empty lines. Grace parked beneath the light closest to the building's east side. It was just a few minutes after ten, an hour after closing.

The restaurants on the south end served up enough noise in the summer night to indicate that the mall doors might still be unlocked. Security lights shined on the glass entrance, but the hallways inside were dark except for the emergency lights. She pulled the handle. Locked. Light filtered from the men's clothing store across the atrium, but they would never hear her knock. She retreated toward the circle of light surrounding her car. The door clattered behind her, and three women exited the building.

"Hold it for me," she yelled, running back to the door, surprised that her feet reacted quicker than her words.

Grace passed the concierge desk, skipped two steps at a time up the stopped escalator and rounded the glass balcony of the second floor to the gates of Honeybee. At the gate, she opened her clutch purse and felt around for the plastic card that opened the gates. Her wallet. Lipstick. Breath mints. Keys. She pulled out her keys—her car and house keys—but in the dim of the hallway, she couldn't find the key card there.

Her bag! Her black leather bag was sitting on the top of the mini-fridge in the backroom, right next to her makeup case and the guest book. She swallowed back the acid in her throat, grabbed the metal gate and shook it.

Her anger confused her, but the emotion swelled harder against her chest. She caught her reflection in the glass of the front window and let her cheek press against the gate. The cool relieved the heat on her face.

A pinpoint spot in the window cast a glow on Lilly's plant. "Lilly, you said I could do it, but I can't. Sure the plant's blooming. But I'm a mess. And my head hurts."

She fished a used tissue out of her party purse and blew.

"Nothing feels like it should. I should be giddy for her. But I'm jealous. Yes—jealous. That sounds selfish doesn't it? It does. But how do I change that?"

****

Grace awoke at 6:30 on Saturday morning with cloudy eyes and a stiff neck. She fell in and out of sleep for another fifteen minutes and then rolled over on her side to stare out the window. Good weather. She rolled over and looked in the full-length mirror. Ugh. She flopped back again, considering how she could match her mood to the weather outside.

Grace intended to leave the house wearing a genuine smile like a new dress to the wedding. That was her top emotional priority, a gift to Trenna and herself. Her actual to do list would lead her to that happy place even if her feelings inside couldn't follow yet. After a few minutes of yawning and deep sighs, she found the shopping bag and envelope she brought home from the rehearsal dinner.

Still in her pajamas, she opened it all on her bed. She unwrapped the cake knife and server from their box and cut a thick purple ribbon from the spool in the bag. She brought the ends together and tied a flouncy bow on the handle of each and slipped them back into their boxes.

In the envelope she found the reservation for the Chase Park Plaza Hotel and the reservation for the flights to and from New York, where Trenna and Max would spend their honeymoon. She made a little travel folder for these and other papers she'd collected of fun things to do and great places to eat in New York.

Finally, she pulled the photograph of Trenna and Max from the envelope. Playful informality replaced the dated formality of the old engagement photographs she'd seen of her parent's friends.

Even though she'd grown to know Trenna well in the past few months, she didn't know the couple together. Trenna had talked endlessly about Max, but Grace didn't get to see the dynamics of their relationship, only hear about them second hand.

This photograph captured their authentic feelings toward each other. Trenna sat on a park bench with her shoulders and profile turned toward the back of the bench while Max leaned over her left shoulder as if he had come up behind her by surprise. The delight in both of their eyes directed itself right back to each other, not at some perceived audience behind the camera. Max's hand rested on Trenna's right shoulder, and she held it with both of her hands. Their hold communicated their surety in each other's love. Marriage would only bind them stronger in the years to come.

She trimmed the photograph for the cover of the guest book and slipped it back in the envelope. She would go back to Honeybee to pick up her makeup bag, the guest book, and her keys and then complete the last item on her list: Pick up the groom's ring from Bernhardt Jewelers in Ladue Marketplace. Beside this task, scribbled in a different ink color and handwriting, was this qualifier, presumably from Roberta—pick up TWO packages. Maybe a surprise bridal gift?

Grace had a special piece of jewelry to wear, too. She opened the top drawer of her bedroom dresser to look for it. Under the cast-off slips and tights and next to her hair clips, she kept several jewelry boxes of various colors. A burgundy cardboard one held a red leather box inside with a heart-shaped necklace that she'd received at her baptism.

A black velvet box hid away the engagement ring from Jeff. "Keep it; if you ever change your mind," he had said the last time she saw him—almost two years now. This one she shoved further to the back without allowing her heart to be stirred like it had been the night before.

Under a stack of Honeybee black hosiery in varying levels of opaqueness, she found the one she wanted. She scooped the royal blue velvet one into her own travel bag to take with her to the wedding.

Grace showered and fixed her hair, and this time her only grimace in the mirror came from her embarrassment of going into work without any concealer for her dark circles or mascara on her light eyelashes. When she left her house for those last errands, she was finally not feeling false.

A beehive of activity met Grace at the Foster's house a few minutes before one. The queen bee herself was nowhere to be seen, but numerous others carried out her demands. Doors stood open everywhere, letting in men carrying coolers from the catering truck and flies that someone would have to swat in the hours ahead. Decorators moved tables and chairs between the rooms inside and the canopy outside, and floral specialists beautified an already decadent landscape with more flowers.

The bustle of movement pushed her toward the entrance of the gardens, between the carriage house and the main house. The gate stood open for the scurrying workers who skirted around a ribbon-and-post aisle without actually stepping in its wide path. It flowed in a stream through rows of white chairs, waiting for the moment of drama and perfection. She ached to walk down that path to the fountain at the end.

Trenna slipped out of the carriage house with her back to Grace and gently shut the door behind her.

"Is that legal?" Grace asked.

Trenna jumped and screamed. Then she saw Grace, giggled, and put her finger over her lips.

"Feeling guilty are you?" Grace said.

"I set the rules for my wedding," she said.

"That's what you think," Grace laughed and flicked her wrist to point out the scurrying workers. "Just don't let the queen know where you've been."

The pair climbed to Trenna's suite of rooms by way of the kitchen stairs, bypassing any questions along the way. No one sacrificed space in the sprawling house.

Grace expected an overly decorated escape but found a dated décor in the suite that was really just two bedrooms connected by a bath, one for hanging out and the other one for sleeping.

Trenna's high school and college diplomas hung over the desk, and trophies and awards lined the matching oak book shelves beside the paperbacks and college textbooks. Two patterned loveseats faced each other in the middle of the room.

"Is it a shrine to your teen years?" Grace asked.

"More like a catchall for the last fifteen," Trenna flopped onto the love seat. "Catching all the stuff I've collected since my purple pony room. There wasn't any need to pack it up when I moved away to college, so I never really moved out. And when college was over, well . . ."

"I'm not surprised you've been hiding out in the carriage house."

"Yeah, Max's got it all set. It feels more like me than any place I've ever lived. Even if it's just next door, I can't wait."

"You don't have to wait." Grace glanced at the clock. "Well, I guess, one hour and 39 minutes. But we're not waiting; we're beautifying. "

Then she looked at Trenna's hair—swept into a loose updo—and her smooth olive skin and green eyes, which looked like they would never even need makeup.

"*I'm* beautifying, and you're dressing," Grace corrected herself and picked up her makeup bag.

Trenna didn't say anything or even get up. She sat in the silence of the room looking at her hands. She clasped her hands and rubbed her thumb on the inside of her palm to her engagement ring and back. Grace paused on her way to the bathroom.

"I'm scared," Trenna admitted without looking up.

Grace returned and sat down so Trenna would know she'd been heard. She didn't have words, so she waited. Often when

Grace took her place on the pink stool, Lilly only spoke a few wise words alongside a few carefully placed questions. While the silence felt familiar, the activity of the approaching wedding seemed far removed from those days with Lilly.

"They say that's natural," Grace finally said.

"Oh, it's not the wedding. Or even the honeymoon or the first few months. But what about in six months? Or a year? What if I find out he's as normal as every other guy? Or worse, what if he finds out I'm not perfect, either? I just can't come back here." She splayed her arms open and took in the whole room, but Grace understood that she meant more.

She wanted to ask Trenna about the last line. "Is he your way out of here? Your way to get free?" Or she wanted to say something funny like, "You've known him a long time, and you haven't found anything wrong, yet?"

But she didn't.

Instead, she said, "It won't be long, and you'll discover he *is* normal. And he will discover you are, too. That's marriage— it's for regular people, not just princes and princesses in a fairy-tale romance. It's a commitment to work on our weaknesses together."

Trenna turned her head. Her eyes were wet with tears. "How do you know that?"

"Do you mean, how do *I* know that? Someone who is highly experienced in the marriage business? Or do you mean how do I know that it's true?"

"Either one."

"My parents, I guess, for both. They're as regular as anyone I know, and they're doing it."

"But how?"

Grace considered the question for a minute. "They didn't pretend with each other or with us. They openly admitted their mistakes. And I saw them grow closer as they did."

"I don't feel like I can make mistakes here." Trenna threw her hands up to take in the whole room. "Maybe it is more that my mom prevents me from failure." Grace stood up and went to the bathroom to find a box of tissues. She grabbed a metal-clad box and held it out to Trenna, who took one, blew her nose, and wiped her eyes.

"Now I'm scared to fail with Max."

Grace didn't speak. She just reached out and held out tissues—one at a time—to Trenna while she sobbed. Grace could here the buzz out the window and occasional shouts from the hallway. The wedding drew closer, but the two of them stood still as if Trenna wasn't the bride upstairs getting ready. Really, only a few minutes passed before Trenna wiped her eyes and her nose.

"Are you scared by how Max might see you?"

"Right now I am." Trenna wiped a finger under one eye. "You didn't mean that, did you? No, you meant how he sees me inside. I'm not scared of that. Even if I'm at fault, he forgives; he moves on."

"Then maybe Max is exactly what you need to see beyond your mother's gaze."

"You're right."

"No, you are. I just asked the question."

"If that is right, how do I change it? In here? In my head?"

"Just believe that he's looking at you through his eyes. Now I have one more question. Are you ready to marry him?" Grace asked.

"Absolutely." Trenna looked at the clock behind her. "I don't know how my mom left us alone long enough to get that out. Thanks for being here."

Knowing the envy she felt the day before, Grace took a deep breath before she spoke. "You're welcome, but you're going to still need my help, you know."

Grace pulled Trenna up, and steered her to the bathroom, where they both stood in front of the mirror and laughed at their rumpled reflection.

"We both need some help," Grace said.

"We'll get there."

They stood side-by-side at those double sinks, washing their faces, reapplying makeup, and trading tips for a tear-free day until Roberta burst into the room with the floral box holding the bouquet. She handed it to Grace and hurried Trenna to her room to dress. She came through the bathroom a moment later alone, "Do you have the pearls?"

Grace handed her the packages she'd picked up from Bernhard's.

"Get Faye—she's downstairs in the kitchen—while I retouch Trenna's hair. She can make the gown lay right."

She followed Roberta's directions and delivered Faye right to the door of the bride's bedroom. Grace stepped in with her, but Trenna was lost in a cloud of white slips and ribbons. Back in the sitting room on the opposite side of the bathroom, she dressed herself. After pulling the zipper in place on the purple satin dress, she perched on the love seat and dug in her bag for her shoes. Her hand brushed against the velvet and metal of the jewelry box.

With the box in one hand, she opened the lid with the other. A folded pink paper fell on the floor and beneath it were three strands of pearls wrapped into a bracelet and fastened with a larger pearl set in a gold clasp.

The first time she read this note was when she unpacked her suitcase during her first week in St. Louis and found the blue velvet box in her clothes. In a whisper to herself, she now reread the cursive handwriting in blue ink on the pink-lined paper.

I'd planned to give this to you when you married, when grandma gave them to me. But you need their beauty now to remind you of yours. I love you, Mom

No sound came from the bride's bedroom beyond, but music played outside the window. She peeked out, saw many guests seated, and checked the clock. She opened the floral box and lifted out the bouquet. Five purple hibiscus flowers surrounded a tight collection of pink peonies. So this was the outcome of the floral debates. She slipped the pearl bracelet from her mother on her left wrist and the corsage on her right and carried the bouquet to the bride's room.

Trenna stood alone in her wedding dress, her head bowed and her hair falling over her cheek. The pearl-topped gown shaped Trenna's silhouette against the sunny window on the opposite side and flowed into the floor to an indistinguishable end. Trenna opened her eyes.

"I asked my parents to wait outside. But I'm ready now."

Grace handed her the bouquet with her left hand. Trenna noticed the bracelet and pointed to the nightstand.

"Oh, wait. There, that gray box. Open it for me."

Inside was a set of pearl earrings. Each had three pearls—the first small, the second medium, and the third large—as if they were falling in bigger drops from the ear. Grace held one up and held it toward Trenna.

Trenna shook her head. "For you. For today and whenever."

Grace reached out and squeezed Trenna's hand. "Thank you."

After Grace put on the earrings, she opened the door and then gathered the train up in her arms. Outside the door, Roberta, Alan, and the bridesmaids waited along the hall toward the front stairs. Trenna stepped forward with Grace following behind, and they descended the stairs.

Chapter Five

While Trenna and Max honeymooned in New York City, Grace traveled north to Minnesota for a family reunion by the lake. Her well-meaning aunts inundated her with questions and concern about her love life, but the trip rooted her again in the community of relatives where she always belonged. Her mom invited her to make strawberry freezer jam in the day, and her brother and sister traded childhood stories with her in lawn chairs by the fire at night.

"How's that plant? The hibiscus." Her mom turned the water on a sink full of strawberries. "Did you find it a home?"

"I took it to work."

"Who did you give it to?"

"I didn't give it away. It's the centerpiece of our front window."

"Really? Don't you trust yourself?"

"It feels right to do it together, to involve the women in a project together."

After a week of catching up with family, Grace appreciated returning to St. Louis and the quiet of the store where she found Lilly's plant blooming. Good, they hadn't forgot it.

"Everyone adhered to the schedule," Sylvia said to Grace immediately. "I reminded them."

There was no way they could have forgotten the plant with her reminders.

"Lilly's plant appears to like the attention." Grace said and turned to add a navy silk shorts-and-sweater set to the rack of spring items. After she hung the short-sleeved sweaters, she faced Sylvia with direct eye contact.

"I appreciate your efforts. However, it's not really part of the staff's job responsibilities to take care of the plant. It's great if they want to help and sign up to do something. But let's be careful how we ask or remind them. We don't want to turn this into a chore or duty, but something they want to do."

Sylvia's smile remained on her face but the edges of her mouth hardened their lines until her smile became a smirk and her green eyes receded into a dull stare. She thrust the hangers toward Grace and left the store.

"Where's she off to?" Beth said, passing Sylvia as she came in.

"I don't know."

Sylvia's hot-then-cold approach to her relationship with Grace and Lilly's plant flip-flopped for the rest of the summer. Likewise, rotating employee vacations came and went in the heat. No one seemed regular nor did any schedule stay routine.

Through it all, Grace stayed steady. She tended the store, Lilly's plant, and her garden without the emotional upheaval of the first six months of the year.

Weeding her garden on humid summer nights was a cathartic release. Her work yielded basil for pesto more than once a week, interspersed with dinners of cucumber sandwiches on multi-grain bread. Her zucchini plant didn't survive, but her tomatoes were turning from green to red. And she brought bowlfuls of cherry tomatoes to work.

Lilly's plant bloomed multiple times in these months and added new leaf and stem growth. Grace took over as the main caretaker for feeding and watering, both of which would need to be scaled back in the fall to give the plant a break for the winter.

During this transition she surrounded the plant with focused attention so she could preserve the spring and summer growth in a cutting. She researched the process and considered bringing Lilly's plant home to remove the cutting, but Chanel and Faye said that even though the plant seemed strong, the trauma of the cutting and the move might bring too much shock.

So on a Saturday in late August after Sylvia left work, she and Chanel closed the store and then lifted the awkward pot off its stool and carried it back to the light of the backroom fluorescents.

"We'd better cover the table, to keep all the dirt contained. Want to set it on the floor while I get some packing paper?" Chanel said.

They placed it on the floor next to a box of UPS labels. Grace reached for the instructions she'd printed to guide her through the process while Chanel spread three or four sheets of tan packing paper over the break table. They bent down together and lifted the plant, which was more awkward than heavy, on top of the packing paper.

"The mess can be cleaned up, but I'm worried I'm going to ruin the plant. Well that—and that the cuttings won't even take root," Grace said, wiping her hands and glancing through the instruction sheet again. "These are just book learning; we actually have to do it. I wish Lilly was here."

"We could always call her. Don't you talk to her on the phone?"

"She called me the week they got to Florida. But we haven't talked since then. I could call, but . . . I know it wouldn't be the same."

Grace reached into the paper bag of supplies she brought from home, remembering the week when Lilly's daughter had come to pack. They had still talked, but the relationship had changed. She held up three knives—a paring knife, a steak knife, and a camping knife.

"So which one should we use?" she asked.

"The sharpest one!" Chanel laughed.

"That would be the paring knife, but I think it's too small to cut into this," Grace said and set down the paring knife and the steak knife, choosing the camping knife. "I found this one in my garage. I cleaned it up, but I'm not sure how sharp it is. But let's try it.

"There are a couple pots in that bag," she directed Chanel. "Will you find those and the rooting hormone? And we'll need to water the mixture to make sure it is moist and put some of that rooting hormone in a smaller container."

Grace looked around the cramped room. "Maybe those Styrofoam cups over there."

While Chanel searched for the supplies, Grace looked over the plant for new healthy green shoots that were about six inches long. She found some at the top and decided to take a few from the front and a couple from the back. She leaned over, held the bottom of the piece she wanted to cut and gently slipped the knife in to make an angled cut.

Something crashed in the front of the store, and the noise jolted her right hand. She missed the stem of the plant and cut into the flesh of her thumb. Blood oozed immediately from the wound.

"What was that?" Grace said, grabbing one of the moistened paper towels Chanel had laid on the packing paper for the cuttings.

"Should I help you or check it out?" Chanel hesitated. Grace sat down on a sturdy box and wrapped the paper towel tightly around her finger.

Grace waved her to the front. "Just go. I'll be fine."

"Hello," Chanel called ahead of her steps.

"It's me," Sylvia yelled from the front of the store.

Grace dropped her head onto her knees and pressed the towel against the pain. She wasn't sure if she was relieved that it was just Sylvia or irritated that she'd have to deal with her again that night. She tightened her jaw, rubbed her throbbing thumb, and listened for some indication of the damage that had been done out front.

In a few minutes Sylvia strolled into the tight space with a smile and an easy-going saunter as if she'd just left for the day. Chanel followed behind her with a distraught expression. Sylvia grasped Grace's injured hand and thrust it above her head.

"Hold it there," she said.

Grace rested her hand on the top of her head, lifted her brows, and said to her, "So? What happened?"

"Oh never mind. We got it all cleaned up. What about you?"

Grace raised herself from the box to stand four or five inches taller than Sylvia. "What happened?" she demanded.

"Now Grace, check your emotions," she said in a calculated, unemotional tone. "You're just hurt. Don't say something rash."

"This is not about me!" Grace burst forth.

"It most certainly is. You've brought a sharp knife to work. You've cut yourself, and now you're reacting to the pain. I simply knocked down the metal sale sign when I came back for my bag."

She turned from Grace and went into the bathroom without shutting the door. Grace motioned with her wounded hand to Chanel and mouthed in an angry whisper, "What was that?"

Before Chanel could respond, Sylvia came back with the company-issued first-aid kit, which contained more gauze and tape than actual adhesive strips. Despite the growing discomfort she felt toward Sylvia, Grace allowed the two of them to wrap her finger with gauze.

"You'll need a stitch or two if it doesn't stop bleeding. I'd go get a tetanus shot, too, if you're not up to date. That knife looks nasty," Sylvia said while she wrapped the last piece of tape.

"I washed it in bleach before I brought it."

"That's not enough. I've seen what those things can lead to—infection . . . or worse." Sylvia cleaned up the scraps of gauze and the bits of tape into her hand and replaced the contents of the first-aid kit. "Well, I'm off to a party if you don't need me any more."

"We don't!" Chanel volunteered for both of them.

"I'm opening tomorrow so you can just leave this mess for me to take care of, if you can't manage." She indicated with a wave that she meant not only the mess of the first aid kit and paper towels, but also the plant and supplies.

"We'll manage," Chanel emphasized.

Sylvia shrugged and left.

Grace dropped back onto the box as if her puppet strings had been cut and she could no longer stand on her own.

"Did it feel like she just diminished any authority you or I have?"

"More than diminished it," Chanel said. "She negated it and took control."

"It's as if she deflected every word away from herself. Was she hiding something more than what she told me?"

"Not that I could tell. She did knock over the sale sign, right into the gate, that's why the crash reverberated. But I couldn't tell if she had been coming or going when it happened."

"Was anything damaged?" Grace questioned.

"The sign fell out of the metal holder and bent in the corner," Chanel said. "But the sale ends next week. I just slipped it back in. Except for a small crease that only we can see, it looks fine."

The two of them sat in silence for a few minutes before Grace reached for the knife again.

"Grace . . ."

"I just want to complete it. I'm not leaving this out for her to take over, too."

"Then let me do it," Chanel said.

Grace handed her the knife, and they traded spots at the table. Grace pointed out the places to cut and then relaxed into the black office chair. Chanel cut each of the parts off the plant, slit the nodules like the picture showed, took off the bottom leaves, and wrapped them all in damp paper towels. Grace took them one by one and dipped each node in the rooting hormone, made a hole in the sand and perlite mixture, and then gently inserted each cutting into a hole.

They worked in silence, which relieved the emotional strain that had built in the overcrowded room. Without further words, they restored the plant to its place in the front window, gathered the supplies, and wrapped the mess up into the packing paper.

With the back room and the floor of the store back in place, Grace took the supply bag in her uninjured hand. Chanel picked up the two pots of pencil-length cuttings.

"I'll carry these out for you. I work in the afternoon tomorrow with Sylvia, and I'll question her a bit more," Chanel said. "You go home and restore yourself to order before Monday."

"Thanks," Grace said meekly. She stood by while Chanel turned out the lights and locked the store and the gate. Together they walked to their cars.

Before Grace closed her car door, Chanel yelled from hers, "She is right about the tetanus shot."

****

Labor Day brought about a change in season and a change in sales patterns. Grace met with Chanel during the second week of September to create a new schedule. Up to that point, she used a rotating schedule every two weeks. After consulting with Sue, the regional manager, she decided to shift to a regular schedule for all employees, like the managers had already adopted for themselves. Each employee would have a consistent day and time to work. She hoped that this would especially benefit the part-time sales staff, and Trenna in particular.

Trenna had honeymooned all summer. Even though she came back from her actual vacation, her hours at Honeybee bounced between four and seven hours a week, depending upon whether the one shift a week she'd requested for these summer months was an evening or a full day. Her focus for her job flitted away with her single status. Gone were the goals she had expressed less than six months ago in the interview, and it disappointed Grace.

From the time she hired Trenna up to the wedding, their relationships as friend and employer had grown in a balanced way, but since then, she'd seen less and less of Trenna as a friend *and* as an employee. She wanted to give her the benefit of the doubt that she was adjusting to marriage but wearing two hats with her had become uncomfortable.

Grace and Chanel were halfway through their morning schedule meeting when Trenna appeared in the doorway to the back room, tanned and wearing a peach cardigan and cocoa silk pants purchased from the new fall collection on the front racks.

"Hey guys," she said, unaware that they were meeting formally and rushed into a one-sided conversation. "Mom's out front shopping with Sylvia's help. Thought I'd come see you while they pick through the sales together. How are you guys?"

Trenna didn't even pause for them to answer. "What's that smell? It's really strong."

"Grace, are these yours?" She'd already caught sight of the basket of tomatoes and cucumbers on top of the mini-fridge and began fingering them. She lifted a tomato and pressed the sides. "They're so red. But, what is that smell? It's not the cucumbers."

"It's the herbs underneath, I think." Grace finally said when Trenna took a breath from her monologue. "Basil and cilantro. Take any of it. That's why I brought it."

Trenna didn't speak, but stood completely still with her eyes squeezed together. Then she clapped her hand over her mouth and fled into the bathroom, kicking the door closed behind her.

"She's puking," Chanel said with a disgusted look. "I'm going to leave for now, okay?"

Grace nodded and rifled through her papers without really looking at them while she waited for Trenna to come out of the bathroom. When she did, all the color that had been in Trenna's face had faded. Dark circles stood out under her eyes and her lips had paled.

They looked straight at each other and then both spoke at once.

"You're pregnant?" Grace said.

"I'm pregnant," Trenna confessed.

Grace got out of her chair and pushed the more comfortable office chair toward Trenna.

"I'm not handicapped. I can still sit over here." Trenna motioned toward the hard chair where Chanel had been sitting.

Grace held out hers. "You look awful. Just sit here."

Trenna agreed and slumped down. Grace examined her face with concern.

"How long have you been doing this?"

"We found out at the end of August, and I've been throwing up for about two weeks. It's morning, noon, and night sickness."

"How did we not notice before now?" Grace asked.

"I really haven't been here much, have I?"

Grace gestured at the schedule. "I was just about to talk to Chanel about that."

"Plus, I don't always throw up, only when I smell or eat something that triggers it. I'm getting better at just breathing through the nausea till it passes. Sometimes it does. Sometimes it doesn't. Today it didn't."

"Do you want something to drink?" Grace said, pulling a water bottle from the fridge. Trenna shook her head, closed her eyes, and took a deep breath. Grace waited until Trenna opened her eyes. Her skin looked brighter.

"I'm sorry I didn't tell you right away. We just weren't expecting it, and I didn't know what to do, who to tell."

"Honestly? I thought you were avoiding me," Grace said. "Or avoiding work."

She looked at Trenna whose eyes were focused on a fly on the ceiling. Grace watched it, too. The moment of quiet felt as heavy as the pasta she ate for dinner the night before.

Grace finally broke. "How do you feel about it now?"

Trenna pulled her legs up into the chair and tucked them underneath her. "I'm getting used to the idea. And so is Max. But my mom certainly isn't."

"She'll warm up to it when she realizes it means grandchildren."

"No, I don't think so." She paused, leaned forward and scanned the doorway.

Grace followed Trenna's search. "She's by the front desk with Sylvia. I can see her."

"We told them the day after we found out, but she's hyper about my health. That's partly why I haven't told anyone else. I don't want to deal with their reactions. This week she insisted on taking me to her doctor, even though I'm not that far along. Plus, she wants to spend every day doing things with me, like before the wedding. I just started feeling some independence, and now she's smothering me, again."

"All that is enough to make you feel sick, even without a reason, isn't it?" Grace said. While the old irritation toward Roberta hardened in her chest, Grace wanted to be cautious with any negative words about her. Of course Trenna could speak that way, but she felt a responsibility to check herself—as a friend, and even more as Trenna's employer. Asking a leading question like this was just on the edge, but it allowed Trenna the opportunity to open up.

"She hovers, but it's even worse than before," Trenna said and stood up to look over Grace's head at the sales floor. At the front counter, Sylvia folded a sweater into a bag for Roberta. "She's been buying me new clothes already—everything with elastic waists. She's asks me every day if I took my vitamins. They make me gag. She comes over as soon as Max leaves for work to bring me crackers or toast. In a way, I guess it's better because I have an excuse to escape to the bathroom whenever she presses me too much."

"What can I do? As a friend? For work?"

"I want to be here more to get out of the house, but my stomach is precarious."

"Don't worry about your schedule. Now that I know, I can still just give you a couple shifts a week. When do want them? Evenings, weekends?"

"After lunch is best, but before the evenings when it gets bad again. Maybe if I could work two short afternoon shifts a week?"

"We can manage that." Grace flipped a page in her pile of papers to read something. "Beth wants to take on more hours, now that her children are back in school."

Grace wrote some notes on the top paper and then pointed her pen at Trenna. "But what about the time when you're not here? Fewer hours won't help that?"

"Short of getting another apartment right away, which we hadn't planned, I don't know." Trenna untangled her legs and stood up. "They're coming back here. I've got to go."

"What about my house?" Grace whispered to Trenna as she moved past her to close the distance before they came in.

Trenna raised her eyebrows and nodded. "A possibility," she

said and met her mom in the doorway. "Come show me what you bought."

Trenna steered Roberta back out to the front of the store and left a few minutes later to go out to lunch.

"Try the new tuna salad at the Landing," Sylvia called after them.

****

Grace lifted the plastic wrap that lay over the new hibiscus cuttings on her windowsill and spritzed them. Outside, her tomato plants produced huge six-foot vines, and she harvested the fruit through the end of September. They had outgrown their cages so she balanced another tomato cage right on top. They teetered a little, but the vines grew into them. Tomatoes wouldn't grow like that during a Minnesota fall; the frost would have grabbed them already.

The good tomato harvest made up for the zucchini that she'd been promised would take over but never even appeared. At least her neighbors wanted the tomatoes.

"Nothing tastes like a garden tomato," Mr. Reynolds said when she brought him some.

The overabundance prompted Grace to invite Max and Trenna for a garden-themed meal, and this time they accepted with the caveat that Trenna may be a picky eater but Max would finish whatever she couldn't.

Grace made Italian pesto chicken with a tomato cobbler she'd found on a popular blog and a chopped cucumber, mayonnaise, and dill salad. She carried her kitchen chairs outside and set them around a card table under the towering elm tree. The blue tablecloth she'd bought for the bridal shower complemented the blooming flowers she'd hoped to also showcase at that party.

Her lifestyle had become a bit introverted since her arrival at Honeybee. She only ever used the barest necessities for her own dinner place setting and never had company to share her meals. If she were going to nurture her relationships like the legacy of Lilly's plant inspired her to do, she would need to have more than just acquaintances.

The gift she'd bought for Trenna was the logical next step in reaching out to her. She tied a bow on the bag, slipped the key in the card envelope, and set them next to her place.

"Lady Lu. Lady Lu. Come in Lady Lu," Mr. Reynolds called from behind the screen of lilac bushes separating their yards. She dragged a chair to the edge of her yard and peeked over. He stood on the top of his concrete back stairs stooped with shortness from age.

"Mr. Reynolds, I saw her slip under our bushes and go behind my shed. Do you want me to see if I can find her?"

"Please."

She didn't have to. Just as she stepped off the kitchen chair and turned around, Lady Lu, ever faithful to the voice of her owner, slinked out of the shrubs, and strutted across the grass, ignoring Grace as if she knew who'd betrayed her.

"She's here," Mr. Reynolds called back when the cat appeared on the other side of the overgrown lilacs. His patio door creaked open.

"Mr. Reynolds, wait."

Grace climbed back up on the chair quickly. One front leg of the chair pressed unevenly low into the soil, and it wobbled underneath her weight. She waved a hand at him.

"Wait. Have you eaten? I mean . . . I'm having some friends over. I don't know if . . ." She stammered like young child making her first phone call to invite a friend to play. "Would you like to come to dinner?"

He rubbed his hands on his belted trousers, nodded, and said, "I'll clean up first. What can I bring?"

"Bring us a good joke," she said, hopping off the chair, which fell back on the lawn behind her. She rearranged the three place settings and added a fourth where her gift to Trenna sat. The doorbell rang. She shoved the card inside the gift bag and tossed it underneath the table.

At the door Max handed a white Tasty Pastry box to Grace, who lifted the lid. Mini chocolate éclairs and mini turtle cheesecakes lay neatly in rows.

"We're all still young enough to eat these," Trenna said.

"We?" Grace asked. "These are only meant for adults who've reached 30—when the calories don't count."

"That's when they do start counting!" Max plucked a mini cheesecake out of the box and held it to his mouth. "So I'm going to get mine in."

"Not fair," Trenna cut in. She grabbed the cheesecake from Max and returned it to the box. "I'll outweigh both of you combined before winter, even without your rules."

"Not even if you try," Max said.

They conversed as easily in the backyard while Grace assessed the coals she'd already lit in her new charcoal grill. Max held a seat for Trenna and gestured toward her neighbor's Victorian house behind her.

"Suitably painted," he said, wandering over for a closer look.

"You have to see the colors he's painted in our second bedroom," Trenna said to Grace. "If that is going to be a nursery, the baby will be either dizzy or perpetually awake. Four different colors on all four walls."

"Do you think you'll stay there long enough for that?" Grace said.

"Until we can find what we want to buy ourselves."

"I would think Max would want to build something or at least remodel."

"He would. But we don't want to move way out to find land for that. The remodel of the carriage house curbed his passion to put his stamp on something. I honestly don't think he's ready to tackle one with me, but he won't admit it."

"But what about living so close to your parents?"

"What do you mean, Grace?" Trenna looked up at her. Grace thought they'd established a comfort level talking about this, but maybe she had introduced an I-can-criticize-my-family-but-don't-you-dare moment.

"Never mind." Grace turned back to the grill. "Looks like the chicken can go on now. I'll be right back."

Grace reappeared at the screen door five minutes later carrying a Pyrex dish with marinating chicken and a handful of Shasta daisies. Mr. Reynolds followed her, decked out in an old-fashioned gray summer suit with a collared shirt and tie.

"Would you like me to start those?" Max reached for the chicken.

Grace welcomed his help. The stress of pulling it all at the same time had finally caught up. Max put the chicken on the grill while she deposited the flowers in a tall glass and introduced her neighbor.

"The Olivers are newlyweds, Mr. Reynolds," Grace said.

"Congratulations on your new marriage, Mrs. Oliver." He daintily took Trenna's hand and smiled widely at Max without letting go. "Maybe you'll earn her by the time you die."

Max laughed and handed the barbecue tools to Grace as he wrapped his arm around his wife.

"Grace told me to bring a good joke, but I need to warm up first," Mr. Reynolds confessed.

They laughed—Grace at the quirky formality he brought, Max at his momentary jealousy toward an older man noticing his wife's attractiveness, Trenna at her awkwardness with Mr. Reynolds' hand still holding hers, and Mr. Reynolds at himself. He released Trenna's fingers and stood behind the chair Grace offered him, resting his palms on the back of it, opening and closing his fingers over the top.

"So, Max, how are you supporting your beautiful bride?" Mr. Reynolds pried.

"I work for an architecture firm downtown. They transferred me from their Kansas City office at the beginning of the summer."

"Architecture, hmmm. I could take you on quite a walk around this neighborhood."

"It seems like a place the new urbanists dreamed of creating but could never quite match," Max said.

"We've lived here more than forty-five years, and there's been no better craftsmanship in the decades since. But of course so many people move in and out, so it doesn't all stay that way. A lot of them have been lost in disrepair. Some try to restore the original. Others just modernize it."

"Which are you?"

"None of the above. I just fix it and carry on."

"I see your neighbor's paint job," Max said, motioning to the house behind them. "Seems like they chose authentic paint colors."

"Nice for a Victorian, but ours—Grace and mine—are just bungalows. Our details are on the inside. The fireplace. The bookshelves. The arched doorways. The moldings."

The late summer evening loosened their tongues, and they grew more comfortable in conversation about outdoor theater in St. Louis and music, then and now. The food filled in the gaps in conversation as everyone praised the dishes, even the cucumber salad, which Grace was sure had way too much salt.

At the end of the meal Mr. Reynolds offered to clear the table, and Max stood to help.

"I like your date," Trenna teased, when they were inside.

"Better than some I've had," Grace replied.

"I kicked this," Trenna said, pulling the gift back from under the table.

"For you. Open it, but save the card for last. "

Trenna pulled out a pregnancy book with a bare-bellied pregnant woman on the front. "I'm glad Mr. Reynolds is inside," she said, giggling.

"Apparently it is *the* book of the moment for expectant moms, or so Darlene says," Grace said.

"I need this. Now I can tell my mom, 'In THE book, it says . . .'"

"What's in the envelope will also help with that problem," Grace promised.

Trenna carefully peeled the envelope and pulled out the card. A key fell onto her lap.

"What'd you get?" Max said from behind her shoulder. She slipped the card in front of the pregnant belly picture while she read it and then handed the book, card, and key to Max.

"Why the key?" he asked as Mr. Reynolds sat back down at the table.

"Just when I want a chance to escape my mom. I can come here and be alone. During the days when Grace works."

"Do you think that's a good idea?"

"I have to be alone sometimes; I never get that at our place," she responded, louder than she probably intended.

"Mr. Reynolds, let's go inside and start on those dishes. Can you help?" Grace proposed.

Trenna got up first.

"Excuse us," Max apologized and followed Trenna.

Mr. Reynolds looked as uncomfortable as she felt. Grace reached for a napkin to distract her eyes from meeting his.

"Grace, marry a man your own age. Then as your beauty fades, so will his eyesight," Mr. Reynolds said. She could only laugh meekly.

"That was my Phyllis Diller joke," he said, pushing his chair back. "I know when it is time to leave. Thank you for the wonderful meal and especially for the company of your youthful voices."

"But we haven't even had dessert."

"Oh, I'm too old to eat like that anyway. Besides, my granddaughter brought me a plate of lemon bars yesterday. They're good, even without chocolate."

He bowed his head to her and grasped her hand, and she squeezed it before he walked down her driveway.

No one was in the kitchen, so Grace started to stack the plates. The front door closed, and Max came through the doorway alone.

"Is Trenna okay?" Grace asked.

"Yeah, she's getting a Tylenol from the car," he said. "She's trying so hard not to take any medications this first trimester, but she has a headache."

"I could have given her that," she said while she dried her hands and leaned against the sink.

"I think she wanted some space for a minute, too."

"If you guys want to leave . . ."

"No, I asked her that," he said, "but she wants to stay. Other than the headache and the emotions from her hormones, she's happy here."

"I guess that's why I offered—the key, I mean," she said. "To give her a place to regroup."

"I know. I've tried to make the carriage house like that, too, but her mom . . ."

"Interferes?" Grace suggested.

"Not when I'm there, she doesn't. But, yes, during the day when I'm at work—especially now."

"Is it just the pregnancy?" she said. "You know—her daughter? Her first grandchild? Wanting the best for them?"

"Some of that is why. You can see Roberta really dominates Trenna," he said, holding the trash can open for Grace to scrape the plate. "But it's more than just a typical mother-daughter struggle. What has Trenna told you about her brother?" he said.

"Ryan? Not much."

"No. Her other brother," he said.

"I didn't know she had another brother. He wasn't at the wedding, was he?"

"No . . ." Max looked around the kitchen corner. "She should really tell you. I think she will—when she's ready. Just know, she's going through a lot and needs your friendship. She walks a careful line, finding the right balance with her mom."

"So why would you object to her coming here?"

"I don't. Her mom might, though. And I want to protect her from that."

Trenna opened the screen door from the backyard, carrying her glass from the table. "May I get some water?"

Grace filled her glass and handed it to her while Max disappeared outside, returning with two chairs. Trenna sat down on the first one he set down. He didn't sit beside her but finished bringing in the chairs and the odds and ends off the table.

"I didn't expect to be so tired. I'm not doing that much," Trenna said.

"Not in an obvious way, but you really are." Grace nodded to the pregnancy book in Trenna's hands. Grace dumped the utensils into the sink and dipped her hands into the hot water. Over the pots on her windowsill, she noticed Max shaking the tablecloth and even folding it.

"Jeff would never have helped like that." Grace sighed.

"Tell me about Jeff." Trenna came up behind her and grabbed a dishcloth. "Was he your boyfriend in Minnesota?"

Grace slipped a knife into the water and ran the dishcloth over the edge. "My fiancé. But I broke it off before I moved."

"Because you were leaving and he didn't want to come?"

"No, I decided to move after we ended it—to start over."

"Well, he obviously didn't do the dishes," Trenna teased.

"No, he certainly didn't."

Even though she'd brought Jeff to every function after they had announced their engagement, her parents still hesitated in giving their full support to the engagement. She'd wanted them to know Jeff like she did, wanted her mom and dad to see how well they fit together.

"I invited him to dinner with my parents. He arrived thirty minutes late, almost an hour after them, but he was super attentive to them, just like we hosted guests many times, talking to them, drawing out there interests, and all that." Grace handed Trenna a serving dish. Outside, Max was scraping the grill.

"When my mom stood up to clear the plates, Jeff insisted he would do it. 'You do this every day at home. Leave it and relax; we'll do it later,' he told her."

The conversation and rapport had progressed better that day than any other time. Jeff and Grace's dad agreed on politics and discussed the governor's election campaign. Jeff had even asked her mom about her work as the Friends of the Library chairman and kept her talking about books, the local book sale, and her favorite classics until they all realized how late it was.

"He charmed them—even my dad, who whispered to me when they were leaving, 'I guess I'll let him marry you.'

"My mom caught sight of the dishes piled on the table and said she wanted to help. But, again, Jeff reassured her, 'Grace and I will clean up together.'"

"But that didn't happen?" Trenna asked.

"I cleaned while Jeff sat on the stool explaining why he was late, criticizing his coworkers, and checking his phone," Grace said. "At the time he felt distant, but I assumed he was just distracted with work."

She didn't tell Trenna about the hints of his false displays that came later that night. He had pulled her against him, kissed the back of her neck, and whispered in her ear, "You're the only company I want. I wish you'd stop worrying so much about what your parents think and let me stay all night. We didn't get any time together. Did they talk forever, *or what?*"

She had pushed back from him, surprised at his complaint, and said, "Wasn't it you who was interested in the conversation, too? I'm exhausted and have to get to sleep." She had smiled at Jeff and kissed him to show that she was just tired, not upset, but he had left angry.

Now, she wished it hadn't taken so long for her to understand what her parents had first suspected. Grace pulled the stopper out of the dishwater and the bubbles sucked down the drain. She handed the last dish to Trenna.

"I guess Jeff simply told people what he thought they wanted to hear, but in the end he only cared about meeting his own desires." That inconsistency now looked like the dishonesty that it was.

"It sounds like he really hurt you. Is that why you broke up?"

"No. It took some time—once we were apart—to realize that about him."

Trenna finished wiping the last plate and laid the towel on the side of the sink. "People are complex, aren't they? I think I'm pretty genuine about who I am, but I don't always share my whole story. Sometimes that has created a lot of assumptions."

"Oh, yes, I assumed," Grace said. "He told me he didn't want a family. I assumed he would change, but I guess that's where he told the truth and stuck to it. In reality, I let go of my own desire for children—to appease him. Ironic, isn't it?"

"But you figured it out and moved on, right? So you haven't lost that chance," Trenna said, reaching to squeeze Grace's forearm.

"I hope I haven't, but I do wonder if I gave more up than I gained." The little sign of affection from Trenna softened her, and Grace reached another arm over and gave her a hug. "Thanks for listening."

"Anytime," Trenna gave another squeeze and then backed up. Grace wiped her cheek with the back of her hand. "Usually, I'm doing all the talking since Max is such a good listener."

"I am?" Max said from the other side of the screen door, with a card table hefted to waist level in two hands. Trenna rushed over to the door and pushed it open.

"Where can I store this?" He held up the table in the tight space.

"In the second bedroom closet," Grace said. "Trenna, can you show him?"

She finished the dishes and wiped the counters before she wandered back to find them. Trenna sat on the bed as if it were a chaise lounge with her back pressed against the wall and her legs stretched out in front of her. Max stood next to the bed holding several medium-sized, matted watercolor paintings, handing them to Trenna one at a time. Grace stayed in the doorway, happy with their comfort level in her house.

"We've been snooping. Should we stop?" Trenna confessed.

"No, go ahead. They aren't anything more than my cast-off attempts from high school and college."

"So they're yours?" he asked.

Grace nodded and plopped onto the foot of the bed, lifting the two they'd already seen—a goldfish in a bowl and a group of pine trees in the snow from her Minnesota neighborhood.

"They're not very good," Grace said. "Amateurish, really."

"Maybe," Max said, teasing. "But they aren't bad."

"Since you think that, I'll just keep them for me." Grace teased back, holding out her hand for the painting he held, a close rendering of an old man's hands. He drew back from her and continued to examine it.

"You're good with people. The focus in this one is better than those of a landscape or still life."

"Oh, I painted it from a photo of my grandfather." She peered over his arm to study it closer. "I just painted his hands because that's what I remember of him. His hands looked old to me, but he was always working when we visited. When I helped him, he always untied the knots I never could or threaded my fishing line. He had working hands."

"Do you still paint?" Trenna asked.

"No. I thought I would, but I didn't pursue it long enough to make it a career, and I haven't gone back to it as a hobby."

Grace gathered all the paintings and stacked them on the small student desk she'd bought at an antique store. In the front room Max found his place beside Trenna, who tucked her feet underneath her on the couch.

"I wanted to major in art, too," Trenna admitted. "But my parents steered me toward business and marketing. More practical, they said. I took a few art classes as electives, though."

They talked about art galleries they liked and their passions that had become hobbies for another hour before Max stood up and steered Trenna toward the door.

"Mr. Reynolds was nice," Max said. "But . . ."

Grace raised her eyebrows at his inflection.

He continued, "I have a friend who may be a little younger than you, but he'd make a nice substitute next time."

"But I'm sure he wouldn't look as good in that suit," Trenna teased. She pulled Grace's key from her pocket.

"I'm sorry that I assumed," Grace said and held out her hand to take it back.

"You didn't, but you are now. I just wanted to show you that I'm keeping it. But only if you agree to help me start painting again."

"Anytime," Grace said, returning the promise Trenna gave earlier about being available to listen.

Chapter Six

The holiday spirit began six months before Christmas in the retail world. First the buyers in Honeybee's corporate office found the right product, and then the marketing team planned how to create a holiday buzz. Sue gathered all St. Louis and Kansas City managers at a regional "holiday" training retreat in early October and pressed them for individual store goals for the coming three-month sales season.

Last year's proactive approach to selling more merchandise to each customer entering The Plaza Honeybee store produced good results—mostly due to Lilly's tenacious holiday mood. Her contagious smile could persuade customers, without flattery, to buy whatever she put together for them. This year Grace knew that her sales team lacked that same quality and the recession had greatly reduced the number of customers who actually entered the store.

The marketing plans were in place, but Sue warned that even with the advertising purchased across different media in their markets, more and more customers were moving online to read, socialize, and shop, not exposing themselves to the traditional marketing paths.

"Our online sales are up, but we're losing the next generation of customers in the mall stores. Each manager will have to justify your store's existence in these three months or changes will come next year."

The whispered voices of women rose in the room as Sue paused for them to consider the consequences of the economy, the digital age, and how both directly impacted store sales.

"Your store locations will be a big factor that you can't change, so you'll have to take them into account. Traffic remains constant in most of our city markets, but our suburban stores are losing out, with one exception—the new store in Liberty, Missouri. It's in a mixed-use development, and that opens us to more of the daytime career crowd. Their sales numbers are now the highest in the Missouri region."

That news stabbed Grace. Higher numbers than hers? She focused on Sue's lips, but the mental noise that erupted in her swallowed all the external sound, making it hard to process what that meant for her.

Sue dismissed for a break, and the managers rose from their seats to chat in pairs. Some walked to the back of the small conference room where the hotel staff had arranged trays of muffins, doughnuts, bagels, and fruit alongside several coffee pots.

Grace sat still. They *had* slid slightly this year, but was it really enough to knock The Plaza store off the number one spot?

Sue turned away from her conversation with a Chicago counterpart. Grace automatically dropped her eyes to the floor and bent forward to rummage in her bag for her phone.

When the path to the back seemed safe, she escaped to the break table and lost herself amongst the other hungry women.

The glossy doughnuts and crusty bagels tempted her, but she selected a banana from the fruit basket behind the pastry trays. As she reached for a small muffin, a hand cupped her elbow.

"You know, those older lunching Ladue ladies are not going to be your bread and butter for much longer Grace," Sue said on her right side.

Grace set the muffin down and chose a glazed doughnut instead. "The Plaza is just shifting to a different crowd—an evening crowd. I expect it will pick up, especially with the holidays."

"Well, that will help when we evaluate the whole St. Louis market next year." Sue took a water bottle from the tray and pointed it at Grace. "Come up with your holiday sales plan with your staff this week. But remember, your customer demographic at The Plaza has aged. You'll have to bring in a new one and keep them beyond the holidays to stay relevant in this new economic climate."

As soon as Grace returned to the store on Monday, she unloaded the news on Chanel.

"Shall we go to lunch and come up with a plan?" Grace asked. Channel nodded, and Grace grabbed the phone to call down to the Landing.

"The Landing's still busy," she said when she set down the phone. "Thirty minute wait. So much for Sue's suppositions."

Grace repeated this observation half an hour later as they weaved through the crowded restaurant.

"She could be right." Chanel motioned toward the bar where a number of professionals gathered. "Look. These are not the social eaters or the 'let's do lunch' crowd that's been coming to The Plaza for so many years. All of these people are going to eat and leave without stepping into the mall."

The waitress seated them at a table, not a booth, and handed her a menu. Grace waved it away. "I'll just have the chicken Caesar salad," she said, and Chanel ordered the special.

"I looked over the numbers Sue gave us this weekend. The number of sales we're making is the same, but the amount has dropped. So if she's right and the daytime traffic is reduced, those shopping in the afternoons and evenings are not buying as much. What about the foot traffic in the evenings? You're here more than I am at those times. What do you see? Who's coming in?"

Chanel's eyes passed over the groups of diners gathered around them talking. "I'm sure we get more of the restaurant crowd then. Families in for dinner. Women out shopping by themselves. Couples seeing a film together. Friends on a girls' night out at Glitters Spa."

"Girls' night out? Are people still doing that?" Grace sighed.

"You obviously haven't been out lately."

"I guess I've just avoided gatherings like that."

"Avoided them? I don't think so," Chanel countered. "You organized one for us."

Grace skewed her eyebrows and twisted her head in a questioned expression.

"Gathering here to decide about Lilly's plant?" Chanel reminded her.

"But that wasn't a girls' nights out!"

"Yes, it was," Chanel laughed at Grace holding herself above female popular culture. "I know this will stretch you, but I think we should sponsor one."

"You're kidding, right?" Grace slid further back in her chair.

"Not at all."

"Honeybee's not big enough for a large crowd all at once, and a small group isn't going to impact our sales."

"We could broaden it beyond just us," Chanel said. "Make it a full mall event."

The waitress handed the salad to Grace and a plate of Asian noodles, vegetables, and pork to Chanel.

"Well, the full mall approach might focus too much of the organization on the mall management, and it may not bring women right into Honeybee."

"So what would you do instead?" Chanel asked.

"Pair up with other stores like the Glitters Spa, Kitchen Gourmet, and the shoe store downstairs. We really could approach any store that targets the women's demographic and invite them to have an open house with us."

"Do you think Sue will see that as collaborating with the enemies?" Chanel said.

"We all benefit when we increase foot traffic that wouldn't be here otherwise," Grace countered.

"Maybe each could offer something—a demonstration, a guest, food, some incentive—to bring people in." Chanel's eyes danced with the new idea. "We'll just have to tailor our incentive with an original idea."

"Whatever we do, we have to focus on our purpose— nurture a new customer base."

"Let's brainstorm with the sales staff at our staff meeting tomorrow. Get them excited and let them give some input, like you did with the plant," Chanel suggested.

"We've lost that excitement for Lilly's plant, haven't we?" Grace said. "It flowered and did well, but then we all forgot about it."

"I don't think so," Chanel said. "It may not be new and exciting anymore, but that doesn't mean we don't still pay attention to it. You know Trenna adores that plant. I think she may talk to it as much as you do."

Grace covered her eyes with her hand.

"We all know that you do that, so you can finally admit it. You come in before everyone else so we won't see you having your conversation," Chanel teased.

"But, honestly, Grace, everyone still cares. Faye makes it an accessory to whatever she puts in the window—like the pumpkin display she did last week. Audrey helps, too. She dusts the leaves every other week. And Beth mixes the fertilizer and pours it into the spray bottle."

"Really?" Grace stretched closer to the table and questioned Chanel with her eyes.

"You didn't know that, did you? Beth never lets it go past half a bottle before she adds more. Even Sylvia asked me how your cutting took. Each of them still wants to be a part of it, even though you've been giving more of the primary care."

"I thought that I wasn't using that much fertilizer. And, I didn't know the leaves needed dusting—since they've been dusted already. But Sylvia, she's so on again, off again, I'm not sure whose team she's on."

"Be careful about those false assumptions," Chanel said. Grace didn't bristle at the straightforward advice. They could talk openly like that to each other, especially about the management of the store.

"I assumed I was doing it alone," Grace said, more to herself than to Chanel. "It's hard for me to see what other people are doing."

"How are those cuttings, by the way?"

"Some look better than others, but they haven't died. I'm still giving them a little water every day, and they should be completely rooted soon. But it's going to take a while before they become a plant as vibrant as the one Lilly gave me."

Chanel leaned in close to the table and pointed her fork toward Grace. "That's the point you need to remember at the store, too. It's going to take time to build a new base of customers. The plant made us more aware, whether anyone verbalized it or not, that how we work together matters. Whether it is to take care of a plant or take care of our customers—it's the same. "

"I never connected the two," Grace replied, straightening the dessert menu that was tucked between the condiments and the sugar packets.

"Well, maybe you didn't consciously think, 'I want them to sell like Lilly,' but we all feel her legacy. The plant just reminds us, 'Be interested in people,'" Chanel said with her fork in the air again. She quickly caught herself and lowered it to finish her noodles. "That's what I imagine, anyway, when I walk by the front window sometimes."

"So, how do we translate that into a sales plan for the next three months? Put Lilly's plant on display in the middle of the store, tie her with holiday ribbon, and give away hibiscus flowers?"

"For a holiday girls' night out?" Chanel questioned with a shake of her head. "The influence is more subtle. Don't make it overt to them or to the customers. Remember, too, it's not necessarily quantifiable. Sue may want sales to go up now, but the results of what you're really doing are longer term."

"For the short term, though, we have to justify ourselves, as she said. So our plan should be what—keep the plant, get their input, and solicit their help for the holiday open house?"

"For the girls' night out," Chanel corrected.

"Do we have to call it that?"

"Absolutely! And use those words when you present it to the staff."

That afternoon, Grace organized her thoughts on paper. Chanel popped in the back room for a markdown pen and warned, "Bring it to them raw. They will appreciate it more if they contribute."

Surprisingly, they did. They shot ideas at her so fast she couldn't even evaluate them on the spot, which Chanel later said allowed for more creativity and a broader scope of ideas. They wanted to reach out to the thirty- to forty-something age group and those who may want to update their style with pieces to add to their core wardrobe. They agreed to host a hands-on style demonstration in Honeybee at each week's event. And towards the end of the meeting, both Sylvia and Trenna proposed online social networking as a way to publicize the event. Sylvia even wanted to go out that day and start spreading it word of mouth.

"I love your enthusiasm. Let's go with that plan," Grace decided. "We can begin the first week of November and run the events right up to Christmas. But I need to work through the details with Sue before we start marketing it."

This project sparked something in all of them that a regular workday lacked—a larger purpose, a bigger goal. Most importantly, as Chanel pointed out, it was their light bulb. They had discovered the idea together and each wanted a part of it.

Sue approved the plan, but countered, "That's not wholly

original; I've heard it's done at a lot of malls and other places. But it's an event that can build traffic."

"Right," Grace said.

"We are working on a short timetable," Sue said. "Why don't I approach the mall managers with the plan myself and coordinate all the details between Honeybee and The Plaza?"

Sue's qualified praise and involvement in its implementation pulled Grace's eagerness back, but she let go of that as the plan developed and spread amongst the other managers. Many stopped by to introduce themselves to Grace and thank her for initiating it. Obviously, the mall management and Sue had given the credit to Honeybee. Knowing that, Grace passed along the praise to her staff, hoping she could now pay less attention to her own insecurities and focus on what others were doing well.

In these weeks of launching the event, Trenna dropped by Grace's house unexpectedly one morning before Grace left for work. She opened the door to find her with a plastic shopping bag on one arm and a large sheet of watercolor paper in her hand.

"Did you really mean it? Can I come over and paint here while you're gone?" Trenna asked.

"Of course. Paint. Hang out. Whatever." Grace opened the door wider to let Trenna in.

"Let me show you what I bought for us, and you can tell me where to put them."

"For us? You really want me to paint, too?" Grace said to Trenna who set the paper on the back of the couch and pulled out a pile of new brushes, mixing trays, and tubes of paint.

"Of course. I need someone to get an artistic representation of my belly. I'm not doing the naked tummy shot in a photograph like everyone else has done—it's not all that attractive. Plus, Max said you're good with people."

"I'll see if I can remember anything. But I still have work, so I can't promise you much." She looked at her watch. "Like right now."

"Can I stay?"

"Sure. Just set up in the second bedroom. You can use the desk in there. And lock up when you leave."

At The Plaza Grace passed multiple posters advertising the girls' night out and saw that nearly every store had a flier in their window, too. The assistant manager of Glitters Spa came by at lunch to brag about their increase of bookings for that following Thursday night. The first of the eight holiday events started in just a week and a half, and momentum was building.

Sylvia had aggressively publicized the first girls' night out, creating an event on Facebook, inviting everyone she knew to come, and encouraging them to share the event. Trenna had done the same in her own professional style. From their reports, the online word was spreading beyond the narrow circle of the West County community. Even Beth's ongoing complaints about her workload and the burden of her busy schedule increased attention for the event when she touted herself as the poster woman for girls' night out.

Faye dressed up the store with a few modifications of the fall line to get them through before the holiday clothes arrived and agreed to conduct the first style demonstration—how to wear a scarf. They ordered three boxes of new scarves, and Audrey worked on a Saturday, even though it meant missing Nick's basketball game, to sort and hang them. Chanel preordered

500 chocolate-filled cookies from Tasty Pastry as Grace had suggested.

"Oh I know Bridget Peterson will be here and, of course, Kassi Kendall. Do you know the Kendalls?" Sylvia dropped these names to a woman in knee-high boots aimlessly flipping through a rack of jeans. "Kassi and her mom have been coming here forever. We're so close. I picked the outfit she wore to Mariah Hennen's party. This is going to be even bigger than that. Do you want me to choose something for you to wear next Thursday?"

In the moment, Grace bit her tongue at the frustration this exchange caused her, but after the store closed it came back to her as she stood at the front window and stared at Lilly's plant. Only a small bud formed on the stem and one leaf had turned yellow, but the other foliage accented the fall blouses and jeans displayed behind it.

On the surface, her initiative to move the staff toward a larger purpose appeared successful. When she considered it deeper, though, it seemed like she'd blown up a balloon and let it go only to be swept into a crowd of other balloons.

While everyone *was* helping now just like they had helped Lilly's plant to bloom, she feared most of the staff were caught in the excitement of planning a party and had lost sight of their original purpose. Sure, they wanted to increase sales, but not just for the short holiday stretch. The real goal was to establish a new core customer base that would carry them into the next year or two. That wouldn't happen with one successful event; the staff had to truly meet the needs of the customers.

She backed away from the window and walked through the mall, feeling distant now from the posters she passed. At home she opened the door on the dark back porch, went inside, and hung up her short silver trench coat. A light was on in the front of the house. The lamp in the second bedroom was on, but no one was there. Four damp paintbrushes lay on a paper towel alongside four paint tubes and a note.

> *Grace, thank you for a few days of solitude this week. Call or stop by tonight, if you'd like. We're just watching an old Woody Allen movie and ordering pizza. Trenna*

She flopped down on the bed in that room and stared at the plaster cracking on the ceiling above her. Should she go? She flipped onto her stomach and read the note again, torn between her own need for solitude and a desire for real friends. Maybe this note showed that was what Trenna had become—a true friend.

Would it feel awkward hanging out at the carriage house with her and Max? It hadn't when they'd been at her place, even after her jealous feelings before the wedding. It wasn't that she desired Max or envied Trenna's life; she simply wanted the relationships she'd sacrificed when she left Jeff. Marriage. Children. Family. Those same desires were still with her, but now the jealousy was gone. Even more surprising, she realized, she hadn't felt it when Trenna announced her pregnancy either.

She suddenly bounced off the bed, excited now to accept the invitation. In her own room she pulled a new sweater from the dresser, changed into the jeans that lay on the end of her bed, dragged a brush through her hair, and then twisted the end to make a shaggy bun. She reached into the top drawer for a clip to secure it and saw that black jewelry box in the back.

Her long hair fell out of her hand as she picked up the velvet box. She hadn't opened it since Jeff gave it back to her that night they said goodbye, and she shouldn't now. She would just wrap it up and return it to him.

She turned the box into her palm, and closed her other palm

over it, rubbing the nap of the velvet against the inside of her fingers. She positioned her thumb on the front of the box, the pressure pushed apart the top from the bottom, and the hinge at the back popped the top firmly up. The white gold and diamond ring she'd worn on her finger for six months and the wedding band that went with it lay between the folds of the black velvet inside.

Two weeks before their anticipated wedding date, she had knocked on his apartment doors and removed the diamond ring from her hand when he answered.

"Whenever you said that you didn't want children, I agreed. What you said made so much sense. But I don't really agree." She held the ring out to Jeff over the threshold. "Marriage means more than just you and me. It means children, too. I can't marry you, knowing we aren't settled on that."

"Really? Now you decide?" He stared at her with only a flicker of emotion—she couldn't tell what kind—visible in the slight flutter of his eyes. She didn't answer.

"If that's what you want." His words felt callous, as if he were the one who had ended their relationship. Wasn't he going to try to persuade her to change her mind?

He didn't. He just said, "All right, but don't leave yet."

She leaned against the supports in the doorway between this apartment where they'd planned their future and the lonely hallway of the apartment building.

He returned with his hand cupped around something. Even though it looked tangible, she hoped it would be an appeal for her to change her mind. She wanted him to fight for this. For them. For their family. She didn't really want to do this. He held out the black velvet box, opened it to show her the wedding band

and handed it to her.

"Keep it—if you ever change your mind," he said without indicating even a possibility of a change in his own desires and shut his apartment door.

Now she stared at both rings—the one she'd worn for so long and the one she never would—and wondered, why *had* she kept them?

She closed the box and put it inside her jeans pocket. No, she wouldn't ever change her mind, but until now, she imagined and hoped that someday he might change his.

She grabbed the silver trench coat she'd hung less than an hour before and headed back out to her car. She opened the glove box and gently tossed the velvet box to the back and shut it again—to ship to Jeff on Monday. Tonight she'd close off the worries of the day and enjoy herself.

****

The scope of those worries about the first girls' night out didn't press on her so much when she returned to work on Monday. She didn't just talk to Lilly's plant in the window— she came in early, opened the door to the front window, and sat alongside the plant to verbally review her priorities for the week. "It's probably important to move forward as things have developed rather than trying to rethink and reconstruct the event," she concluded and gave the plant a slight turn to show off a better angle.

Every day leading up to the event, she did the same thing, with more assurance that the holiday GNO events would be successful, not only in the short term but as a means of long-term growth, for her and the company. The retail market was stiffer and tighter. She suspected that they had not only lost customers who had aged out of their clothing line but also customers who had traded the upscale boutiques and department stores at The Plaza for discount stores. The company had been sending fewer products in the shipments, and the inventory next year would be even leaner. The hints Sue dropped about the new multi-use developments in the exurbs made Grace think they were reassessing store locations, too, and the mall's decreased traffic wouldn't help that. There were only so many women like Roberta Foster left to carry them.

A partial shipment of new holiday clothes arrived unexpectedly on the morning of the first girls' night out. Beth and Grace shuffled clothes from the front racks to the back. In the middle of this disorder, Roberta came to shop.

Reluctantly, Grace gave her handful of sale items to Beth, along with the red marker, and weaved to the front of the store where Roberta intently searched the new clothes on the temporary rack.

"Grace, bring Trenna out here and have her help me weed through these new things."

"It's just Beth and I here," she answered, wiping sticky hair off her forehead with the back of her hand. "Trenna's working tonight, with the rest of the staff for the girls' night out."

"Well that's ridiculous, she's not at home. She left an hour ago; I'm sure she's here."

"I'm sure she's not," Grace said impatiently. She looked around her at the overfilled rolling racks and the empty front racks, sighing at the thought of putting the store back together in six hours. She changed her tone, but her tiredness gave it an edge that sounded bothered. "What else can I find for you today? Are you looking for something in particular?"

Roberta held up a revealing black evening dress. "What's girls' night out?"

"A promotional holiday open house for women with giveaways, demonstrations, food, and mingling across the whole mall. They're every Thursday night for the rest of the year," Grace said and pointed at the poster on the door.

"Why didn't Trenna invite me?"

"Maybe she thought you already knew."

"Well, I didn't. How could I?" Roberta handed Grace three other black evening outfits and pulled out her cell phone. "Put these in a room for me."

Grace retreated with the clothes to the dressing room and returned to the markdown job she'd transferred to Beth. Roberta passed her, leaving a voice mail for Trenna, and closed herself into the dressing room.

"Those are all too young for her," Grace whispered to Beth. "If you have a minute when she comes out, see if you can steer her toward something else."

When Roberta left with a silky black stretch skirt and an embellished print top. Beth shrugged at Grace. "I tried."

Customers continued to interrupt the work of merchandising the new inventory all day. "Sorry about the mess," she said to four women who came in all at once, trying to cover her embarrassment at the still-empty front racks. We're having a big event tonight."

"I know. We're having our girls' night out today, instead," one of them explained.

When they left, she called Faye and Trenna to the rescue. Trenna was painting at Grace's and promised to clean up and come over. Faye arrived from the Clayton store within the hour and quickly set up new display racks in front, while Beth finished sorting the new sale items. Grace fielded the increasing flow of customers.

She finished ringing another sale at the cash register and handed the hanger of the garment bag to the customer. "Thanks for coming in."

A man walked in with two large covered trays. "I have 500 cookies. Where do you want them?"

Trenna appeared right behind him, and Grace pleaded, "Will you please find a place?" Trenna efficiently took over, carrying the plastic-wrapped trays to the back, one by one until all ten had been unloaded from the delivery cart.

Faye brought side tables from the back of the store, erecting a center island for the refreshments and demonstration. Although the store appeared more cluttered, both Faye and Trenna assured her they would work quickly to bring it into shape. They disappeared while Grace paced through the store—hanging clothes, refolding sweaters, and sorting accessories. Faye returned, dragging behind her a set of mustard–gold drapes from the stock room. Trenna held a pair of scissors.

"Are you sure?" Grace couldn't imagine how this would look any better.

"They hung in the front window ten years ago," Faye said before she cut one of the drapes in half and handed both halves to Trenna. "No one will miss them if they haven't used them yet."

Trenna steamed the material and covered the small round side tables with each half, bunching the excess material at the bottom so that it ballooned. Faye covered the main rectangular table up with the other drape. Then, she returned to the stock room and brought back another cast-off—the top half of a naked mannequin, which she handed to Grace.

"Dress her," Faye said.

"In what?"

"Something neutral. And no collar."

Everyone remained busy with little and big preparations. By 5 p.m. Grace and Faye dropped exhausted onto the top of the two stairs that led to the raised level. Trenna slipped her hand under the plastic wrap of the cookie tray and handed out cookies.

"What if 500 women actually do show up?" Grace said.

"That's a rhetorical question, right?" Faye said, brushing the crumbs off her lap and passed around the tray of cookies again.

Even if they didn't feel prepared when Sylvia, Chanel, and three other part-time saleswomen arrived a few minutes before six, they looked it, having changed out of their standard work clothes and into a step above dressy casual.

"Lines of cars are backed up looking for parking spots," Chanel reported. "They'll be flooding us soon."

"Did you see all those women outside Glitters Spa? They've set up a free facial in front of their salon. That's what they're all in line for—a facial, right there," Sylvia said. "Can you imagine? I wouldn't do it in front of everyone."

"Have you considered putting *her* out front?" Faye whispered to Grace after Sylvia moved across the store to talk to another sales associate. Grace laughed.

"I'm serious," Faye hissed.

"That's what I was afraid of," Grace whispered and then raised her voice for the others to hear. "Despite a little chaos today, we've already had good sales. Thank you, everyone, for your help. Remember, our busy preparations aren't just for the event itself. Focus on the exchange you will make with each woman inside—or outside—our door."

As if her words were a welcome, five women walked through the door, and the sales staff scattered to greet them. Faye flung a few scarves around her neck and gathered several more women around the mannequin to show them how to tie a square scarf. Grace took Faye's advice and steered Sylvia outside to greet and welcome those who were "just looking."

Outside the store, the energy of women's voices drew her into the crowds rushing in and out of the stores on this level. From the balcony she eyed the smooth male model in a tuxedo greeting the ladies with free cologne samples outside the menswear store. Groups of women gathered around him, and others chatted in pockets of threes and fours in the center court decorated with lit potted plants tied with holiday trim.

The crowd coming out of Kitchen Gourmet circulated toward her. The diverse groups of women scattered along the mall were younger and dressed more casually than those she encountered on a regular shopping day. Grace didn't recognize many familiar faces from her regular clientele.

"This is good," she said and headed back to the store, nodding to Sylvia. "You can't get new customers out of the same old bunch, can you?"

Sylvia shrugged and said, "Not likely."

Inside, fifteen to twenty women wandered amongst the racks, eating cookies and tying scarves on themselves and each other. One woman who'd just relocated from Chicago had come with her neighbor and was now buying two scarves. She also wanted help choosing between a pale yellow cashmere sweater and a green one.

"It complements your hazel eyes," the neighbor told her, pointing to the green one. The woman bought both of them with the scarves, and Grace invited them to come back the following week when they would host a mini fashion show of their new holiday clothes.

"Cross your fingers that the rest of the clothes arrive in time," Chanel, who was in charge of the show, mumbled behind her.

"Can you believe how many people are here?" Grace said. She wasn't going to worry about next week before this night had even passed.

"Sylvia said she's counted more than 100 who've come through the door so far, and it's not even seven yet. Most of them are just popping in for a cookie, but I'd say that a third of them have stayed to shop, or at least listen to Faye."

"Food matters, doesn't it?" Grace moved back into the mob of women streaming in for the cookies Audrey was distributing. "Would you like to learn some different ways to accent with a scarf?" she asked the curly-haired pregnant woman who had two cookies in her hand and one in her mouth.

When the crowd peaked in the eight o'clock hour, Grace felt the press of people in the front of the store that pushed against each other. She gestured to Chanel and Trenna to lead women into the empty spots in the side and the rear of the store.

"Did you check out these sales racks back here?" Trenna, despite her petite size, led the crowd with her influential tone as if she were a shopper herself letting the crowd in on her secret find. A horde followed her, and when they were occupied, she returned to the front to lead another group to the raised level on the other side of the store.

With an hour left to go before the event's close, Grace walked to the front doors again to relieve Sylvia. Two women dressed in scrubs underneath their wool winter coats chatted casually with Sylvia just outside the door. From what Grace overheard it was gossip, more than anything, about a fellow staff member in their doctor's building. She edged closer to the door, still greeting others as they came in, where she could hide from Sylvia's view but still see the women.

"She'll be at the office party. But oh . . . you won't be there this year," the brown-haired woman closest to the door said to Sylvia.

"You never should have left, Sylvia," her tall friend added.

But Sylvia was focused on something else. "See that woman coming up from the first floor?"

The two women— obviously Sylvia's former coworkers— turned their heads and laughed crudely. "Hah. Someone should have told her this isn't a cocktail party," the tall friend said.

"Or the cow's night out," Sylvia added.

Grace couldn't see beyond the door, so she casually stepped out from behind it just as Roberta Foster rounded the balcony in that too-tight black stretch skirt with the print top and black peep-toe heels. Her plump figure bunched the shimmery fabric in bulges around her middle, and the skirt pulled across her hips. She flushed in embarrassment for Roberta who normally commanded the respect of shoppers at The Plaza but now walked awkwardly alone through the crowd of women toward Honeybee.

Sylvia caught site of Grace at the same time Grace recognized Roberta.

"That top and skirt would look so much better—on someone taller," Sylvia backtracked.

Grace gave Sylvia a disappointed look and said in her loudest and most cheery voice, "Roberta, how nice of you to escape your busy evening and come and see us. Come in and have a cookie with me."

Behind her, Sylvia snickered to her former coworkers and said without even a whispered voice, "I think she already had a few before she came."

"Right this way," Grace spoke loudly to Roberta to cover the laughter behind her, hoping she hadn't heard. From the straight look on Roberta's face, Grace couldn't tell if she had, but Roberta declined the cookie Audrey offered.

Grace led her further into the store where the crowds had thinned. Trenna spotted her mom and came forward immediately. Grace left them as soon as she could and strode angrily back to Sylvia, trying to check her expression before she stepped out the door and encountered her. The women she'd been talking to had moved on down the mall, talking to another group of women in scrubs by the shoe store.

"I'll relieve you, now," Grace said. Sylvia backed up toward the opening to the store. "You can go home."

Sylvia drew down her upper lip and pulled it tight against her front teeth, tipped her head at Grace, and disappeared through the racks of clothing to the backroom. Grace stood at the entrance to Honeybee with a plastered smile the rest of the night, especially when Sylvia brushed past her with her coat and purse.

"I'll call you," Trenna said to her as she escorted Roberta out a few minutes later.

Grace sighed. She didn't know what to say to Roberta or what she would do to Sylvia—beyond that immediate reprimand—to manage the damage done to this faithful customer that Lilly, and then she, had nurtured. Even though her relationship with Roberta dipped in the awkwardness of her friendship with Trenna, she'd always treated her professionally and honored the example Lilly had set.

Despite the energy Grace found early that evening when she saw the mall and store fill with women, she left Honeybee deflated. The crowds dispersed slowly, and the stray groups of women carried their conversations down to the restaurants or the parking lot.

Colleen, the manager of Kitchen Gourmet, waved to her and pulled their doors shut. Grace walked past the display windows and picked up the scattered trash. She didn't even shift her eyes toward the plant in the window. She was afraid that there, too, she might find that her plant endeavor had been swept up with the others, coming down to sputter at her feet.

Chapter Seven

Grace didn't consult Sue or Chanel about what to do with Sylvia. She didn't even ask Trenna about Roberta's reaction. Grace just acted on her gut feeling as the manager. This wasn't her problem; it was Sylvia's to fix. When Sylvia strolled into the backroom the next day, Grace confidently met her with an ultimatum—apologize or quit.

"Oh, Grace. You can't be serious. You, yourself, have scoffed at Roberta's weight and her inability to know what looks good on her."

"She's always put together."

"Because you—and Lilly before you—and who knows how many other saleswomen in this building, dress her from her underwear up. She never puts together her own outfits. She doesn't know how. That was obvious last night."

"Sylvia," Grace raised her voice and pointed toward her. "Enough. I expect you to apologize to Roberta, in person when she comes in or on the phone if she doesn't come before next Thursday's event. We didn't invite all the women of suburban St. Louis to The Plaza last night so we could lose our oldest customers." Grace walked out of the backroom, leaving Sylvia scowling still holding her purse and coat.

"We sold a lot of scarves," Chanel said cheerfully as Grace reached for the previous night's sales report.

"We already knew that," Grace said. She caught the condescension in her words but didn't know how to rephrase it.

"We're three percent above a normal weeknight evening."

"Is that all?" Grace said under her breath. Could it be that the stressful busy evening didn't bring anything more than that?

"Grace!" Chanel scolded in a motherly tone. "Recognize the improvement. We have an increase in sales. Sylvia's slip up didn't take that away. One person's mistake doesn't color the achievements of the whole staff."

"I know you're right, but her treatment of Roberta points to a bigger issue. Sure the numbers of people in here caused the sales to rise, but we need fifty people buying more than thirty-dollar scarves. We need the Robertas of this place. Can't you see the symbolism of her actions? We sought new customers while simultaneously turning our backs on the ones we already had."

"Are you going to close the door on the new ones because they don't spend as much?" Chanel accused.

"That's not it at all," Grace defended.

"Isn't it?" Chanel left the counter with a returned sweater.

Had Sylvia's misstep blocked her ability to see the good in last night? Was a problem with one masking the positive efforts of all? She didn't think so. What happened was a serious error and might destroy years of what others had built.

At home that night Grace found another invitation for a dinner and a movie at the carriage house, but she was too tired this time to make an effort. Grace opened the fridge and closed it again.

She filled a glass of water from the tap and drank it quickly without even adding ice, the edge of the counter pressing into her hips. Her stomach gurgled a sickly sound from the rush of liquid into emptiness. She leaned over the sink, allowing her head to rest on the cool protruding tap.

The moonlight that bounced from the window distorted the stainless steel in the sink so that it appeared to be moving. With the glass in one hand and the other on the side of the sink, she stared into that deep drain hole like a tunnel of her own mixed emotions.

She rested there, exhausted by thought and energy spent. Were all her and the staff's efforts the night before worth it? She just wanted to use her time for the right purpose and have it matter—and be received.

Lady Lu called out in a helpless whine, and Grace lifted her face to the window. The cuttings, not the kitten, stood in her line of sight. She reached out a hand, lifted the plastic wrap covering, and touched the soil. Dry. The water bottle next to her was empty. When was the last time she'd misted them? Had she left them too long? How often had she neglected them until they were dry?

To see more clearly, she flipped on the light above the sink. Three of the cuttings had new growth of small leaves on them. The others, though, didn't have any and probably wouldn't make it. Maybe she could transplant the growing ones into pots of their own. She filled her spray bottle, misted all of them until the soil was more than moist, covered them again with the plastic and went to bed early, only eating a handful of cashews.

Sleep cleared away the fight within her mind, and she woke to the prospect of being able to transplant the cuttings. Her

Saturday walk in the crisp fall air took her to the hardware store to buy some pretty pots for the transplants. Even though the Halloween decorations had been stripped from most of the homes, she found some stray candy wrappers in the gutter as she turned onto Lockwood. The city had already brought out the holiday flags on the lampposts. She expected holiday décor in November at the mall, but the old-fashioned part of her still wanted these neighborhood stores to observe the not-until-after-Thanksgiving rule.

Everyone wanted an extra dollar, and as a retail manager, she understood the game. The sooner the customers began shopping, the more retailers could make. As Chanel pointed out so crassly, the number of customers, not just how much they spent, also mattered.

She walked past Tasty Pastry, but the apple fritters she saw through the window drew her back, not having eaten yet. The store's owner, a short round, Danny Devito–looking man stood behind the counter.

"Thank you for the cookie order to Honeybee at The Plaza. We only had 50 cookies left at the end of the night," she reported. "I think we took our count by the number of cookies eaten, not the number of women coming through the door. We're doing it all over next week. Any suggestions?"

She sampled the pumpkin chocolate chip cookie, which he handed her along with her apple fritter, and ordered five hundred. She bought four glazed clay pots from the clearance rack at Ken's Hardware and stalled in front of the window at The Floral Shop on the way back home. They had removed the hibiscus and set up their Christmas display. In the corner were three miniature pine trees potted in glass pots.

Grace pushed open the door to The Floral Shop. The same woman who'd helped Trenna with the bouquet found her. Grace pointed to the display. "I've never seen anything as unique as those pots. Do you carry them?"

"No, sorry, but I can get you the website where we found them." She scribbled down the website address and gave it to Grace.

At home, Grace flipped down the screen on her laptop in disgust. "Seventy-five dollars a piece!" The clay pots would have to do. In the shed she had a bag of potting soil, at least half a bag, which should be enough to transplant all of them. She came out of the shed, loaded with supplies and ambled toward her back stairs. She stopped beside the garden she'd abandoned when the temperatures fell at the first of the month. Tomato vines stretched like lazy limbs over the path, and the crumpled leaves covered the herbs. She set the bag of soil on the top step and moved back the colorful leaves. Her basil plant was alive and green, obviously protected from the earlier frost.

"Maybe I can salvage you, too." She returned to the shed for her shovel, distracted now by the garden and dug around the base of the plant. She awkwardly carried the plant inside to her table, dropping dirt along the way, and plopped it in the first pot she found. Wiping her hands on her jeans, she grabbed several plastic kitchen bags from under her sink and laid them on the table. Now, to fill those other three pots.

She brought the cuttings down from the windowsill and carefully loosened the soil around the perimeter of the first pot with a butter knife. Her hand stretched out to catch the new tender plant as she turned the pot on its side, allowing the sand and perlite to spill onto the plastic bags and the young plants to fall into her open hand.

Two of the three she held had formed new leaves, and they also had those stringy new roots on the bottom. She separated all three, laying aside the one that hadn't rooted. She laid the other two out on the table and then filled a pot with soil. She hadn't read up on this transplanting part, but she assumed it would be like transplanting the tomatoes into her garden.

She worked as quickly as she could to fill the soil in two pots, make a small hole in which to insert the young plant, and then placed one in each. Their transition from Lilly's plant to her windowsill to this new pot might have roughened up the plant and weakened the root system or they could have grown stronger and more independent with each step in the process. She wasn't sure which would happen, a complete failure or a remarkable success.

Grace carefully repeated the process, but this time she filled the remaining pot with soil before she poured out the other cuttings. From the lack of growth on all but one of the plants, she knew she would only have one more to transplant. This one she babied so that its roots wouldn't be touched more than a minute with the heated air in her kitchen.

At the end of the planting project, she had three new pots with baby hibiscus plants and a fourth with the summer basil she'd brought inside. She carried these to the windowsill and reassessed the light. The filtered sun that came through had been just right for their start, but it probably wouldn't be enough for their winter needs.

She left the basil plant on her kitchen table and walked around her house with a plant tucked under either elbow and holding one out in front of her. At every window, she analyzed the light. Now that the leaves were off the Esplins' trees next door, the midday light in the front bedroom of the house was good, and the rarely used table in the second one would be out of the way for a group of them together. She set them on the floor, grabbed a plain white flour sack dishtowel from her kitchen, and spread it on the table.

When the plants were in place, she watered them and fell on the bed in the sunlight. The warmth on her face felt like the day in the early spring when she'd napped in the sun on her living room floor. That was the day she'd prepared Lilly's plant to go to Honeybee. Then, she had looked through the glass of her coffee table at the plant. Now, Lilly's baby plants had come home, and she visualized what they might have looked like in those glass potters. Maybe she would have been able to see the roots grow, as well as watch the new branches appear.

She'd written in the red leather journal those first days and wished she could record these first moments, too. At the store, they'd all neglected writing much about the care of Lilly's plant anymore, hadn't they? That's what she meant when she said to Chanel, "It's hard for me to see what other people are doing."

When she went back to work on Monday, she'd bring the journal home and pick up the record where they'd left off. While she could see that all of them had contributed to helping Lily's plant grow and bloom, she didn't believe the majority of the staff understood the underlying idea that the nurturing they gave the plants was the nurturing they needed to give the customers.

Chanel had said not to make that influence of Lilly's plant overt, but she knew it should be the basis for the girls' night out that she and Trenna were planning for the first part of December. That's where they would start brainstorming—with the foundation of that plant.

With this hope of better relationships all around, Grace smiled at Sylvia when she greeted her the next week. Despite her effort, they stood uncomfortably side-by-side at the sales desk until two women came through the front door a few minutes apart.

The first woman wore black dress slacks, a white blouse, and too much makeup for a woman her age, with foundation and powder settling into her wrinkles. The second, much-younger woman wore jeans and a tight sweater. The physical and social distance between them made it obvious to Grace that they were not together.

"I'll take the one in front; she's one of our longest-running customers," Grace said, attempting to move out from behind the counter to help the wealthy, older patron.

"Don't you trust me?" Sylvia hissed.

"She knows me, Sylvia. She trusts that I know what she wants."

Sylvia gripped the side of the counter and stood solid in her place, neglecting to help either customer. Grace directed both to different racks and came back to find Sylvia at the front entrance. From the mall hallway outside the store, Faye directed the mall maintenance workers to set up a platform for the fashion show.

"Three feet closer to the balcony," Faye motioned to the workers. "We want it to be seen from the atrium court below."

"They've got to have a reason to come upstairs," Chanel agreed.

Grace rested a hand on Sylvia's shoulder. "Why don't you come in during this lull of customers and call Roberta?" she suggested.

"You don't have to pour syrup all over it to get me to swallow my punishment," Sylvia breezed past her to the phone on the front desk and pulled out the phone book.

"Her number is in our customer database, too."

"This is fine," Sylvia bent stubbornly over the directory.

Grace stood on the opposite side of the counter, although she faced the group out front who were now covering the edges of the platform with black fabric while Sylvia dialed.

"Roberta Foster, please," Sylvia said and waited. "No message."

Grace mouthed to her to leave a message, but Sylvia ignored her and hung up the phone. "Why didn't you leave a message?" Grace asked.

"What kind of message would that be?" Sylvia asked.

"Something anything—that would prompt her to know you didn't mean it."

"But, I did mean it," she said, flicking the phone book closed. "And I still do."

"But that's not an apology. An apology is from the heart; it's more than words. It's remorse," Grace said, coming around the counter to stand between the counter and the wall. Sylvia shrunk back from Grace's approach.

"You may be my manager and my employer, but you are *not* my mother," Sylvia said, leaning in a few inches from Grace. "My remorse is mine and mine only. I will meet your demands for the words but you can't demand that my heart is attached to it."

On the day of the next event, Audrey and Chanel practiced walking on the platform. Grace moved in and out of the store, assembling outfits on the rack beside them. Chanel handed

Audrey a tan suede coat, and she pulled it on just as Sylvia came out from the back of the store.

"Are you modeling the clothes?" Sylvia asked Audrey.

"Chanel asked me."

"Trenna's modeling, too," Chanel added.

"But she's pregnant—and short," Sylvia complained.

"She's just barely showing. People should know we carry petites. The two of them will attract that younger audience we want," Chanel said, lifting her eyes to see Grace watching them.

"I'm still young," Sylvia said.

Grace followed her to the backroom, but Sylvia ditched into the bathroom. When she came out, Grace stood up.

"You're not going to block my path, again, are you?" she asked.

"Sylvia. What can we do to resolve this?"

"Withdraw your unrealistic expectations."

"Unrealistic?" Grace said. "This is about good customer service."

"Whatever."

Over Sylvia's head, Grace saw Trenna and Roberta enter the store. Sylvia turned to see what had stopped their conversation.

Sylvia grunted and left the backroom. Grace followed casually behind until they reached the pair standing in front of the counter.

"Mrs. Foster, I am happy you came back tonight," Sylvia said with affection and took Roberta's hand. "I regret the words you overheard last week. I was simply playing to the audience of other women. Please accept my apology. It was out of line with the service you've received and will continue to receive here."

Sylvia released Roberta's hand, moved behind her, and smirked at Trenna and Grace.

"Is there anything more we can do for you tonight?" Grace asked, at their side.

"I would like to stay for the fashion show and preview some of your holiday outfits. As you saw," she looked around for Sylvia, "the one I chose last week didn't fit very well."

"I'm sure Sylvia could help you find something tonight, and whenever you come in. Couldn't you, Sylvia?" Grace put her hand on Sylvia's elbow. Sylvia squirmed and folded her arms across her chest, overlapping her hand on top of Grace's. A sharp digging pain shot into Grace's right hand.

"I would love to, Mrs. Foster. Let's start right here." Sylvia released her nails from Grace's hand and steered Roberta toward a shelf of cashmere sweaters.

Grace rubbed the pain out of her hand, but it lingered even after she recorded the incident in Sylvia's employee file. She couldn't say anything to Trenna, and after Chanel's reaction with the last confrontation, she wondered if she could even discuss it with her.

The Thanksgiving holiday moved them into the height of the holiday shopping season with Sylvia withdrawing her enthusiasm for any group goals and replacing it with an increase of sarcasm toward Grace. The girls' night out events had slightly smaller crowds than the first night's window shoppers, but even Chanel admitted to Grace that they were more eager customers.

Sue noticed the increase of sales and called to congratulate the whole staff on their success. Grace didn't assume it would be smooth sailing for the rest of the holiday season; she'd still have to work longer hours with increasing stress for the next month.

At least now that stress came from a busy store, not an empty one, and they'd shown their worth again.

Despite Chanel's early suggestion to leave Lilly's plant out of the GNO events, Grace proposed an idea to Trenna to make the hibiscus a central part of the December events. At the first staff meeting of the month, Trenna and Grace met at the store earlier than the rest of the staff. They moved one of the round tables into the store's entry foyer. Together they hauled Lilly's plant out of the front window display where it had been now for eight months and set it in the center of the table. They dressed up the yellow pot with a silver bow and scrunched a purple scarf around the base of the plant.

"I brought Lilly's plant into the store last spring to remind us of one of the store's longtime employees, Lilly Klein, and her contributions to the store. Many of us have helped, and the plant has grown," Grace said when the staff assembled around the plant. "Likewise, your contributions of ideas and work the past two months have helped the store traffic to grow. Thank you for your effort."

Grace moved to the side of the table to give a clear view of the plant. "Now, we've moved the plant out of the front window display to this central spot where we can remember our purpose with each customer who walks through the door. Lilly said, 'Time given to nurturing relationships doesn't sacrifice the essential—it is the essential.'"

Grace motioned to Trenna, who came forward.

"Lilly's plant represents the nurturing gift in each of us, wherever we are in our lives. For our last girls' night out, we want to honor that quality in our customers and for them to honor it in each other. It is intangible but produces growth when it is given and received."

Grace could watch the staff's reaction more clearly when Trenna was talking. Most were engaged in the idea. Faye was nodding her head in agreement. Chanel looked right at Grace and caught her eye, which was positive encouragement; she didn't want Chanel to feel looked over as the assistant manager on this. Beth cracked her knuckles but cocked her head with interest toward Trenna. Sylvia rolled her eyes and moved behind Bridgette, a new full-time associate, with a tightened jaw.

"The plan is to leave the plant here throughout December," Trenna continued. "Talk about it with customers. Share what it means. On the last Thursday event we will invite women who come to take a seed packet of flowers from under our hibiscus 'tree.' They can write any name and message on the back and give it to a friend, coworker, daughter, sister, mother, mentor— someone they've nurtured or who has nurtured them."

"HOW CUTE!" Sylvia immediately said in a loud, sarcastic voice from the back row. "Now we're not only in the business of selling clothes, but we're selling sentimentality. I won't buy it."

Trenna opened her mouth, but Grace held her hand out toward Trenna. Grace moved forward in the semi-circle of women in front of the plant.

"Sylvia, you don't have to buy it. It's free." Grace gestured to the plant. "Lilly's plant is now at the center of the store. People may ask about it. Others may not care to participate, and that's fine. I hope you will use its position and message to generate interest in the coming weeks. Any other questions or concerns?"

After the meeting, Chanel sought out Grace. "I told you to not do this, but I was wrong. If you can do it in this way, it will still be subtle, tasteful, and inspiring to those who want it to be."

Sylvia gestured angrily at Beth who stood dumbly silent, still cracking her knuckles. Chanel lowered her voice. "And those who want to make it more or less than that—well, I'll back you up to Sue on whatever you say in answer to that."

Despite Sylvia's reaction, most of the staff took a renewed interest in the plant in its new, more prominent location, and the women who came into the store responded. They talked and shared stories, changing interactions between employees and customers beyond simply, "Can I help you?"

The final event brought what Grace had envisioned from the start. Trenna's younger cousin Elyse, who was also a talented violinist, sat in the front of the store and played live holiday music. She not only played solos for an hour herself, but she rotated with two fellow musicians she had asked to play with her. Women mingled in the store with festive drinks, good music, and conversations surrounding Lilly's plant. Best of all, they bought merchandise—for gifts and for themselves.

"Do you have an earring back for this set? It's missing," A woman with black hair dangled a pair of cubic zirconia pendants in front of Grace. "I want them to give with my seed packet, but only if you can find a back."

Grace disappeared into the backroom with the mini concert as a backdrop to the women's voices. As she opened the drawer of jewelry odds and ends, the music ended and she could only hear the buzz of louder women's voices. One voice sounded distinctly louder than the rest.

Grace peeked out the backroom door. Sylvia's sleek auburn hair stood out amid a cluster of blonde and brown and weaved through the assembled women. Curious at the gathering around Sylvia, Grace quickly pulled a new packet of backs from the drawer and then weaved her way through the talking women.

Chanel met her half way with an outstretched hand. "The earring back? I can finish this." In her eyes Grace read a warning that could only be spoken with one word, "Sue."

The regional manager stood right beside Lilly's plant, and Sylvia stood right beside her. The women that surrounded them seemed familiar, but Grace couldn't immediately grasp who they were. Then she recognized Barbara and Renee from the Clayton store. While she was trying to put names and faces to the others, Sue looked up and greeted her.

"Grace, I brought some of our sales staff from the other St. Louis stores to see what you've done here, and Sylvia was explaining tonight's theme to us."

Bet she was. Grace pushed her hair behind her ear and wet her lips. Smiling, she moved forward to extend her hand and position herself between Sue and Sylvia.

Sue made cheerful compliments—not the sour snubs Grace expected—and mingled with Grace's staff and the customers who continued to come. At the close of the night, Sue gathered all the Honeybee employees again around the table displaying Lilly's plant.

"Lilly left a great legacy in this store, and I appreciate that you used the theme of nurturing relationships and growth tonight. It communicates exactly what I want to say tonight to all of you employees of Honeybee, but especially the staff here at The Plaza. You *are* growing. While we won't have final holiday numbers until after January first, this season looks better than last in every store. You've met the expectations the company set for you in October. As a result, the Honeybee stores will expand in the St. Louis market this year. We have just signed a lease for a new store at the Wild Horse Creek development in Chesterfield."

****

The restaurant hugged the corner of the street on the first block of Clayton's Demun neighborhood. The buildings on the street, like hers in Webster, held a semi-urban charm. Sadie's itself was no bigger than a few parlor-sized rooms grouped together with an arched doorway between them. The intimacy enhanced its old-school white tablecloth quality. Grace hid the heavy gift bag behind her coat and followed the maître d' over the carpet to where Max and Trenna sat at a tiny rectangular table for four.

Max stood for her. Nice manners. The maître d' had already pulled out the slim chair for her, and she slipped into it, setting the gift bag on the empty chair beside her. He handed them menus and left.

"Charming place," Grace said.

"I've celebrated every birthday here since I was ten," Trenna said.

"It's too quaint to be pretentious, but did you like it when you were that age?"

She nodded. "I was weird."

"You still are," Max joked. Trenna pushed him playfully.

Grace slipped her coat off her arms and shrugged it to the back of her chair. "Thanks for the invitation. It caps the week— no, the month."

"Last night went well, didn't it?"

"Unexpectedly so. Sue even told me privately afterwards that if our store holds our sales through the end of the week without too many returns after the holiday, we will be the top-grossing store this quarter—not just in St. Louis, but in her whole region."

"Back to number one, like you hoped. A good reason to celebrate," Trenna said and turned to Max. "Should we tell her or just wait?"

"Hmmm . . . how about the gift first and then the other surprise?" he said.

Trenna nodded, reaching under her chair. "After that month of build up I wanted to get you the right Christmas gift." She lifted a large package wrapped in brown paper and tied on all four sides with a black velvet ribbon.

"Something that would be worth tying this seed packet to." Trenna twirled the packet of bluebells tied to the bow so that Grace could see as she handed the package to her. "Merry Christmas and thank you all in one."

"Wow," Grace said and started to set it on the chair beside her.

"No, open it now," Trenna protested.

Grace pushed her chair back so that she had more room to slip off the ribbon and then the brown paper, which crumpled loud enough to disturb the atmosphere. She uncovered a wood frame beneath the wrapping and turned it over.

The watercolor painting on the front showed a small round wood table beside a window. The walls in the background receded in the shadows, but sunlight from the window shone on the top of the table. In the glow were three blue pots atop a plain white cloth, each holding a small plant, just barely peeking over the top. The tallest one was also the fullest with new growth on the top and the sides. A still life from her own spare bedroom.

"The cuttings from Lilly's plant," Grace said.

"Really?" Trenna asked.

"I didn't tell you that's what they were because I hoped . . ." Grace paused.

"Then that makes this an even better gift," Trenna said.

"It does. You've captured them so well, Trenna. Thank

you." Grace set the painting on the chair beside her and reached for the heavy gift bag there.

Grace stood with her hand supporting the heavy bag and set it in front of Trenna, who peeked inside. The tissue paper and ribbons blocked the view so Max pulled the bag off the bottom while she brought out an oblong package covered in tissue paper out the top. A silver bow and a seed packet of cosmos tied it all up.

Max cut the bow with the scissors on his Swiss Army Knife. Trenna folded back the paper and revealed a miniature plant about eight inches high in a glass pot. She grinned and pointed to the picture propped up in the chair across from her. "It's one of those, isn't it?"

"Yes, the only one that survived," Grace confirmed.

The moments of realization descended upon them, warming the moment even more than it had been with just the first gift. That's when the tissues came out and both women excused themselves to the ladies' room together. They left the restroom more composed, and Trenna led them back to the table. She stopped abruptly, and Grace ran into her.

Trenna turned around and said, "I forgot something; let's go back."

"You forgot something in the bathroom. What did you forget?" Grace said.

"Umm . . . my lipstick. It's on the counter."

They returned down the hall. Trenna looked on the counter and then opened the stall door. "I thought it was in here."

"In the stall? Look in your purse," Grace said. Trenna opened her clutch purse and rifled through it. She pulled out a silver tube of lipstick and held it up.

"Mystery solved," Grace said. "What's up?"

"What do you mean?"

"You did not leave your lipstick; you didn't even get it out when we were in here," Grace reminded her.

"Max has a surprise, too. It's at the table. I just wanted to warn you."

"So warn me."

"I did. Your surprise is at the table."

Grace rolled her eyes and led the way out this time. She scanned the table as soon as they reentered the dining room. Max had cleared away the gift wrap and ribbons, and the table was empty except for the menus. He was seated in the same place, looking toward them. She didn't see anything. He waved with a goofy smile on his face, and Trenna grabbed her hand and led her through the maze of the tight dining room again. Then Grace saw the surprise—a dark-haired man sat in the fourth chair at the table and turned to show her the most eager grin she'd ever received from a blind date.

Chapter Eight

The start of the New Year and success at work opened Grace to new possibilities. Transferring to manage the new store could be a real option and with new prospects for relationships, she could even imagine loving again.

That first setup warmed her to that. He invited her to the symphony the next week. His crisp button-down, tie, and dress slacks combined with his gracious opening of the car door attracted her. On the third date they went to the Gateway Arch since Grace hadn't ever visited it. A little egg-shaped elevator traveled up the side to the top, and he rested his hand on her back when it shifted and shook. The warmth of his hand through her knit top relaxed her. From the top, they peered at the city below, picking out the stadium, his office, and the Old Courthouse.

"We should wander through the Cathedral," Grace motioned toward the historic Basilica after they emerged from the south leg of the Arch. But she wished she hadn't. That's where he revealed that he didn't believe in God or religion. Although Grace hadn't been to church since her move to Missouri—and not much more during her engagement to Jeff—she didn't want to fall for another man whose beliefs didn't fall anywhere close to hers.

The failed attempt, though, only ignited Max's efforts to bring Grace back into the world of dating with Max suggesting every available friend, colleague, or relative he knew between the ages of twenty-five and forty. The thrill of this was not lost on Grace who had missed the anticipation of preparing for a date and the engaging conversations that could arise when meeting someone for the first time.

So for the first three months of the year, Grace marked not only her thirty-first birthday but she also marked her calendar with new dates. Although her stomach fluttered for a few, none of them progressed enough to stick. Still, Max called with another setup in March.

"Haven't I gone through all your friends? I might be better off with online dating."

"So do that, too," he encouraged.

"Remind me again why you've made this your mission?" Grace asked.

"Trenna says you're happier when you're with people. Someone needs to prod you."

"And I can't do that?"

"If it were up to you, you'd hibernate at home." He was right. "Besides, you can't give up yet. I have another one—a project manager who works at a large construction company."

Mike, the project manager, met Grace after work on a weekday evening. He had light blond hair like hers, but his curled up on the ends. His broad construction worker shoulders matched evenly with her eye level.

They went to the Landing for dinner. He ordered a steak and talked about the farm he left in Iowa after his divorce. Between bites of salmon she tried to visualize them as a couple ten years ahead or even ten days, but she couldn't.

"I'm in Chesterfield every day working on this new development," he said, vigorously cutting his steak. "I'm too tired for much of a social life after that. I just go to my townhome and watch TV."

She imagined him sitting on the couch with a man-sized frozen entrée on his lap and the remote control in his hand. She still couldn't picture herself sitting next to him.

"Do you build homes?" she asked, trying to sound interested.

"Oh, we're not home builders," he said with his mouth full. "We specialize in large commercial developments. Well, I guess we do some residential. It's mixed-use but mostly retail."

"Mixed-use?"

"Well, lifestyle centers, really—townhomes on the perimeter with walking trails that lead to a village of restaurants, small businesses, and retail shops in the interior."

"Like the Wild Horse Creek development in Chesterfield."

"Yeah. That's the one. You know it?"

She leaned in toward the table, interest growing. "Not really. But I'd like to go out there. Would you take me?"

"Tonight?" He tore the flimsy covering off another tub of butter and spread it on his slathered baked potato.

Grace checked her watch. "It's probably too late. Saturday maybe?"

"Sure."

They arranged to have lunch at a restaurant that had just opened in the first phase of Wild Horse Creek. She met him at The Plaza again, knowing it would be even further to her house. She told him to meet her on the steps near the west parking lot.

He said he'd be driving a red pick-up truck. When he arrived that weekend for their outing, his oversized American truck stood out from the foreign luxury vehicles that filled the lot, and she quickly climbed in.

While country music played on the stereo, she struggled to find a common topic. They passed hospitals, private schools, and businesses, all set in a landscape of emerging green. In between, new housing developments stretched out like they were reproductions of the suburbs surrounding The Plaza, just thirty years newer.

"Why is everything made of brick here?" she asked, not seeing that as much in Minnesota.

"Tradition. Availability. Here in West County—it's also a showy facade."

Grace liked the brick bungalows of her Webster neighborhood, but these newer brick homes weighed heavy on the rolling hills with their immense size. The suburban landscape tightened into closer new development as they traveled toward the Missouri River and exited at Chesterfield Airport Road. Car dealerships with huge glass windows, chain hotels, and retail strip malls exploded on both sides of the freeway.

"Welcome to the Valley," he said with a wave out the windshield. All of it seemed new. Freshly painted crosswalks spanned dark asphalt roads. Modern streetlights channeled threads of traffic into new chain restaurants and stores. While the traditionalism of her usual part of town comforted her, this contrasting new infrastructure energized her.

"Twenty years ago, this was supposedly empty with just the airport and a prison out here. Then, the whole thing flooded."

"With development?"

"With water," he said.

"They must have built some kind of flood system or taller levees since then." Grace noted the miles of strip malls and acres of box bog retailers. The traffic matched the frenzied pace of development.

"They have."

"Will it be protected, though? Why do people . . . why do you keep building here?"

"Land." Mike turned at a construction trailer with a field of dozers and graders parked beside new foundations with steel framing rising from them. Stretched out on the other side of the road from the construction site was a massive new development—all of it in monochromatic shades of stucco. Narrow streets wove through the mini "town" and intersected with main roads filled with cars and people. They parked in the last available stall in the parking lot.

"No brick?" she said.

"Too traditional for here. But plenty of places to eat and shop."

"I thought the mall was dying."

"The indoor mall maybe, but this place certainly isn't," he said.

The well-kept exterior encouraged heavy pedestrian traffic even though the temperatures were just warming up for spring. Thick piles of new red mulch freshened the early spring landscaping and planter pots of new pansies, the first annuals Grace had seen yet this year, marked the sidewalk at every crosswalk.

They walked two blocks past a trendy burrito bar, an upscale men's clothing store, an ice cream vendor, and a shoe store with ten pairs of red shoes in the window. Offices and living spaces rose above main level storefronts.

Grace stopped him at the new Mother and Me store, which was also opening soon at The Plaza. There she found hand-knit blankets for Trenna's surprise baby shower, but Mike paced uncomfortably when she lingered at the matching cutesy outfits that were reminiscent of the ones her mother had sewn for her and her sister.

At the Asian restaurant on the corner they waited for forty-five minutes for a table. They bounced between the semi-circle wooden bench on the sidewalk and the red leather couch in the vestibule.

"Did you help with this phase, too?" Grace asked.

"No, they finished that up just after I moved here. I worked on another project, the one where I met Max, and then they moved me over to help with the new phase."

"I like it better than I thought I would."

"Max mocks these developments, but I don't mind them. He says it looks like they're trying to rebuild the character of the older streets in Clayton or Webster without the money or craftsmanship to do it right."

Once she had a menu in hand, the spring energy she inhaled outside prompted her to brave a spicy pepper dish instead of her usual chicken salad. Mike had another steak. After lunch, he brushed her hand as they weaved toward the door, but she snuck it quickly into her pocket.

He filled in the awkward lull. "Anywhere else you'd like to look?"

"What about phase two? Can you show me anything there?"

"Well there's not much, and we don't meet OSHA requirements either."

"Our company is building a new store out here, I think. You can point it out from the street, couldn't you?"

"Honeybee?"

"Yes. Would it be on the plans?" she asked.

"It might."

They walked toward the construction zone, through the parking lot, and crossed the street next to the construction trailer. Mike took out his keys and opened the door.

"I'm really not supposed to allow . . ."

"That's fine; I'll wait here," Grace said. She paused at the bottom of the stairs, outside the trailer, while he went inside. He came back and stood at the top of stairs, inside the door, and unrolled a large sheet of paper.

"From what I can see, I think it's in on the east side of Block 10."

Grace stepped up on the bottom step, and Mike sat down on the top one with the site plan in his lap and pointed with his pen. When she leaned over to look, she stood directly in front of him, closer than she wanted but eager for more information.

"How big are those spaces?" She pointed to the spaces in Block 10.

"Oh, maybe 2500 square feet," he said. "It depends how they finish the interiors."

"Really? That big? Ours at The Plaza is only 1500."

"Seems like this will be quite a bit bigger then."

He set the paper on the floor next to him, removing the physical barrier between them. Before she could step back and give herself more space, he reached out and put his hands on her hips. He drew her body closer to his and half rose up from his spot with his mouth directly in front of hers. She grabbed the sides of the doorway and pulled to the side before he could kiss her. Mike scowled, grabbed the plans off the floor, and disappeared inside the construction trailer.

He said nothing on the ride home. The silence unnerved Grace, but she didn't speak either. When he pulled over at The Plaza, she quickly reached for the door. "Thanks for taking me."

"Wait," he said. "Am I reading you right? You came out with me. You asked me to take you there, show you around. I did, but then you stopped it."

"When we were alone, you . . . I'm not sure I'm interested."

"Then what interested you today?" he asked. "You talked in this animated, interested way. Like you cared about me or at least my work."

"Maybe it was just the place, those stores, all those people. Something seems to be happening out there—unlike this place," she gestured to the building beside them that looked more like a museum than a mall.

"So you like the place, but not me?" Mike grunted.

"No. Not like that," she said, not wanting to offend. "I'm just not ready to make it physical. I guess you can call me, again, and we'll see. Thanks for lunch."

Grace escaped inside rather than toward her car. Trenna would be working this afternoon, and Grace needed an outlet to talk. She self-consciously looked down at her jeans on her way through the mall. She would never wear jeans to work, but she wasn't there to work.

"I thought you had a date." Trenna raised her eyes in a wide expression and wobbled toward her.

"Over now," Grace said. "Who's here?"

"Sylvia and Audrey," Trenna said. "Chanel will be here within the hour to take over for me, but I'm not sure I can make it that long."

"Are you sitting down enough?" Grace said, pointing to the chair beside the register.

"Nothing's comfortable. Not sitting. Not standing. Not walking. I'm too short for this little girl inside," Trenna said, but she sat down anyway.

"Maybe you want to rethink your last day," Grace said, stowing her purse under the counter and entering her password into the computer.

"You're not going to work are you?" Trenna asked.

"Not really. I just wanted to catch an update on the corporate site for the Wild Horse Creek store," Grace said. "I just saw it—well, saw where it's going to be, anyway."

She scanned the site and found an artist's rendering of something that looked very similar to the stores she saw that morning with a headline of "Coming Soon."

"Trenna, it's going to be nearly double the size of this store," Grace said, excited for one new prospect that might just work out.

Sylvia came out of the back room. Grace lowered her voice, "The website says it opens in September. I'm sure that Sue will consider me to manage it; we just need to keep our numbers up."

"That would be great, if it happens," Trenna said. "How was your date?"

"Fine, I guess. After lunch, when I asked to see the plans for Honeybee, he took me right to the construction trailer, which was nice. But then he wanted to move faster than I want."

"Max said he's eager to marry again soon and have a family. You want that, too."

Grace made a face. "I'm not really that attracted to him."

"Then why did you go out with him a second time?"

"I wanted to see the store—or at least know more about where it would be and what it would look like." She played with the mouse with the browser still open to the rendering of the new Wild Horse Creek store.

"Grace," Trenna started. "That sounds just like what you told me about Jeff. Putting up a false front to get what you want. That's not you."

Grace bit her lip and backed up to lean against the wall. His flattery *had* destroyed her trust. But was she doing the same thing?

"Grace, everyone is going to have weaknesses—including you. Every marriage is going to have struggles. You're the one who told me that. Remember? I think you said, 'Marriage—it's for regular people, not just princes and princesses.'"

Grace's own words quoted back to her sounded amplified in her head. "You're probably right. So what's up with you, beyond being overly ready to be finished with this pregnancy?"

"Max and I are making a birth plan, and we've had a change of heart. I stayed with my mom's OB/GYN because I didn't know anyone else. But at my last appointment, I saw a certified nurse midwife in his office, and I really liked her. I'm thinking of switching to have her deliver Jillian."

"Hmm. That would be interesting. Does she deliver at Mercy, too?"

"Yes," Trenna said. "But we're considering . . . We want to have a home birth."

"Isn't that . . . messy?"

"Not really. We can also do it in water. That's what we want to try."

"What changed your mind?" Grace said, trying to soften her confusion.

"For me, having a baby is part of the nurturing process, like Lilly's plant was, or is, for you. I want a different, more natural, connection with my daughter than I have with my mom."

"What did Roberta say?" Grace asked. "Is she okay with that? Right next door?"

"We haven't told her. Besides, it's not her choice."

Grace understood, but what about the repercussions, the consequences of a home birth? Had Trenna fully considered all of those? She wouldn't personally want that additional risk outside the security a hospital could provide.

Sylvia appeared from behind the tall shelves and leaned across the ledge of the counter. "Grace, I didn't know you were working today." She peered at Grace's jeans and looked back and forth between Trenna and Grace.

Trenna eyes silently asked, "Where did she come from?"

"No, Sylvia, I'm not working," Grace answered, logging off the computer. "Just checking on a few things, and then I'm leaving."

"I finished up that sizing you were doing, Trenna." Sylvia took a couple steps toward some sweaters on a low table. She folded the top green one, fluffed the collar on the blue one, and turned back toward them. "Oh, by the way, I think it's really great that you're going to birth at home. I had an aunt who did that a long time ago. My sister is pregnant and considering it; she says it's coming back in style."

Sylvia turned toward three women who walked through the door. Grace squeezed Trenna's shoulder and said, "I'll support you, whatever you choose. Okay? Just be safe. Now, I'm going home to rake off my garden and see what's growing underneath the leaves."

Despite the abundance of shoppers over the holiday, the foot traffic had dwindled in the last few months. Today it was deserted. Even on a Saturday, the only crowd on the second floor was a group of giggling preteen girls coming out of the overpriced bath shop with a spritzer bottle passing between their hands, trying to spray each other. One of the girls ran down the hall after another.

Around the corner, Grace stopped at the front window with a new display of jewel-tone spring ensembles. Lilly's plant sat on a low table in the foreground soaking up the rays from the atrium. The hibiscus was full of growth but lacked any blooms. "Maybe it's time for a new spot for both of us."

****

Two solid weeks of April thunderstorms—interspersed with drizzles—drenched St. Louis. Grace finally bought a giant golf umbrella at the luggage store, but when she tried opening it in a narrow parking space with a luxury SUV parked too close, she feared scratching the vehicle and herself. Instead, she ran inside wet as usual on another drizzly morning.

More than a few older women were already gathered around the doors of boutiques in expensive outfits, overdone makeup, and plastered hair, which didn't seem to be touched by moisture. They were unable to meet each other for garden club meetings on their patios or for golf at the country clubs but were perfectly able to open their umbrellas to get inside completely dry.

Grace rushed to Honeybee, opening the gate and the doors, as she flung water off her trench coat. She made a short stop in the dimly lit bathroom, hung her wet outerwear on the hook behind the door, and squeezed her hair into the pool of water that had formed underneath her. Then she mopped the puddle with a wad of paper towels.

"The rain still brings out the old faithful, doesn't it?" Sylvia said when she arrived five minutes later.

"It's a good thing, too," Grace said. They were grateful to have this shopping demographic still intact—for now. They might not be as eager to go out in the rain if this were Wild Horse Creek, but that didn't stop her from checking the corporate site or her company email periodically for updates. Future shoppers probably wouldn't shop in brick and mortar stores as much as a pastime but rather as a destination to find something. She wanted to be a part of their search.

Sylvia brushed her elbow at the computer. "Just need to clock in."

"Just a minute; I'll finish up here," Grace said, instinctively turning her shoulder so that she could close out the page with the "Coming Soon" headline. Had Sylvia seen it?

Later, while they waited for their customers beside the dressing room, Sylvia pounced, "Do you drive very far to work?"

"Not so far," Grace said, wondering where she headed with the insinuating tone.

"Oh, I have to fight the traffic every day from St. Charles. That's why I was late this morning. The rain came down in sheets on us, right when we were driving past that new development out in Chesterfield. It would be so much closer to just stop there."

Thankfully, Grace's customer leaned her head out of the dressing room. "Can you bring me that linen blouse in a size ten?"

Roberta's group of friends came in after lunch. Each woman carried at least two bags a piece of clothing and accessories for their grandchildren from the new Mother and Me store that opened downstairs that morning.

"Where's Trenna?" Roberta asked. "I have to show her the outfits I bought for my girls."

"She's not working today," Grace said.

"Oh." Roberta plopped in one of the easy chairs beside the dressing room. Her two girlfriends fumbled through the racks, criticizing everything they saw until they finally found something they could each try on. Sylvia took them into the dressing rooms.

Roberta sighed, resigned herself to waiting, and unwrapped her tissue-laden shopping bag.

"They have that store at Wild Horse Creek, too." Sylvia came out from behind Roberta's chair and waited for her customer to finish in the dressing room. "I took my sister there last month to buy her first baby outfit; she's due just after Trenna."

Roberta smiled at Sylvia as if she were patting her on the head and held up the toddler outfit in a paisley print for both of them to admire.

"I dressed Trenna in this exact material when she was two," Roberta crooned. "It may have even been a romper like this one. I bought a matching one for her, too."

Roberta pulled out a jumper without any obvious waist. Sylvia started to laugh but coughed to stifle it. Just the day before Trenna had been pining for the black pencil skirt that had just been marked down even while she whined about already outgrowing her maternity clothes.

"Well, maybe if Trenna keeps her pregnancy weight for a

couple of years, it will still fit her by the time her baby has grown into her outfit," Sylvia said.

Grace shot her a warning look.

"I just meant maybe Trenna would be pregnant again," Sylvia said, defensively.

Sure you did, Grace thought. But the comment didn't seem to bother Roberta.

"Oh, I never did lose all my weight when the babies were born. It just kept adding up, one at a time. But Trenna will be different. She's already showing her individuality about this baby, and I'm sure it will continue."

"Yeah," Sylvia said. "What do you think about that? A baby in a bathtub."

"No, dear, I don't think we got her one of those, yet." Roberta leaned over in her chair and pulled off a shoe and began to rub her foot. "Maybe you could give her that for her little surprise shower next week."

"I meant for the birth," Sylvia corrected. "You know? The water birth at home?"

Roberta stopped rubbing her foot and sat up in her chair, rolling up from her spine, one vertebra at a time. By the time she lifted her head, her face was no longer perplexed as Grace expected, but an atrocious purple with broad eyes spread under an angry brow.

"She's giving birth at the Mercy Hospital birthing center. What gave you the idea that she was birthing at home?" Roberta demanded.

Grace intervened. "What Sylvia meant . . ."

"I know what I meant, Grace," Sylvia insisted. "Trenna told us about her birth plan—a water birth at home."

Roberta's cheeks flamed red, and her mouth exploded. "NO! SHE CAN'T!"

She struggled to climb out of her chair, looking absurd with one shoe still lying on the ground. She hobbled forward and returned back to the chair for her purse.

She pulled out her cell phone and hit a number. She waited. Roberta dialed another number. "Max, where is she?"

Grace was unsure whether to stand and listen, repack the contents of the shopping bag, or interrupt the conversation with Max somehow.

"Go do something," Grace scolded Sylvia like a three-year-old.

Sylvia moved toward the dressing room, "Is everyone good in there? Do you need any different sizes?"

"The birth plan—it's NOT happening," Roberta commanded.

Roberta waved at Grace for her to clean up the Mother and Me clothes. Grace dropped to her hands and knees to gather all the layers of tissue that Roberta's stomping heel had shred on the floor.

"You know she can't," Roberta screeched with high-pitched volume.

Grace shoved it all in the bag along with the clothes. At this point, she honestly didn't care how she treated the outfits or her "best" customer.

"He can't clear her," Roberta said, shaking her head. "He doesn't know the history."

"We'll see." She abruptly ended the call and fell into the chair with her breath coming out in heavy pants.

Grace, who was still under the clearance sweaters looking

for another stray piece of tissue, feared Roberta might be having a heart attack and crawled on her knees to her.

"Are you all right?"

Roberta nodded but continued to pant. Her breathing finally slowed, and she sighed. "What do you think of this? You can't think it is a good idea."

Grace leaned back against the wall next to the overstuffed chair. Should she answer as a manager to a client she wanted to keep happy? Or as the best friend of this woman's daughter who understood why Trenna wanted to do it? Or as a woman who had her own misgivings about a home birth?

"I think it's unusual, but lots of people do it just fine," she finally answered. "I researched it a bit after she told me, and if she's having a normal pregnancy, it should be fine. They've prepared an alternate plan if something happens."

"If something happens, it will be too late to do anything about it," Roberta said.

"That's not necessarily true. From what I read, the midwife always has a back-up doctor and hospital written into the plan."

"Believe me. If something happens, it will be too late for a back-up plan." Roberta's eyes widened and held on to Grace.

"Roberta, can I give you some advice? Let her choose for herself."

"But the consequences . . ." Roberta closed her eyes dramatically.

"They always hurt more when we can't control them, don't they?" Grace said. "But they will hurt beyond that if you don't give her some space to live."

Roberta opened her eyes and said, "You mean well, Grace, but you don't understand anything about this. Apparently, neither does Trenna. She just better be prepared to tell me herself why she's doing it. Where is she all the time, anyway? Do you know?"

"She paints at my house," Grace admitted. "She's there today, I think."

Chapter Nine

When Grace arrived at home that evening, the paint tubes lay uncapped on the desk. Several brushes were still in the mucky brown water, and the tray held residual paint mixings. Watercolor paper lay on newsprint with a few lines of a pencil sketch. Nothing had been painted.

Grace called Trenna's phone. Straight to voice mail. She called twice the next day and three times on Thursday. She checked the schedule. Trenna worked two more times—that night and Tuesday, which would be her last day and the day of the surprise shower.

Chanel arrived at 5:15. Knowing that Trenna was scheduled for six, Grace stalled her departure. Chanel looked quizzically at her standing by the front counter making idle chit chat. Grace regretted the pretext and left. She sauntered through the corridors of the mall, browsing in shops that she hated, scanning the shoppers for her overly pregnant friend.

In the parking lot she peered into every approaching vehicle for the yellow VW convertible and then sat in her car, unwilling to turn the key and lose her chance to make amends with Trenna. Two women approached the lot in front of her car and whispered to each other. To avoid suspicion, she turned the key in her ignition and reluctantly backed out of her space.

At the stop sign Trenna's familiar yellow car streamed through the intersection in front of her. Grace honked and waved, but Trenna's eyes pointed straight ahead without glancing toward Grace.

Trenna continued to ignore Grace's calls over the weekend. Alone in the backroom on Monday, Grace tucked the gift-wrapped blankets inside her bottom desk drawer and dialed Faye.

"Got a minute?"

"Yeah, but let me first put the belt on this red crepe dress, which, by the way, I hope you get in a shipment soon."

"Faye," Grace said, hesitating. "I've been thinking. Should we go through with it still? The baby shower?"

"WHAT?" Faye yelled. Grace held the phone away from her ear. If anyone had been in the backroom, they would have heard her, too.

"But she doesn't respond to my calls," Grace said. "Trenna's going to think I'm trying to make everything all right with this surprise party, even though it has been planned for months."

"I can imagine it will be hard with Trenna, but what are they going to think if you call everyone and cancel the night before?"

Grace nodded. "They would think that was weird. You're right. I'll see you tomorrow."

"At nine?" Faye asked.

"Yeah, at nine in front of Kitchen Gourmet."

She rolled back and forth in her chair. Honestly, it *would* be easier to curb the staff's disappointment then face Trenna, who clearly didn't want to talk with her. Reaching in her top desk drawer, Grace retrieved the blank card that lay tucked under the ribbon of the wrapped blankets.

She slid the card out of its envelope. The right words didn't come to mind, and she dreaded writing a cheery statement, which would diminish their friendship and accentuate her mistake with Roberta.

The front cover was one of those black and white photographs with just one object in color. The two young girls in black and white held a doll wrapped in a pink blanket. Inside, the card read, "You're no longer just playing house."

She picked up her favorite pen and wrote, "But I appear to still be playing games with our friendship. I'm sorry. Love, Grace."

She blew on the card to dry the ink, slipped it into the white envelope, tucked it under the ribbon, and slid the whole package back into her drawer for the next day.

****

A crash exploded outside the window of Grace's room. She sat up in the dark of the night. The wind howled outside. Probably just some close lighting and thunder. She listened closely for something else to indicate an emergency but fell back on her pillow before any other noise came. The darkness quickly lulled her back to sleep.

Hammering awakened her, a noise that sounded different than the earlier one. Her clock showed 7:06, but she pulled a pillow over her face to block out the light that now streamed through her window. The noise returned, louder this time. She didn't have to strain to know someone was knocking on her door.

Grace fumbled for several minutes in the closet for the old pastel blue robe her mother gave her five Christmases ago.

Her feet on the cool wood floor wished for the worn, matching slippers she'd given to Goodwill that very month.

"I'm coming," she called to the knocking. Unlatching the chain, she undid the dead bolt and opened the door to Mr. Reynolds.

"You have a tree down."

"I do? Where?"

"Alongside the driveway toward the back of your house. It's lying on your garden about two feet from your house. A limb grazed your rear bumper. You're lucky it didn't crash through the whole car or your house."

The noise in the middle of the night.

"I have to work today. Can I leave it there until I get the landlord out here?"

"Not if you want to get your car out," he said, shaking his head. "We'll have to move it."

"How?"

"I have a chainsaw."

"Do you know how to use it?" She stood at least four inches taller than him and couldn't visualize this frail gentleman with a chainsaw.

"Of course I do."

"Then, I'll get dressed and come help."

Grace wondered what to do about work. How long would it take to clear a small tree? She dressed in jeans and a sweatshirt from the dirty laundry basket and then phoned Chanel, who sounded like she was still sleeping.

"I can work for you this morning, but I'm closing with Trenna tonight," Chanel said. "If I'm going to stay for the party, as well, I can't work straight through."

"I'll be there as soon as I can," Grace promised.

She hung up, opened her kitchen door. The small tree beside the garage wasn't the one that had fallen. The large elm from the middle of her yard lay on its side in a diagonal path to the driveway and crushed her new garden beneath it. The chainsaw whirred above the destruction on the ground. Adrenaline quickened her steps, and she pulled on the work gloves from the shed.

After just an hour, her promise to Chanel looked premature. She phoned Faye for backup and returned to the mess of a yard, climbing over the stump where the tree split from its foundation and jagged shards protruded.

Mr. Reynolds sawed the tree while Grace stacked the logs behind the shed until they could be split or hauled. They worked in the residual mist of the storm to clear away the obvious mess. In between loads, and when Mr. Reynolds needed to rest his back, Grace phoned her landlord with messages about the downed tree and requests for help. By afternoon, the two of them had taken care of the majority of the tree and its scattered debris with still no word from the landlord.

While he wiped the blade of his chainsaw, she grabbed her purse, pulling out a check and a pen. "You'd offend me if you sign that," he said, shaking his head. "I won't take it if you do."

He motioned to the stump. "Just keep on your landlord to come take care of that and the wood behind the shed or he'll forget about it."

It was after three before she laid her dirty gloves on the table and called work.

"Honeybee, Trenna speaking."

Grace gulped. "Trenna, It's Grace. I've had a problem here today and . . ." She wasn't sure whether to describe the problem, ask for Chanel, or take a chance after six days of silence to apologize right then.

Trenna decided for her. "I just got here. Let me get Chanel."

"Grace, is that you?" Chanel answered.

"Yeah. I'm sorry I didn't get back to you. It took longer than we expected just to get the tree out of the way so that I could back out my car. My back bumper and the trunk were damaged . . ."

"We're okay here," Chanel said like she meant it. "We covered you. Faye actually took the morning shift, and I came in a bit early for this one. Go take care of your car—and yourself. We'll see you tonight."

"Thank you," Grace said, overwhelmed by the day of immediate needs and those who helped her to meet them. With all that help, she pulled into the parking lot at The Plaza hours later with clean clothes and plenty of snacks for a crowd of women to eat.

On top of all the other stressors, her Tasty Pastry order for Trenna's favorite mini cheesecakes had been lost. They only had those that were in the case, two dozen instead of four. They apologized and offered to substitute an alternative for free.

"Anything chocolate," she said, gladly accepting their suggestion of mint brownies.

At Schnucks she grabbed veggie platters as well as a few pints of ranch dip and four more bags of chips. At this point she didn't care if she or the food looked glamorous. She brazenly left her car unlocked in the fire lane, sprinted up the stairs to the second floor, and ducked behind potted plants and columns so that she wouldn't be seen from the doors or windows of Honeybee.

Audrey and Beth huddled behind a center sofa waiting to meet the others. She waved them over to her, and the three of them ran back to her car to unload the food. They waited at the curb while Grace parked, then they all carried the food back to the second-floor meeting place, stacking it precariously by the corner of the Kitchen Gourmet entrance.

Colleen, the very store manager Grace feared to meet with her stockpot of soup, closed the store doors and eyed them strangely. Grace cocked her head toward Honeybee, mouthing "surprise party."

Colleen nodded and smiled.

Eight minutes quietly passed—the eight minutes when Grace knew that Chanel and Trenna would close the store's front doors, pull down the gate a third of the way, ring up the last sales in the register, replace all the clothes on the racks, and tidy the store for the morning—until the other ten women from the sales staff appeared.

Faye arrived behind the group carrying a bunch of helium-filled Mylar balloons and wiggled in between Audrey holding the veggie trays and Grace with the white boxes of pastries. With all of these women here to support Trenna, Grace hoped the surprise would soften the rift she'd created between them.

The main lights turned off in front of Honeybee.

"That's the sign," Faye said, leading them single file along the edge of the store, no more than a foot away from the outer wall of Kitchen Gourmet, then to the outer wall of Honeybee, and finally in front of the front window.

As the last person in line, Grace passed by the window alone, catching sight of Lilly's plant perched in its familiar place. Healthy green leaves filled its branches, but no buds had formed in months. Ahead of her, Faye ducked under the gate and herded the women into the pocket between the gate and the front doors. They rustled loudly with the crackle of gift bags filled with tissue paper and shushed whispers as they tucked themselves into the tight space. Faye tried to make room, tangling herself in the strings of balloons instead. Grace ducked under last of all and nodded. All together, they pressed their weight on the doors and burst into the store.

"Surprise," everyone yelled.

No one reacted in the dim light of the store. Then, Chanel scurried toward them.

"She's in the bathroom," Chanel called in a loud whisper. "Go hide, and I'll turn on the lights when she comes."

They piled their gifts on the center table, where Lilly's plant had been during December, and scattered behind the racks of clothes. Grace set the food on the front counter and ducked behind it alongside Chanel, who kept her eye on the path coming out of the back room and her hand on the light switch. Grace's stomach growled, and Chanel elbowed her. A shadow wandered through the darkened store.

"Chanel, did you already go?" Trenna said with hesitating concern, just a step away on the other side of the counter.

The lights flicked on. "Surprise!" the women yelled, louder than the first time.

Just as Grace popped up from her hiding place, Trenna grabbed the ledge right in front of her with nails pressing into the counter. Although Trenna replaced her grimace with a smile, her fear-filled eyes told Grace what she hadn't known about her friend—Trenna did not like surprises.

Loud talking, hugs, laughter, and questions pierced the air for ten minutes while everyone debated how and where to set up the party. In the end, Beth dragged a chair for Trenna to the front, next to the center table, and most of the others dropped down on the carpeted section of the floor just in front of her as if they were little children waiting for a librarian to read them a story.

The others—Faye, Grace, and Audrey—created a food buffet on the front counter and passed plates of treats to the seated women. Audrey handed one to Trenna, who held it on her lap while her eyes wandered over the group of women who surrounded her.

"Open presents. Open presents," Beth begged her. Although in the center of it all, Trenna appeared to be on the fringes of her own party.

Grace stood tensely herself on the opposite side of the talkative crowd not knowing what to do. Should she approach Trenna or wait for some indication from her feelings? How had her good intentions with Roberta so quickly torn apart their friendship? She *had* tried to smooth the road between mother and daughter, and Trenna couldn't fault her for that. Hadn't it been Sylvia, anyway, who had revealed the birth plan without permission? But did Trenna even know that?

Sylvia commanded the most comfortable place with a prime spot in a comfy chair to the right of the center table. From this position she jumped up to deliver new gifts to Trenna, carried on a side conversation with three of the recently-hired saleswomen, and even produced a notebook and pen to create a list of gifts and their givers. From her spot, Grace could only offer a trashcan from behind the desk for the remnants of ribbon, tissue, and torn wrapping paper.

"Audrey, the burp rags are *too* cutesy. Where'd you find them?" Sylvia asked as Trenna handed them to the women on her right. "Hold them up so I can take a picture."

Trenna pulled open a flowered gift bag and brought out a mini purple sweater set from Chanel. "It's lovely," Trenna said and winked at Chanel.

"Oh, is that a three- to six-month size?" Sylvia grabbed the outfit from Trenna's hands. "Don't you think it will be too small for the baby by the time its cold enough to wear it?"

"Does she think her help gives her the right to judge every gift Trenna unwraps?" Faye whispered to Grace.

Beth took over Sylvia's spot and grabbed the biggest, most awkwardly shaped gift from underneath the table.

"No, that's my gift." Sylvia lunged at the present. "I want her to open it last."

Trenna *did* unwrap it last and remarked courteously at the bassinet and every item that Sylvia herself pulled out of it—soaps, lotions, cloth diapers, and baby blankets—baby blankets that looked identical to the ones Grace had purchased at Mother and Me.

"They look extra soft," Trenna said. "Thank you, everyone."

At this word the women stood to stretch their legs and socialize. Sylvia's voice called loudly over the murmurs.

"Grace, I must have missed writing down your present," she said. "What was it you gave Trenna?"

The flush on Grace's cheeks burned bright. The huddle of associates waited for her response. Honestly, she'd left the gift in her desk drawer, but now that Sylvia had given her the same blankets, she didn't want to even go collect hers.

"Sylvia," Trenna spoke up from her chair in the middle of the hubbub. "Grace has a special private gift for me."

Trenna looked up to Grace with a slight grin and then returned her eyes to the women gathered around and said, "This means a lot to me—and not only your gifts but also your friendships. Thank you for including me in your life here at Honeybee."

Was this an apology? An acknowledgment? Reconciliation? Whatever it was, Grace appreciated the words.

Beth clapped loudly, and the others joined her. Audrey hugged Trenna, and Grace lost her friend's face in the group of women wanting to touch her, especially her belly. It was the quickest shower most of them had ever attended, but no one stayed around just to extend it. Sylvia left first, followed by everyone except Trenna, Faye, and Grace.

"I'll do this," Faye waved her hand over the remnants of the buffet. "Why don't you help her with the gifts?"

"That's a great idea. I'll go get a cart or a box." Grace headed to the back room, passing Trenna talking on her phone outside the dressing rooms.

"Yeah, I'm going to ask her tonight," she said. Probably Max.

In the back, Grace forgot what she'd come to collect and ached to sit down for the first time since that morning's crisis. As she did so, the cuff of her trousers caught on the handle of her bottom desk drawer. She pulled her pant leg off the handle that had come loose on one side and now dangled by one screw.

This was the drawer with Trenna's gift. At least now she could add that to the gifts out front. Inside, the card lay taped to the underside of the ribbon, but the wrapped blankets were not there.

"I'm leaving," Faye called from the doorway.

"Bye," Grace mumbled, in shock. "Faye, wait."

"Yeah?" Faye said, walking in as far as the break table.

"I left Trenna's gift here, and it's gone," Grace motioned to the drawer. "The card is here, but the gift isn't."

"Maybe someone came and got it for you. Did you see it in the pile?"

"No, but remember what Sylvia said?" Grace said, remembering the exact same knitted blankets she gave Trenna.

"Sylvia!" They both said her name at once.

"Her blankets. They *were* mine," Grace said. "She didn't just buy them from the same place; they were actually mine."

"Grace, be careful . . ." Faye said. "You're accusing an employee of stealing."

"What else could it be?"

"Well, I think you may be right, but be careful with your accusations. You don't have any evidence except Trenna's blankets."

"I have the receipts," Grace said.

"But that only proves what you bought, not what she didn't buy."

"I know. And that's exactly what she wants. She insinuates and sneaks around here like she's hatching a plan. I want to lay it all out for her—or Sue. Either way, she would deny it. And like you said, I don't have any evidence."

"Are you recording them? The instances when it happens?"

Grace unlocked her filing cabinet next to her desk and pulled out a file folder. "Every one. Date, instance, every time. Well, not the ones that seem to just be personal."

"What do you mean by that?"

"Just some personal comments she's made." Grace didn't want to reveal the jabs about Wild Horse Creek.

"Personal becomes professional—or unprofessional—when it's brought into the workplace," Faye said.

"That's my problem. I want to share who I am as a person, but in a professional way. How can there not be some overlap in our relationships?" Grace asked. "Like with Lilly. Her mentoring and our friendship. Personal but professional."

"Ah—the work and friendship mix," Faye said.

"Yes. It worked with Trenna, too, until this misunderstanding. Those negatives cause me to falter—like the hold Sylvia's trying to get on me," Grace sighed and motioned to the empty drawer. "Or the lack of a resolution with Trenna."

"You've done well with Trenna, trust that. I think this misunderstanding will probably smooth over. But with the rest of the staff, you are more manager than friend, and you're trying to be more friend than manager. You don't hang out with them socially, but you want them to like you. You think if they do you'll be more successful."

"Isn't that true? Isn't that how Lilly had so many customers? She was interested in them, really cared about them. She met their needs, and they kept coming back," Grace said.

"Lilly didn't have to manage them, though," Faye said. "That's a different position. It's easy as a leader to want everyone to like you. So you give in and overlook some things, like with Sylvia, and then she manipulates you to get what she wants."

"It's not that I want them to like me . . . It's hard to explain," Grace said, honestly. "But when I did stand up to Sylvia, like making her apologize to Roberta, it made things worse."

"It will for awhile because she's testing you. Like my boys," Faye said, and glanced at the clock above Grace's head and started backing up. "The boys I need to rescue from their babysitter."

"What do I do?" Grace felt helpless solving the "Sylvia problem" alone.

"That's what we're all figuring out, isn't it?" Faye said. "With Trenna, be her friend. Listen to her. Just listen a lot. Kiss her baby. Baby-sit so she can go out with Max. With Sylvia, hold her accountable. Write down what she's done, consider what action to take, maybe get Sue's take on it, and follow through. Be the leader." Faye hugged her—which she didn't do very often— shrugged into her spring jacket, and walked out as Trenna knocked on the open door.

"May I come in?"

"You still work here, don't you?" Grace grinned, rising from her desk.

"Well, not officially," Trenna said. "I clocked out before you all surprised me."

"Why don't you sit down while I find some boxes for your presents?" Grace said, gesturing at her own desk chair.

Trenna slid down onto the soft leather, pulled her arms across her chest, and rested her chin and cheek on her right hand.

"You don't like surprises, do you?" Grace asked gently.

"No, not really."

"Is that why you've been avoiding me? Because I was responsible for that other surprise, too?" Grace said. Trenna wrinkled her forehead in confusion.

"Your mother showing up at my house?" Grace reminded her.

"My mother's actions are never a surprise. I suspected she'd show up sometime," Trenna said. "Whenever I try to keep *my* actions and intentions to myself—that's when we clash."

"So, you've been upset at her, not me?"

"You did confuse me," Trenna admitted. "I opened the door, thinking you left your key, and there she was, staring at me. I tried to sort it out, but I couldn't. She started talking about my plans for the home birth, and I couldn't figure out how she knew. I only told you."

"Sylvia told her," Grace said. "Remember she overheard us talking about it?"

"She accused me of hiding in our friendship," Trenna said. "Hiding what, I don't know."

She paused and looked around the room. "But with you and with Max, I'm not hiding. I'm more myself, living more like myself, choosing more of what I think is right for me. I continue to feel like it is all wrong to her, never the right thing."

Grace still wasn't sure where she stood. She reached into the almost empty drawer and pulled out the card with the ribbon hanging from it and handed it to Trenna.

"Open it."

Trenna slit the top with her fingernail. She laughed at the picture on the front and opened the card. She closed her eyes and waited a minute.

"I'm sorry, too," Trenna finally said. "I just didn't know if you were on her side or mine."

"I saw the look in your eye tonight that told me it wasn't me, that there was something more," Grace said. "Max alluded to it that day when you guys were at my house for dinner. Why are there sides between you and your mom? Do you want to talk about it?"

"Talking it out doesn't always help," Trenna said. "Not with this."

"That's fine. But if or when you want, I'm learning to listen," Grace said. "Anyway, I have a gift, too, but Sylvia stole . . . my idea."

Trenna protested, "No. I wasn't just covering for you when I said that. I have a specific gift request. But, it's very personal, and it has to be the right time."

Trenna hesitated, not sure how to say what she wanted to say. "I told Max that I wanted a doula, but we researched it and decided we didn't want another stranger at the birth. We're still considering a doula to help us postpartum since I'm not going to be at a hospital, but what I really want at the birth is a sister—someone who knows how to support my emotions and me. Max suggested you."

Grace wasn't sure how to react.

"That is a big gift," she said with a long pause, "Considering that I don't know anything about childbirth."

"I know you don't, but you've supported me woman-to-woman through one of the hardest transitions of my life. I needed that. Especially now . . ." Trenna stopped and rubbed her ribs at the top of her belly. "My mom declined my invitation to attend."

"So, I'm second choice," Grace teased.

"No, but I wanted her there, too. To heal our misunderstandings."

"Okay." Grace nodded her head.

"Okay? You mean 'okay, you'll do it' or 'okay, something else'?"

"Yes. I'll do it. But I'm not sure what I'm supposed to do. I've never given birth," Grace confessed.

"Neither have I."

Section Three
Flowers of Grace

Chapter Ten

G race opened Sylvia's folder on her desk. "Chanel, will you call Sylvia and ask her to come in and meet with me today? We need to have a one-on-one."

"She won't be back until the end of April," Chanel reminded her. "Two Mondays from now."

Skipped away on a spring trip to Florida. "Ugh," Grace grumbled. "I can't stew about this that whole time."

Instead, Grace wrote a written description of the most current incident with Sylvia beneath the other two major incidents. The first was the suspicious return she made when Chanel and Grace took the cuttings from Lilly's plant. The second occurred when she insulted Roberta and assaulted Grace with her fingernails. Now, this third incident was the stolen gift.

Grace could separate these three incidents from the more subtle insinuations, negativity, and disrespect toward her. While she couldn't record the smaller but equally insubordinate actions, the larger, more obvious errors in judgment and wrongdoing— according to the company handbook—gave Grace the authority to put Sylvia on employee probation. She filled out a formal probation sheet and slipped it back in the file folder. She would communicate her decision to Sylvia as soon as she returned and then file the paperwork with the regional office.

Once she made that decision, her anxiety receded. Beyond the day-to-day managerial responsibilities, customer relations and sales, she planned to clear her mind of work concerns to learn everything she could about childbirth in the next three weeks.

The doula organization Trenna planned to use for her postpartum care wouldn't train nonprofessionals, but Trenna invited her to an appointment with the nurse midwife.

On the day of the appointment they sat in the cubicle-sized room with only two chairs, a small desk with a rolling stool, and the exam table with stirrups. Grace felt the horrible lack of privacy, and no one was even undressed.

"Is Max coming, too?" Grace said.

"No, he's been before, and he'll come again next week," Trenna said. She noticed Grace fixated on the stirrups. "I've become a lot less inhibited through the process. I'm sure I'll regain some privacy after it's over, but, honestly, I'm getting used to it for now."

A stout fifty-year-old woman opened the door. Trenna kicked Grace's leg with her foot.

"That's her," she whispered.

"Carol Gregory." The midwife shook Grace's hand and sat down at the desk next to Trenna's chair.

"So you're going to help at the birth. I'm sure you have a lot of questions. I can answer them for you today, but here," she handed Grace a stack of brochures. "You'll probably also want their birth plan. Right, Trenna?"

She pulled a piece of paper from Trenna's chart and held it up to Grace who leaned away and slid back her chair. Carol laughed and handed the paper past Trenna to Grace.

"No pressure. It's just a copy. I'll keep the original," she reassured her. "I'll take care of the medical; you help her cope. Any questions?"

"Where does that leave Max?" Grace asked.

"He's going to be right there, too," Trenna said.

"You're part of Trenna's support team," Carol said. "Since she wants to have a natural childbirth, she'll need both of you— and you'll need each other if the labor and delivery is long."

Grace searched the brochures and the web for more about home births, water births, and natural childbirth. From the public library she checked out *Spiritual Midwifery* by Ina May Gaskin and read until midnight nearly every night, feeling like she'd opened pages into a new world of womanhood but received very few answers. Book learning could only prepare her at a certain level for what would actually happen. It seemed pretty scary—for her and Trenna—to simply "figure it out along the way," as her dad often encouraged.

****

Sylvia returned from Florida overly tanned and giddy. She bounced into Honeybee, throwing false affection toward everyone she met, including Grace, as if her trip had released her from responsibility for her actions.

"We stayed in this exclusive resort, very private but still hip. I saw that woman who used to judge *American Idol*," Sylvia said in an over-emphasized tone to Beth who sat idly listening to her at the break table. "My friends said we might have a celebrity sighting. The day after we arrived, I turned a corner by the restaurant, and there she was—just leaving."

"What did you say?" Beth nodded at her, mesmerized.

"Oh, I thought about singing for her, but that would have been tacky. Those people go there to get away. I didn't want to mob her."

"Beth, would you help Audrey with the mark downs, please?" Grace said, as she rose from her desk.

Sylvia hopped off the table to follow her, but Grace held up her hand.

"May I speak with you, Sylvia?"

She shrugged and dropped into a chair on the opposite side of the narrow hallway filled with racks of plastic-covered clothes.

"We might be more comfortable at my desk," Grace said, pulling another chair from the backroom table to an empty space next to her desk. Sylvia stayed where she was, even when Grace sat down. Since this nonverbal cue seemed to be a tactic to reduce some of her authority, Grace rose to retrieve the paperwork from the filing cabinet and remained standing, passing the file between her hands as she spoke.

"I've identified a pattern of behavior that escalated at the party before you left. You pointed out my lack of gift, as if to embarrass me, after you made a spectacle of presenting your own. While this is not an issue I can address from a managerial perspective, I have received a report of a stolen item that exactly matches the gift that you gave Trenna."

"I bought those blankets myself," Sylvia tried to justify.

"Do you have a receipt for them?" Grace said.

"I never keep those things," she said. "What evidence do you have that I took them from your desk?"

"Sylvia, you made this easier on me than I thought you would." Grace took the probation paper out of her file folder, leaning over the desk to make some notes on it. She held it up for Sylvia to see what it was.

"I did not mention what the stolen item was or where it had been stolen. But you knew. You're now on employee probation for three offenses—the unexplained incident when you returned after hours, the derogatory comments about Roberta and physical assault with your nails when I asked you to apologize, and the stolen gift. Probation will last six months. Another incident and you're fired."

"We'll see." Sylvia defiantly smirked.

"I am sending this to the regional office today." Grace tapped the top page of the paper. The phone rang. They both stood with eyes locked, neither willing to retreat.

"You may go," Grace said confidently, setting the probation papers in the file on her desk and reaching for the phone. The only thing she regretted was not asking Chanel to witness the conversation.

"Honeybee at The Plaza, Grace speaking," she answered.

"Grace, is your cell phone turned off?" Max said.

"Has something happening?" The nerves squished inside her stomach.

"Her water broke, around 10:30 this morning. I was going to call you, but she knew you were at work and told me just to wait. She said it would take awhile."

"Do you want me to come over now?"

"We're at the hospital."

"The hospital? What happened?" Her voice caught, but she continued. "Is she all right? What about the baby?"

"She's fine. The baby's fine—as far as we know," he explained, but his pace and tone increased. "We didn't wait long. The contractions started quickly and painfully right away. I tried to comfort her, clean up the amniotic fluid, and call the midwife. Honestly—the reality of delivering at home overwhelmed us."

"I'll come now. Are you at Mercy Hospital?"

"Yes. No. The birthing center on the hospital campus. That's what the midwife recommended. Trenna can still labor or birth in the water, if she wants."

"I'm leaving now." She hung up and scanned the office. She had already finished the schedule for the coming week and posted it. The summer shipments might come in the afternoon, but Audrey knew how to unpack and inventory them if they did. Mondays were busy days but not as bad as the weekend; Chanel could manage the customers with Sylvia and Beth.

She pulled her bag and keys out of the cabinet, searching for her phone. Dead battery. Figures. She tossed it back in her bag, which she threw over her shoulder, and left with Sylvia's file still open on her desk.

The birthing center reminded Grace of a nursing home. A false prettiness with flowers everywhere—the curtains, the wallpaper borders, the prints on the upholstery, and the paintings on the walls—as if decoration could mask its true nature. The antiseptic smell gave it away.

Muffled moans came from the half-closed door in room 115. She knocked gently and peeked inside the door. Trenna reclined in a bed with an IV attached to her arm and a wide blue band strapped across her belly. Both of these tied her to machines that beeped incessantly. She squeezed her fists tightly together and grimaced. Max stood on the far side of her bed with a hand on Trenna's shoulder.

"Is it painful?" Grace asked. What a dumb question.

Max nodded. Grace waited, feeling helpless just watching. Trenna's muscles relaxed, and she sat back, smiling weakly at Grace.

"I feel trapped," she said.

"I can see why you didn't want to be here," Grace waved to the machines that decreased Trenna's mobility.

"Not by the place, by the pain," Trenna whimpered.

"Max said they have a tub where you can labor or even deliver. Is that an option, yet?"

"She needs to be further along," Max said to Grace.

Trenna tightened up her face and hands again. Another contraction pulled her out of the conversation and back into pain.

"Soon." Max stroked her hair. He supported her, physically against his chest, wrapping his arms around her. As the pain intensified in her eyes, she bit her lip and pulled her shoulder free from his hug. He backed off and just stood beside the bed. After a minute, she relaxed back against the pillow.

"I'm sorry," Trenna told him. Max kissed her forehead and laid a damp washcloth on it.

"Will you see if Carol can do something?" Trenna whined to him.

"I'll go see what she says." He motioned to Grace. "You're up."

Grace traded spots with him and sat beside Trenna on the bed. She handed her the washcloth, again, but Trenna shook her head and pointed to the water bottle on the rolling cart. After she sipped a bit from the bottle, she held it out for Grace.

"The pain is horrible. Worse than I thought it would be. Fear took away all of my confidence to do this according to my plan." Trenna shivered, reaching for the blanket that lay at the end of the bed. "I thought it was painful at home, but that was discomfort compared to what I feel now."

Grace pulled the blanket up for her and sat beside her on a chair. Trenna turned her head on the pillow. "Do those sound like ridiculous reasons for backing off my plan?"

"They sound like reasonable reasons," Grace said. "You can make a new plan."

"Delivery at home seemed like such a good idea at the time."

"This sounds like a good idea, now."

Trenna closed her eyes, pressing her lids together.

"Another contraction?" Grace asked, but Trenna remained silent. Grace could see the physical tension in her body and hear the anxiety in her short breaths.

Carol opened the door with Max following behind her. "Let's see where you're at," she said, pulling on her rubber gloves.

Grace moved just to the other side of the room while the midwife examined Trenna. Max joined her by the window while Carol explained to Trenna what she was doing.

"The pain disconnects us," Max whispered. "She cuts herself off during the contractions, but then after, she says she feels alone. How do I help?"

"We just don't leave her," Grace said. "We just stand beside her, continuing to reassure her that we're here."

Carol pulled off her gloves and dropped them in the waste can.

"You can labor in the tub, now, if you want," she said to Trenna. She motioned to Max and Grace and instructed them in preparations.

Max helped her take off her hospital gown, and Grace handed her the halter suit to cover her top and a towel for the bottom. Max wrapped another thick towel around Trenna's shoulders while she waited on the edge of the bed for the nurse to unhook her IV and the fetal monitor. Another contraction began, and she tipped her head forward. Max rushed to the front of her and pressed her cheek against his chest.

"Listen," he whispered in her ear. "I'm here. Listen to my heartbeat."

He stroked her head, and she shook in place. Grace reached out to massage her lower back. She was surprised to feel all Trenna's muscles tensed, as if she were trying to fight the pain with her own strength.

"The warm water will relax you," she said, knowing that to tell her to relax might be easier said than done.

The midwife returned, opened the partition, and revealed the inflatable tub lined in plastic with a hose flowing into it. Max helped Trenna climb off the bed and led her to the tub.

"Oh, this is nice," Trenna said, feeling the warmth of the water on her feet and ankles. She sat down in the water, which rose above her belly. She sighed. "It takes all that pressure off my ribs. I haven't had that in months."

"Now, give it some time when the contractions come," Carol said. "Let yourself relax into it. Release the pain, rather than holding all of it inside. Coaches, this is a good time to help her focus during the contractions—on something in the room or something she brought. Trenna, let the buoyancy of the water relieve some of that pain. Then we'll see if you want to deliver here."

"Oh, I do. I can do it," she squeaked, probably more to convince herself, because another contraction had begun.

"Grace," Max said. "There's a box on the dresser over there. Will you open that and bring it over here?"

He was pointing at a white pastry box, taller than it was wide.

"Oh, you want a snack while she's doing this, huh?" Grace teased as she opened the white box.

"Yes, but that's not what it is."

Grace looked inside.

"You brought the plant," she said, lifting the glass pot with the small hibiscus out of the bubble wrap padding that protected it. "It's grown and even has a small bud on it. Did you know that, Trenna?"

Trenna didn't answer or even look. Grace set the plant on an empty cart directly in front of the tub.

"Focus on that bud," Grace encouraged. "It will be open about the same time you take your daughter home."

But Trenna wasn't interested in the plant. Her contractions had intensified. Max sat on the floor behind the tub, and Trenna pushed back against him in pain.

"I can't do this," she moaned.

"Yes, you can," he whispered.

"I've got to get out. I can't get comfortable."

"How about changing your position?" Carol suggested. "Try to lie on your side."

Trenna turned in the tub, this way and that, not finding a way to adjust that would relieve the pain. She pulled herself into a ball, rocking back and forth, as she shook and cried.

"I can't do this," she gasped.

"This isn't good," Grace said. Trenna should have hired the professional doula.

"Trenna," Max asked, "Isn't the water helping?"

"Not as much as I thought it would."

Grace and Max looked at Carol.

"Give it some time," Carol said. "You've been in here less than fifteen minutes. Give it some more time."

"I'm in PAIN. I hurt. I can't do this," she stood up in the water.

"Whoa," Carol said. Max stood with her. Grace held out a towel.

"I want an epidural," Trenna said. She pushed the towel away and crumpled slowly back down to her knees in the tub.

"Maybe if you try to relax and breathe through it instead of turning inward toward the pain. Focus on the plant," Grace suggested.

Trenna faced her with fury, "I don't want to focus on the plant! I want it to be over. I want drugs."

"Is that what you really want?" Carol asked.

Max turned Trenna's face toward him and pushed the stringy wet hair out of her eyes. "This is your choice. Tell us what to do," he said.

"I can't do this."

Max took the towel from Grace, pulled Trenna up, and wrapped it around her. He looked to Carol and nodded before leading Trenna back to the bed.

"I'll set it up," Carol dried her hands and quietly left the room.

Grace hung back, not sure how to help without intruding. Trenna lay curled in a ball in a damp towel while Max hovered over her. She retrieved Trenna's hospital gown and bathrobe from the closet beside the dresser and laid them on the end of the bed. Max smiled his thanks weakly, and Grace slipped out the door, shutting it softly behind her.

Down the hall to the left, Carol consulted at the nurses' station in the center. In the other direction, a sign on the wall pointed to the lounge. She entered the empty room filled with more of the same floral-print couches, a vending machine, and a counter with a coffee pot and Styrofoam cups. A large picture window hung where she expected another landscape print, but the trees and people moving about outside didn't appear any more real than a watercolor.

She collapsed on the couch, dropping her head between her legs to stop the pain in her head. Trenna wanted this to be a time of nurturing and bonding, not chaos.

A door to one of the unisex restrooms along the wall opened. She lifted her head to see a little girl of three or four with shiny black chin-length hair pull the door closed behind her.

"I washed my hands by myself." The girl showed Grace her wet hands.

"Did you? What a good girl you are," Grace said in one of those overly cheerful high-pitched voices that she hated but that she expected all people used with children.

Grace looked behind her at the other side of the room and checked her tone before she asked "Is your Mom with you?"

"She's with our baby." The girl wiped her hands on her purple tights.

"Do you have a baby?" Grace said, with a more normal voice this time.

"Do you?" the girl mimicked.

"No, but my friend will soon."

The other restroom door opened, and a man exited. He motioned to the girl. She waved at Grace and followed him down the hall and around the corner. The reality of this little person startled her. In just hours or minutes Trenna would give birth, too. Her baby girl would grow just like this little girl. She would talk and live and laugh and learn. She would also feel and cry and hurt, like her mom was experiencing now. All that pain would deliver this creation.

After a rest, Grace returned to the room. Max sat in the recliner beside Trenna, who slept peacefully. She handed him a king-size Snickers bar and a water bottle.

"What's the plan?" she asked.

"The anesthesiologist gave her the epidural already."

"So we just wait," Grace said. "Is there any possibility of waiting for it to wear off so she can try the water birth, again?"

"No, she needs to progress, not wait." He shook his head repeatedly while looking out the window. But then he stopped and turned toward Grace, his olive eyes rimmed with red. "Grace, she thinks she failed."

Grace felt her friend's disappointment as if Trenna herself had conveyed it, even though she was sleeping.

"Do you want a break?" she asked Max.

Max shook his head, again.

"Take a break, just a short one," Grace insisted. "Walk up and down the hall; it will help."

Max stayed put, and Grace sat in the chair on the other side of the bed. She picked up a magazine and flipped through it. After about ten minutes Max stood and nodded toward the door. Grace acknowledged him without speaking. At the same time that the door closed behind him, Trenna stirred under the covers. She opened her eyes at the ceiling but quickly turned to where Max had been sitting, then over to Grace.

"Hi. He needed a break." Grace smiled at her.

"So do I."

"I know you do."

Trenna pushed down the covers, but she couldn't get them off her legs.

"Do you want them pulled down?"

"Yeah, I'm hot."

Grace turned back the blanket and handed her the cup of ice chips. "Can you have these?"

"That's about all I can have, now." She tipped several into her mouth, chewed them all at once, swallowed them, and then took another to hold in her cheek.

"I wanted to do it without medicine; I wanted to do it on my own," she said with the ice cube slurring her speech.

"Are you upset with yourself for changing the plan?" Grace said.

"All the books say, 'Be flexible.' I was flexible in the planning process. But to come to the hospital—okay, birthing center— and to not deliver at home, to get the epidural and not have a water birth, that's not what I planned."

Grace felt the truthfulness of Trenna's words in her own life. Her plans had also changed, hadn't they? Things had not turned out exactly as she planned, either.

"This was the first major choice of my life that I could carry out all on my own, and I didn't even get to do it the way I wanted," Trenna whined.

"It's not over," Grace burst out. "I'm sorry if I'm interfering, again, but you're in the thick of it, not at the end. You haven't failed; you're not even finished."

She waited for Trenna to snap at her, again, but she didn't say anything.

"What you're saying is you wanted to do it—give birth—the way you chose," Grace continued. "But you're giving birth, even if it isn't the way you planned. You get to do something I've never done, but something I want to do. You get that chance."

Grace's voice grew emotional, and she sat back in her chair, not wanting to push her loss on Trenna. The tears that wet her face surprised her. Trenna stretched her arm up on the side of the hospital bed and held out her fingers. Grace grasped them.

"You're in the thick of it, too. It's not the end for you either," Trenna said.

The epidural had diminished Trenna's pain into a slight pressure and achiness in her legs, and Grace lightened the mood with the story about Sylvia and the baby blankets. Sharing her work tensions in a lighthearted way with her friend who knew the personalities of her coworkers was easier and more appropriate now that Trenna didn't work for Honeybee anymore.

Max and Carol returned to the room to find Trenna laughing at Grace making fake kissy faces in imitation of Sylvia. The pelvic exam showed that active labor had progressed quickly, and Carol prepped the room for delivery.

Max rolled up and down on the balls of his feet, then grabbed his cell phone.

"No, not yet," he said. "You can come over after the delivery. We'll call you then."

Grace remembered that she was responsible for photographs and regretted not having taken any during labor. She threw open her purse and couldn't find her camera. Her cell phone would not do. Trenna pointed to the luggage bag, where Grace found Max's digital SLR. She hurriedly tried some practice shots of Trenna posing with her wristband and pointing to the fetal monitor, glad the heavy atmosphere had gone.

"Trenna needs to work, now," Carol said to bring them back to reality.

A woman next door yelled, and fear flashed in Trenna's eyes. Grace retrieved the small hibiscus plant from the cart beside the forgotten pool of water and moved it to the dresser.

"Focus on the bud," Grace said tentatively.

"Ready?" Carol said, positioned at the foot of the bed. "Max, watch the monitor and squeeze her hand as the contraction begins. Trenna, you can push anytime you'd like."

Max and Trenna drew an invisible curtain around themselves. They locked eyes—their focus only on each other. Grace pulled the camera to her face to give them privacy and watched the birth through that lens.

Max's hand covering Trenna's clenched fist. His tenderness. Her strained forehead above expectant eyes. Trenna's flexed bare foot. The sunset from the window. Carol's gloved hands. The matted hair of a newborn head. A wrinkled red body lifted up to Trenna's breast. The clamp and scissors to cut the cord. The clock—7:44. The first big cry. Flailing arms and legs on the scales. A hospital band wrapped around Baby Girl Oliver—4/27.

The cap on her head. The blanket around her. A man-size hand beside a tiny new one. Trenna holding her daughter. Max holding his girls.

"Put that camera down, Grace," Trenna called her to them. Grace pulled the camera strap from around her neck and set it on the nightstand. She hesitated at the side of the bed.

"You can sit," Trenna said. Grace perched on the edge of the bed, and Max lifted the baby out of Trenna's arms and handed her to Grace.

"Meet Jillian Grace Oliver," he said as she felt the cozy body come to rest on her forearm.

Chapter Eleven

G race now understood spring. New life blossomed, promising growth and renewal for tired and depressed souls. It was much more than a new bud opening in bloom, even on a hibiscus plant; no symbol of nature compared to a newborn. Just breathing in the sweet-smelling concoction of new baby smell awakened youthful energy and desire.

Every part of this experience didn't smell as good. The mustard-yellow diapers mixed with a lack of sleep, advice-giving grandmas, and the realization that this little person had needs—many of them not known—that a family would now provide without much of a manual or any formal training.

After the first week of phone calls with Trenna, Grace also understood why her mom delivered an obligatory pot of chicken wild rice soup to every new mom she knew within the first week of birth. That soup worked in Minnesota, but not in the temperamental bursts of a Missouri May.

She took a chicken wild rice salad instead, which she layered in her large Tupperware bowl and carried to work with her, like the day she'd carried her stockpot to work for Lilly's recovery.

"Whose bowl is taking up so much room here?" Sylvia complained when she tried to stow her food container in the mini-fridge.

"It's mine. A salad to take to Trenna and Max," Grace said, trying extra hard to not answer defensively.

"How nice of you," Sylvia said in the same sarcastic way she'd ended their last conversation and shoved her plastic container in the freezer section before stalking out of the backroom.

The niceties of life had disappeared in their exchange. Maybe that's another list to keep in the file—day-to-day jabs that Sylvia made at her. She could write them down and then forget about them. Grace opened her file drawer and thumbed through the employee folders for Sylvia's, but it wasn't behind Beth's where she expected it. It was probably petty of her to note every cross word expressed anyway. She turned her attention back to the inventory report she was making for Sue.

An hour later Chanel poked her head in the door.

"We're gathering money to buy chocolates for Trenna. Sylvia's taking her break now so she can go to Bissingers before you leave. Do you want to contribute?"

"Why's she going?" Grace asked, confused but curious. She pulled some money from her wallet and paused as she handed it to Chanel.

"I guess she had the idea. She said you're taking them dinner and proposed we add chocolates for dessert."

"That's weird," Grace said. Chanel shrugged and turned to leave with the five dollars Grace had given her.

"Chanel, did you use the employee files this week? I'm missing Sylvia's. Could you have it?"

"I doubt it; I haven't looked at those since we reviewed the schedules after the holidays."

"I probably misfiled it after I used it last Monday," she concluded.

At the end of the day, Sylvia produced a fancy sampler box from behind the counter. It was too big to fit in Grace's bag so Sylvia set them right on top of the bowl. The chocolates slid to the left and then the right as she walked through the mall. Grace tipped her chin down on top of the box to keep them in place just as Colleen bounded down the mall stairs beside her.

"Let me get the door for you," she called, running ahead, and held the door to the east parking lot. Despite feeling the blush in her ears spread to her cheeks, Grace accepted the offer, knowing how ridiculous she already looked and how helpless she'd be without it.

As she drove, she imagined she was a younger version of herself, with windows down and music on the stereo. Whatever worries work brought, Jillian's birth produced a joy-inducing effect.

Roberta answered her knock at the carriage house door.

"She's nursing. Don't talk; she will get distracted," she whispered in her big voice.

Grace didn't know if "she" referred to Trenna or Jillian. She quietly deposited her salad bowl, the box of chocolates, and a fresh loaf of French bread on the counter in the kitchen. Roberta followed, picking up the chocolates, unwinding the gold stretchy thread, and lifting the lid.

"Oh, nuts are my favorites." Roberta chose a dark chocolate turtle and took a bite, but she grabbed Grace's arm as Grace moved toward the couch to greet Trenna.

"Keep these away from her," Roberta said, shoving the box of chocolates in the microwave.

Trenna rolled her eyes from the couch.

"Believe me," Roberta said to her daughter. "The baby will

always know when you eat chocolate. I could never eat it with you."

"Excuse me, I'm going to wash off all the work germs." Grace disappeared into the bathroom to tune out Roberta's advice. The step-by-step of Trenna's new motherhood journey didn't interest her as much as just holding the baby. Roberta appeared more concerned with Trenna's recovery than eager to spend time with Jillian. Grace didn't mind taking her place.

In the living room, Trenna was burping Jillian on her shoulder, and Grace held out her arms. She supported Jillian's neck while she positioned the baby's chest and stomach across her forearm in a football hold that her mother often used.

"Oh, Grace, don't do that; she's much too young," Roberta said.

Grace self-consciously turned the baby onto her chest and rubbed her back. Trenna excused herself to go to the bathroom.

"Well, I'm just so glad she decided to go to the hospital after all. I feel so much better about the delivery once they called and told us they were there," Roberta recounted to Grace in mock whisper. Trenna returned to the living room. "I would have come, you know, Trenna, when you moved to the hospital. I would like to have been there with you."

"I know, Mom, but the plan just evolved that way," Trenna said. Grace stroked the baby's cheek. Jillian gave a little burp and spit up on the cloth rag on her chest.

"Thankfully, it all turned out well for everyone," Roberta said and left.

Grace resituated herself on the couch. "She's falling asleep. Do you want her back or want me to lay her down in her crib?"

"The bassinet is on the floor on the other side of the couch."

"The one that Sylvia gave you?" Grace asked.

"Yes, it's not contaminated is it?"

"No, I guess not," Grace joked. She laid Jillian down on her side in it and pulled the blanket up to her chin. "She's already changing. Don't you think?"

"Max says her coloring is lighter, and her hair even seems lighter to me. Maybe she'll be a blonde."

"Are you ever afraid you'll mess her up?"

"C'mon, Grace. You're asking a perfectionist that? Of course I worry. I'd love to keep her just like she is. But I think that's what made my mom the way she is—trying to protect me from life. I don't want to do that, either."

They chatted beside Jillian until Max came home after six. Grace stayed to serve them dinner, but Jillian woke up, wanting to eat again before Trenna even tasted her salad.

Grace wasn't sure she was ready to lay aside her fork, or book, or conversation every time a baby cried. Max held Jillian while Trenna finished her dinner. After they ate, Grace cleaned the kitchen for them, stored the leftovers, and took her bowl home.

Grace kept up a weekly or biweekly visit until Jillian was ready to venture out. First, they took her for a walk in her new stroller in Tilles Park. When Jillian turned one month old, Trenna brought her to Honeybee. Even though it was the first time Trenna had taken her out by herself, she carted the car seat on the side of her like a pro.

Jillian preferred the safety of Trenna's arms to the car seat, and Trenna lifted her out so Beth, Chanel, and Audrey could see her whole body. Jillian wasn't smiling at them, yet, but her cheeks had filled out and her eyes brightened when Grace leaned over and spoke directly to her.

"Let's go look at cribs next week. I still haven't chosen one, and she's beginning to move around when she sleeps," Trenna said to Grace at the end of their visit.

"How about we go to Wild Horse Creek? I have Friday off next week. We can go during the day. I'll drive."

Maybe she could check the store's progress. She hadn't returned to the development since Mike took her. He'd never called back nor had she called him.

"I need a change," Grace said the next week when they were on the freeway. "My career and the store are on a plateau. I want to be out here where the shoppers are. If they're going to open in September, Sue will have to decide in the next couple of months who's going to manage it. I want to be at the top of the list."

"If that's what you want, I'm sure you'll do well," Trenna said.

They parked in the lot closest to the new phase of the development, but the machinery from across the street spread the noise into their corner as if they were right alongside the steamrollers laying the new asphalt. Trenna hurried Jillian into the stroller, covered her ears with a blanket, and pushed it quickly toward the quieter main street shops.

They'd come for cribs but the abundance of new stores sidetracked Trenna, who wanted to stop in every one. After they'd checked out several of them, Jillian began to fuss. Trenna lifted her out of the stroller, and she quieted. Grace pushed the stroller while Trenna walked along with Jillian in her arms, peering into windows. That only lasted for another block before Jillian wailed again.

"She wants to eat," Trenna said.

"Where can you do that?" Grace said, looking for public restrooms or a private restaurant with booths.

"I don't know. Some women just nurse on a park bench, but I'm not that skilled, yet. Let's go back to your car."

They traipsed back across the parking lot where the noise had dimmed but had not gone completely. Trenna climbed into the back seat and shut the door. Grace unpacked the stroller, flattened it, and leaned it against the trunk, staring toward the second phase of the development that now had facades and not just steel framing. Neither of them had really accomplished their purpose in coming—shopping with an infant proved a bigger struggle than they imagined.

Two men with hard hats crossed the parking lot behind two rows of cars that separated them. One stopped in an empty stall and shielded his eyes against the sun. He was staring at them. Grace looked around the front. Could they see into the car? She moved in front of the back window to shield Trenna. He left his companion and began walking toward her.

"Grace?" he called and took off his hard hat.

"Mike. Hi. Good to see you." She waved in a way to not invite him any closer to her, but he continued. She rushed forward to prevent him getting very far, hoping he didn't mistake her speed for eagerness.

"What are you doing out here?" he asked when they reached each other.

"Just shopping with a friend. Max's wife," Grace explained. "We're looking for cribs, but we're taking a break."

"You could join us for lunch." He motioned to his friend to join them. She glanced toward the car, hoping Trenna would be finished and rescue her.

"No, thanks. We might just leave, anyway."

But he persisted. "I'm working on the shell of Block 10. That one where your store's going."

"Oh?" Grace said, hanging between the end of the conversation and a desire to leave.

"The shell will be finished by the end of the month, and then their contractors will come in to finish it to their specifications. It's going to be in a prime spot—across from a new Brazilian grill."

Grace nodded, sucked in by the information but trying not to show it.

He moved closer. "How about dinner tonight?"

Grace crossed her arms over her chest. "I don't think so. But thank you."

His coworker pointed to his watch. Mike shrugged, "See you around then."

Grace shot to the car as quick as she could. Trenna sagged down in the back seat but peered through the bottom half of the window like a kid spying on the neighbors from his driveway. "Was that Mike?" Trenna asked when Grace opened the door.

"Yeah. Awkward but informative."

Jillian was back in her car seat, sleeping peacefully now.

"Whenever I look at her sleeping, I only see peace," Grace said. "I imagine that if I breathe quietly alongside her long enough, I'll be transported from this ridiculous state to another world. Maybe there my path will actually lead me to where I want to go."

"Do you want to just go home?" Trenna asked.

"Yes. It seems safer there," Grace said.

****

Jillian flashed her first smile at the Fourth of July parade in Webster—at her parents, not the community floats. After a barbecue dinner in Grace's backyard, she napped. They filled a plate with extra pork steaks, corn on the cob, and potato salad for Max to take to Mr. Reynolds. He had a summer cold and didn't want to pass it along to the baby.

They carried her to the fireworks in a sling and returned through the crowd of people to tuck the sleepy baby in her car seat. Grace hugged Trenna and kissed Max on the cheek. She fell into bed without even washing her face. She slept hard while she dreamed the day all over again.

> *There wasn't enough charcoal. She needed to go buy charcoal, but every time she went to the store, she forgot it. She finally brought some home from the hardware store, but she had to walk through the parade to get to her house. Max and Trenna waved to her, but she kept walking with this big bag of charcoal. She carried it to Mr. Reynolds's house. But he wasn't home. Someone else answered the door, a young man—the one who worked at Ken's Hardware. He told her, "Mr. Reynolds never got over his cold, so he moved to Florida. He met Lilly and they married."*

Grace woke up, went to the bathroom, and went back to sleep.

> *She hauled the charcoal up and down her street, back to her house, and into the backyard. It broke open and spilled, a fine black dusty mess with charcoal lumps. The phone in her pocket rang. It was Lilly calling to tell her that Mr. Reynolds had died, but then the phone cut off. She hung up and waited for Lilly to call her back, which she did. But she couldn't find her phone when it started ringing. It kept ringing and ringing. She couldn't find it. She had taken it into the kitchen to wash her hands when the line went dead, but now it*

wasn't there. It still rang. She couldn't find it in the drawers. She couldn't find it on the table, or in the bathroom. But all the time, it kept ringing. She ran all over her house, opening drawers and searching for her ringing phone. Everywhere she went she left black handprints without finding her phone. "Lilly, I'm coming," she called over and over until the phone stopped ringing.

Grace opened her eyes. Light filtered through her blinds.

"Was that real?" she said, but her phone sat on the nightstand where she set it after the fireworks. She reached over and picked it up it. One missed call. Trenna's cell phone number. No message. She hit redial. Max answered.

"Max. What's up?"

"Grace . . . you called back."

"Yeah. Did Trenna call here?"

He gulped.

"Max?"

"Trenna's gone," he whispered.

"What?" Grace struggled to swing her legs around to the floor and sit up.

"She's dead," he said. "She woke up about 2 a.m. and got out of bed. I thought she went to feed the baby. I went back to sleep. A noise startled me awake at 2:13. Those numbers won't leave my head. I keep seeing them. 2:13."

Grace slipped onto the floor next to her bed. Her shoulders shook against the frame.

"Where's Jillian?" she asked.

"Grace, Jillian's fine. She's fine. I went to her room, and she was sleeping," he said. "But Trenna wasn't there. I walked out to the living room and back down the hall. No lights were on, except I could see a crack of light under the bathroom door."

"I called to her. But she didn't answer me," Max cried. "I knocked at the door, but she didn't say anything. I opened it, partly, but the door stuck on her bare foot. I didn't want to hurt her foot, but I needed to get in. I could see her hunched over the tub, but I couldn't see her face. I called to her. But she didn't answer. I pushed and cut her foot against the bottom of the door, but I got in.

"She wasn't bleeding, but she wasn't breathing. I remembered everything about CPR—everything. I don't know how I remembered, but I did it perfectly. Except, she never came back."

"Did you call somebody? An ambulance."

"I guess I did. I called her parents. They called 911. I don't know when I did it. All I see in my mind are those red numbers 2:13."

"Where are you? Where's Jillian?"

"Roberta has her over at the house. Trenna's dad is at the hospital. Arranging stuff. I'm in our kitchen."

"You need someone with you. I'll come," she said, not knowing what help she would be. Tears wet her eyelids, seeping yesterday's sunscreen into her eyes and burning them.

"No," he said. "My parents are on their way. They left home a few hours ago. I called them from the hospital. I just wanted you to know."

"Max?"

"Yes?"

"I'm so sorry. Please let me help with anything you need.

Food? Jillian? The funeral? Anything, all right?"

"I will, but I'm not doing anything myself. Roberta's taken over with Jillian. Trenna's dad said he'll manage the funeral and burial. I don't know how he can do this all over again, but he says it helps him."

"All over again?"

"When Sam died."

"Sam?"

"Trenna's older brother. Didn't she ever tell you about what happened?"

"No."

"It happened just after I met Trenna, before we started dating. It was sudden, too. "

"Oh Max. I am sorry for you, all of you. Let me know what happens. Or I'll call you later. Okay?"

"Yeah," he said and hung up.

Grace pushed end on her phone and pulled her down comforter off the end of her bed. Despite the humid St. Louis morning, she shook with chills. She draped the blanket over her and fell onto her knees, bent over in a ball, with her forehead pressed flat against the wood of the floor. She shook against that hard floor until she felt like she would crack like the boiled egg she repeatedly tapped against the counter the day before when she made potato salad.

Not even ten hours ago they stood together in her driveway, still chatting about the way that Jillian sucked her thumb when she slept, how they wished they hadn't done that as kids, and the number of years it took for braces to straighten their teeth.

Max climbed into the driver seat while Trenna fastened the car seat.

"I'd like to find that nasty stuff to paint on her thumb that my mom painted on mine when I was three. Do you think that stuff is safe for infants?" Trenna fell into the front seat and pulled her seat belt across her shoulder.

"No. I'm sure it's not. She's only two months old. Just let her have her thumb. It calms her and makes life a lot quieter for you," Grace told her.

"But what if I let her have her thumb now and it becomes a habit she can't break? What's that going to mean down the road?"

"It's going to mean that she won't be sucking her thumb when she goes away to college," Max piped up. "At least that's what my dad always said about our bad habits."

"I want to know if I'm making the right choice. Not giving in for the moment with bad consequences down the road. How do I know that as her mom?" Trenna pulled the door closed but talked through the window.

"I'm going." Max started the car.

Grace's tears fell remembering the little eye roll Trenna gave Max when that happened. Her tears pooled on the floor and soaked her forehead, which was still stuck to the wood, sticky with sweat and now wet with tears. She tried furiously to remember that smirk Trenna gave him that seemed so full of love while still teasing him.

Max had pulled forward a bit to prove he was going. Reluctantly, Trenna waved her hand but Grace could hear her voice streaming from the window as they pulled down the driveway. Grace couldn't imagine the next part. Her mind emptied of images but filled with numb heaviness. She lay still on the floor in a spot of cold tears and slept.

Chapter Twelve

S udden death sounds like a lost cell signal. Except the silence at the end never ceases. The chance to call back and say, "Sorry my signal cut out, but I wanted to say goodbye," never comes.

Silence surrounded her under the cocoon of down. She lifted the edge of her blankets and saw her phone on the floor outside her makeshift tent. She stretched her arm outside and picked it up. Again she scrolled down on her missed calls. The first one at 7:35 this morning. She lifted her eyes to the time on the right corner. Now it was 9:58 a.m.—9:58!

She'd slept at least two hours, and she worked today! It was a rare weekend shift to fill in for Chanel who had gone to Chicago to visit her husband's parents. Sylvia was opening, but Grace was supposed to be in before 10:00 a.m. to have two in the store when it opened. She couldn't go in today, but she didn't have a choice. Who could she call when she was late already herself? Grace dialed Honeybee.

"Honeybee at The Plaza, Sylvia speaking," Sylvia said an overly cheerful voice.

"Sylvia. Something's happened. I'll tell you when I get there, but I will be late. Just go ahead and open. Stay up front, and I'll be there in thirty minutes."

She pushed herself into forgetting the early morning call from Max, grabbed her hairbrush, and smoothed her long hair into a professional bun. She dressed in a simple black skirt and red knit top, finally slipping on black Mary Janes.

In the full-length mirror everything passed her brief inspection until her eyes came to her face. She couldn't go without washing her face and applying makeup, which slowed her down. With the screen door still slamming behind her, she opened her car door at 10:20.

The drive to The Plaza took fifteen minutes from Webster Groves, but if she took a short cut she could make it in twelve minutes. Just as she pulled away from the traffic light and turned on Lockwood, she heard a train whistle. The car a few yards ahead of her crossed the tracks, but then the lights flashed and the arm came down in front of her.

She counted every car that went by to keep her thoughts off the shock of the morning. Six. . . seventeen . . . forty-three . . . seventy-five . . . ninety-two. She could do this, one hour at a time if she could act professional. One hundred and thirty-three cars and another engine on the end. She crossed the tracks into the small municipality north of Webster, making all green lights at the intersections.

With the intersection of Litzinger and McKnight—the cross streets at Tilles Park—ahead, her eyes fogged at the memory of their walks around that park. She sped down the hill as if she could fly by the road to the Foster's and past the park without seeing them. She hadn't counted on her short cut to bring her past these spots. She looked in her rearview mirror to see how much damage her tears had caused and saw the flashing lights of a police car a few yards behind her. She pulled over and stopped.

"May I see your license and registration?" the officer asked. She opened the glove box for her registration, and her fingers stopped on the black velvet box she'd never shipped.

At 10:56 a.m. she walked into Honeybee. Sylvia was on the phone in the front.

"No, Sue, she's here now. Okay. I'll catch you later." Sylvia set the phone down.

"Oh, I'm so glad you're all right. Where have you been? What happened?" Her words sounded as dishonest as any enemy who might come at her with a real weapon.

"Sue. You called Sue?"

"I was worried you were in an accident. You're never late."

"That's precisely why I want to know why you called the regional manager to tell her the one day that I am?" Grace said without even pretending to check her angry tone or her volume.

Sylvia shrunk back from the front counter and deliberately stepped to the side, rather than approaching Grace.

"Grace. I think you'd better lower your voice. You sound angry. I know you don't mean to direct that at me. Just take a minute to think before you speak."

"What kind of self-righteous words are those?" Grace abruptly strode into the back room. Sylvia was right, which made it worse. Both of them knew the manager shouldn't lose her temper, but Sylvia set the bait that infuriated her even more.

Grace knew she wouldn't do well at work alone with Sylvia and rummaged for the list of employee numbers to make a plan for the rest of the day—and the week. She called Sue first, at home, and then on her cell.

"Grace. This is not a good time," Sue said. Grace could hear the noise of the pool and children in the background. "I'll be in on Tuesday; we'll talk about your conduct then. I shouldn't have to be called like this from one of your employees."

"Sue. Let me explain something."

"On Tuesday. My family is here, and it's loud."

"One of our employees—a former employee—died last night."

Sue didn't talk immediately. "Excuse me a minute, Grace." Grace heard her talking behind her hand.

"Who was it, Grace?" Sue inquired when she returned to the phone. The background noise had diminished.

"Trenna."

"The one with the new baby?"

"Yes."

"You were friends, too?"

"Yes."

The silence came again, but now Grace wasn't sure what to say.

Sue continued in an even more professional tone, "Where's Chanel today?"

"In Chicago until Thursday."

"Call in Faye. She'll come and help. She can manage the store this week; she's done it before. Just until Chanel's back, and you can function. Then we'll talk."

The conversation ended more sympathetically then it began, and Grace was left in the back room alone with Sylvia's voice carrying back to her. "Would you like me to get that in a size ten instead?"

Telling Sue about Trenna's death wasn't therapeutic. But she wasn't ready to confront Sylvia or explain what had happened—and especially not to apologize.

She dialed Faye, knowing they couldn't talk it out like she and Trenna had learned to do for each other. Grace hadn't realized how accustomed she'd become to that verbal release—to open up and talk through her emotion until she came to a point of understanding or resolution.

"Faye, something's terrible happened. I need your help."

Grace cried through the explanation, and Faye said she could be there within the hour and that she would call the other employees when she arrived.

"No, I'll do it," Grace said. "I owe Trenna the dignity of her coworkers hearing about her death from me. It will cut down on getting the details of her death wrong. Granted, I don't have many details, myself, beyond what Max told me. I haven't spoken to him or Roberta since this morning. I'm sure they're trying to cope."

"How are you coping?"

"No one this close to me has ever died. I grieved when Jeff and I broke up. And I felt Lilly's departure even more. But this stabbed me. I flip between the searing sharpness of its reality and a drain of physical momentum to even function."

"Do they know the cause?"

"No. I'm sure everyone's as perplexed as we are. I feel so isolated from what's going on over there, but I don't want to intrude."

"When I get there, you can go over, offer some words of comfort or something, couldn't you?" Faye suggested.

"I'll think about it. Faye?"

"Yes?"

"Thanks for bailing me out. I didn't handle Sylvia well," Grace admitted.

"Sylvia didn't know, but even so, she's always making a mental list of weaknesses to expose at her will. Don't take all the blame yourself."

Grace made the rest of the phone calls in a professional manner. Beth's family was at church, and she was able to leave a voice mail. Not a great way to find out but all that Grace could manage. She called Chanel, even though she was on vacation, to give her a heads up in case she might want to come home early to attend the funeral. She called Audrey, who cried for nearly ten minutes before Grace suggested they talk again in a few days.

"She was so young," Audrey said between sniffles. "How could this happen? What about her baby? How can a baby grow up without her mom? Trenna loved her to pieces. Who will hold her the same way? Who's going to sing to her?"

Grace wished she'd waited on that call and told Audrey in person. But honestly, Audrey was socially immature enough to ask all the questions everyone else held inside. She tried her best to offer some comfort without emotionally losing it herself.

When Faye arrived, this normally reserved woman came right up to her, wrapped her arms around her, and wrapped Grace into a tight hug. Grace let Faye hold her weight. The heaviness in her head didn't recede, but the sincere embrace loosened the block that had grown between her chest and esophagus.

Grace pulled back, let out a strong breath of air, which sounded nearly like a sigh.

"I've called everyone, but I haven't told Sylvia. Will you? I can't even look at her."

"Of course."

With arrangements made at the store, Grace drove toward the Foster's, not sure if she would stop or not. She slowed at the brick entrance; the driveway was already lined with expensive cars. A middle-aged couple, elegantly dressed in black, was exiting the last one with a covered casserole in hand. She saw them wave to a woman ahead, carrying flowers. She, too, was dressed in black.

Grace pulled her car onto the shoulder of the road and flipped down the mirror on her visor. Her red collar peeked up around her neck. This morning it felt like the only thing that could bring her any color; now it felt completely wrong for the event of the day. Clearly, she couldn't go in with this red shirt and draw attention to herself. Plus, she hadn't brought flowers or food.

Up at the house the front door opened. Roberta appeared with Jillian in her arms. The woman carrying the flowers kissed her cheek and briefly embraced them both. Roberta waved the casserole-carrying couple inside. Then, the door closed, placing Grace on the outside, again. She started her car and left the Foster's house. She'd call Max later for the funeral plans.

At home her petunias on the front porch drooped, and she fell down beside them to pluck off the dead blossoms.

"You need water, don't you?" she said, now comfortable conversing with her plants. "Probably some fertilizer, too."

Grace didn't have the energy to climb off the edge of the porch to fill the watering can. Now that she had sat down, she couldn't get up, again. Her feet sweltered in the leather shoes, so she pried them off. She pressed her bare feet against the hot cement until her toes burned.

Life continued along her street. A teenage boy across the street and three houses down washed his car and dried it. A set of identical twins raced by on their bikes with bags from the pet store hanging off their handle bars. Mrs. Hancock walked by with her hand tucked into the crook of her husband's elbow, and he steadied her when they crossed over the root-lifted sidewalk in front of Mr. Reynolds' house.

She half hoped he would come outside. His cat lurked in the front bushes and peeked out at her. She felt like the girls at college who would leave their dorm doors open for any social opportunity to happen by. She wasn't looking for sociality, just an amiable voice without the effort of seeking it out. She wasn't even going to tell him what happened, just listen to him talk about his cat or what he had watched on TV—anything to make life seem normal. But he never came out; only his cat stirred.

"Come here, Lady Lu," she called and held out her hand to be licked, but the cat hissed and went back under the bushes. "I can't even comfort a cat."

She went inside and wandered into the second bedroom where she lifted the watercolor painting of herself from the wooden student desk. Trenna's supplies—brushes, paints, a tray, and paper—that she used to keep in a neat stack to the side of the desk were all gone. She'd asked Grace to pack them in a box after Jillian was born.

"For when I have more time," Trenna had said.

Grace finally did that last month and took the box to the carriage house. But she hadn't come back since and given the room a thorough cleaning. Only a few things remained—a white plastic cup with residual paint in the bottom, some sheets of sketch paper that had fallen underneath the desk, a roll of paper towels beside it, *and* the pink stool.

Trenna co-opted the stool from the store in a search for a chair to fit the right height of the desk. A normal-height chair couldn't fit under the desk with someone sitting in it, but the stool fit Trenna's petite frame. Grace sat on the stool, now, and held her portrait.

"It doesn't really look like you," Trenna had said the day after she painted it, pointing out all her failings in her amateur attempt.

"But that's watercolor," Grace told her, but they continued to disagree.

They had taken it over to Mr. Reynolds' house on a gray February late afternoon for his opinion. The light in his overfilled den didn't help, and they insisted he turn on more than the faux Tiffany lamp at his side to get a better look.

"No," he said. "The light is just right for these old eyes. I have all I need to see."

But they both noticed he adjusted his glasses and held it out while he studied it.

"Can you tell who it is?" Trenna asked.

"It is the flower of femininity," he answered, meaning he couldn't tell.

"But who is it?" Grace said.

"It is both of you," he said.

They looked at each other. They didn't see any obvious physical resemblance in them or in the painting.

"Femininity is more than the physical appearance," he told them from his faded recliner. "It's what's behind the eyes, the lips, the hands, the expression. That's what you've captured here. It is Grace in form, but it is both of you in spirit."

Neither of them could see that from their spot on a decades-old flowered loveseat, but they nodded politely.

Even now as she sat on the pink stool and held out that painting, she still couldn't see what he meant. When she accepted Lilly's plant she thought she understood how to nurture, but today she didn't even have the courage to go inside the Foster's house. She didn't have the sensitivity to speak at all to them, let alone the right words. She didn't have any strength to give to anyone.

****

"She was your best friend," Faye said over a plate of pasta primavera at the Landing.

"So many people knew her better and could say something more meaningful," Grace said, picking at her chicken tostada salad, which no longer appealed to her.

"If that's true then Max wouldn't have asked you to do it."

"It's clear that Roberta's not in control of this one. She wouldn't have asked me. I can't even imagine what she's thinking right now. " Grace stirred the salsa and guacamole, making a putrid brown mess in the middle of her salad.

"Why don't you ask her?"

"What? I can't call her and ask her that. I haven't even called to offer my condolences. I don't know what to say to her personally, not just at the funeral."

Faye pointed to the escalator in the atrium through the window of the Landing. "You don't have to call; she just walked by."

Grace shrunk down in the booth.

"Avoidance isn't going to make it more comfortable. She's hurting just like you. You have that in common. Build on your common need. Don't plan it; just speak from your heart." Faye paused. "Do they know more from the autopsy?"

"I called Max's cell phone this morning, and his dad answered. He said they still were checking some other medical history. Why would her heart just stop like that without anything wrong?" Grace twisted back to look out the window for Roberta, but the escalator was empty now. "The weird thing is her brother died suddenly, too. An accident, I thought, but maybe something else. It's surreal."

"Remember that when you have a chance to speak to Roberta. She's bound to feel that—and more. She *is* her mother."

"I know."

After lunch, Grace trailed behind Faye toward Honeybee, even though she wasn't working. They stopped at the window display out front to talk about a plan for the fall merchandise that was expected to arrive in the next few days.

"The hibiscus is overgrown," Faye said bluntly.

"It doesn't really fit in here anymore, does it?" Grace admitted. "I liked it when we had it on the stool, but now it's not part of the whole. It looks more like a screen than an accent."

"A backdrop, maybe?"

"Well, however we describe it, I should move it. Everyone's kind of lost interest in it, anyway, including me."

"It's got a lot of foliage this year, but I've only seen one bloom. Maybe it needs to be cut back," Faye suggested.

"I can do that today."

"No. If a shipment comes this week I'm going to want more space or a different set up. Then you'll want to move it, not just cut it back."

"I can at least trim it," Grace peered eagerly in the window, imagining its new shape.

"I really think you should wait," Faye said. "Till you know what you're doing. Until you're feeling better."

"What else am I going to do?" Grace walked with determination into Honeybee. "Go home and cry over a dead friend?"

Sylvia raised her head and the dark gray skirt in her hand and held it toward Grace like an officer stopping traffic. Faye grabbed Grace's arm and put a finger to her lips. But their reactions to her words couldn't deafen their impact on the customer who stood on the other side of the rack. Roberta walked out and stood face-to-face with Grace.

"I needed an emergency outfit for the visitation tomorrow and something for the service on Friday. Not much black left in my closet to choose from."

"I'm sure Sylvia will show you to the right pieces," Grace said to fill her embarrassment. "You know I didn't mean to say that it in the way it came out, don't you?"

Roberta took Grace's hand. "We all express our grief differently."

"I'm sorry for your loss," Grace said with a sincere expression. "I'm not sure how you can cope with it. I feel such a sting."

"I'm not really trying to cope. I allow myself this chance to grieve. It's a process, you know? We're just at the start of it," Roberta said.

"But how do I do that? Just cry?"

"Yes. Some of that. Remember. Learn."

"But what about right now? And the future? What about

Max and Jillian? What about them?" Grace felt Faye's hand on her shoulder signaling that her voice was too high pitched and too loud for this conversation.

Roberta continued to smile and speak in a controlled tone. "Max said you agreed to say a few words at the service. We're happy you can participate. Please come over to the house anytime you want. You will be welcome." Roberta turned to Sylvia. "I'll take that skirt and this black belted one."

Faye escorted Grace to the dressing rooms and shut her in one of them.

"Stay there."

A few minutes later, she brought back a bottle of water. "Now, you don't need me to tell you that you can't bring all that emotion to the surface in front of her."

"I told you I didn't know what to say."

"I said, 'Speak from the heart,' not from a blocked artery," Faye said.

"I've got to do something. That's what I was trying to say when I walked in. I can't just sit around and do nothing, hoping I will heal. I have to do something to let it out."

Grace opened the door of the dressing room and strode through the store. Roberta had left. Grace went to the front window display, undid the latch, and yanked the plant toward the door. She tugged harder, but it had become so heavy that she couldn't move it very far.

Faye was right behind her, laughing. "I'll let you do that, but promise you won't take it out on the poor plant."

They carried it together back to that dressing room and set it on the triangle seat in the corner. Grace went to work pruning it. She started at the bottom, cutting new growth from the sturdy stems. But then it looked top heavy. She trimmed some new growth coming out at the top but then broke off several branches to make it look even. The mess around her grew as her tears blurred her attempts to improve the plant.

Audrey knocked on the door. "Is someone in there?"

Sylvia knocked on it five minutes later. "Do you need some help?"

Grace could hear the bustle of customers trying on new outfits in the rooms around her. But she kept quiet.

Then Faye walked in. She looked at the mess on the floor, then at the plant, and laughed.

"It's not funny," Grace said.

"I'm not going to let you cut my hair. Ever. Not even my bangs."

"What are we going to do with it now?" Grace asked helplessly.

"What do *you* want to do with it?"

"Do you think it will grow back?"

"Probably. But I'll have a hard time using it in the front display again."

"I know. How about I clean up the worst of it and leave the plant here until after the funeral. It should be fine for a few days. Then I'll take it home." Grace scooped some leaves into her palm and held them tight so they wouldn't fall.

Pruning the plant served as an emotional release that rejuvenated her ability to cope with basic conversations. She even stopped by the Foster's house and played with Jillian in the big house filled with company. When she became fussy, Grace took her to the carriage house and put her in the swing while she prepared a bottle of formula. She gathered her in her arms and fed her in the rocking chair until she was asleep. When she pulled the bottle away, Jillian's sleepy milk mouth held a contented expression.

No one disturbed them until Max's mom, Michelle, quietly checked on them. Together they put her in the crib Trenna had finally purchased, trying not to jostle her or the bed in the process. Her eyes opened half way but fluttered closed again. They covered her up and went back to the living room together.

"You're very comfortable doing that."

"Well, I babysat a couple times for Trenna."

"Do you think Jillian knows she's gone?" Michelle asked. Finally someone acknowledged what she kept reviewing over and over in her head.

"I don't know. Trenna's been with her constantly since she was born, except when she went to her six-week checkup. They went to a movie a couple of weeks ago—their first and only date since she was born. I stayed with her both of those times."

"We've been here since Sunday morning. She fusses all through her bottles and doesn't sleep longer than two hours, but I don't know if that is normal or not."

"You've raised four kids, Michelle. How can Jillian not feel it?"

"Babies don't usually have separation anxiety until six or eight months. She's a little young for that."

"Maybe she misses the normalcy of a routine," Grace suggested. "She seemed fine when I took her away from all the company and brought her back here."

"I think you're right. My children acted out whenever they got out of their routine," Michelle recalled. "They need that, especially when there's a crisis. You're going to be a good mother."

They sat in the dark, with only a nightlight on in the hallway and a light over the stove in the adjoining kitchen. Michelle couldn't see the tears that flowed for the hundredth time that day. But she was embarrassed this time that they weren't for Trenna, or even Jillian who'd been left behind, but for herself and her own ache.

Max opened the door, and the security floods outside brightened the space. She hurriedly wiped her nose on the back of her hand and blushed at the guilt she felt being in Trenna's home with those thoughts in her heart at such a time.

"Is she asleep?" he asked quietly.

"Yes, and I'd better go." Grace moved off the couch to leave.

"No, stay. We haven't really talked since—since Sunday. Not really even then." He sat down, thankfully, next to his mom.

"Did you and Alan decide on a cemetery?" Michelle asked.

"Well, there's the old one behind their church where her family is buried. That's what Alan is expecting, but I like the one in Des Peres on the other side of the park. It's quieter, more remote. More like Trenna would want."

"You said on the phone that the arrangements help Alan get through. Have you found that, too?" Grace said, hoping she wasn't approaching an uncomfortable place for him, but not knowing how she could avoid it.

"It helps. To think of what she would want. To really consider who she was," he said. "But it's hard to do. I keep asking myself that when I express an opinion, 'Is that really what she would want? Did I really know her?' Especially when it conflicts with her parents' preference."

"It's my struggle, too, as I consider what to write, what to say at the service. Did I know her well enough when I didn't know her that long?"

"I think it's the depth of relationship she was seeking, with you, and with me. That's what made you her best friend," he said.

"But what now?" The words sounded selfish when she uttered them and just fell in the space between her and Max. She hoped he would retrieve them without all the emotion she felt behind them.

"I haven't told the Fosters, yet, but I want to go back to Kansas City." He squeezed his mom's hand. "I'm going to ask to transfer back, if they have something open. Jillian and I need to establish our own space, our own routine. I believe Mom is in a better position to offer support for that than Roberta is right now."

"When would you go?" Grace asked, already missing the time with Jillian in the future.

"When it feels right. The Fosters have had enough shock. I'm not going to uproot everything immediately."

"Let me know if you need a sitter before then. I need to store up time with her." Grace picked up her keys and rose from the couch.

"I will."

Max stood with her. He had his arms around her before she could even move toward the door. He wrapped her in a hug so tight and so comforting that Grace held her breath. She hadn't felt such a physical support ever before relieve so much of the anxiety inside. But she also felt his anguish rock against her from the depth of his gut, up through his chest and onto his shoulders where he shook.

"I miss her," he cried into her hair. "Oh. I miss her." Grace just held on, not knowing who was supporting whom, until he straightened up, smiled with only the corner of his lips but not his eyes, and backed a few feet away.

****

The visitation, the evening before the funeral, did not comfort Grace.

"What is the purpose of seeing a person stripped of vibrant life, lying in a casket?" she wondered aloud to the other women from Honeybee who rode with her to the funeral home. "How does that bring relief? How does that ease our grief?"

Grace looked over her shoulder at Beth, Sylvia, and Audrey, but no one answered her concerns; Beth and Sylvia were staring out the window. Audrey, who was scrunched in the middle of this five-passenger car that really fit four, had her arms wrapped tightly around her body as if she was in imminent danger herself.

Faye shushed Grace from the front passenger seat, and then twisted her neck toward the back. "Audrey, have you ever been to one of these before?"

"No," she said. "I didn't want to come, but my mom said it was important for me to be there, since we worked together. Do I have to look at her?"

"Only if you want to," Grace said, more aware of Audrey's immaturity with the situation than before. "You can just express your respects to the family. We won't stay long."

And they didn't. They came and went from the funeral home as quick as the receiving line would allow. The Fosters received relatives and friends in a line preceding the casket, but Max and his parents mingled with guests in the room, seemingly shut out, like she felt, from the official family presence. Grace didn't spot Jillian anywhere amongst the crowd of people she did not know.

Their group remained clumped together through the formal receiving line, but then Beth and Audrey fell back toward the entrance and left Faye, Grace, and Sylvia to view Trenna's body in the casket. Sylvia was ahead of Faye, with Grace trailing. Those in line before them murmured, "They made her up real nice," and "She looks so peaceful."

They moved forward behind them, with Sylvia reaching the casket first.

"It's not her," she said.

Faye extended her neck to the side to see around Sylvia's back, and Grace looked over Sylvia's head to see. The body that lay in the casket resembled her friend in a way, but it wasn't her. Her face was overly outlined with colors that she wouldn't have worn, and her skin seemed bloated but still hollow. Life had left, and this wasn't Trenna who remained. Grace focused on Trenna's hands, crossed on her middle.

The same group of women, plus Chanel, gathered in the vestibule of the Foster's church the next morning to wait for Grace who had driven alone from her house. Audrey reached out to Grace first—with a purse-sized pack of tissues. "So you'll be prepared," she said.

Sylvia stood at the door perusing the faces of the assembled mourners. She turned toward the receiving table, as if she were going to sign the guest book, but, instead, Sylvia lifted her hands to straighten the collar on her black fitted jacket in the reflection of a brass urn.

"I didn't know the Fosters knew so many important people. This is *the* crowd."

Grace opened her mouth to respond, but Faye beat her to it. With a condescending lilt in her voice, Faye said, "I even saw the Channel Four weatherman come in all by himself. He went in that door and sat halfway up the aisle. Maybe he'd let you sit beside him."

Grace smirked behind Sylvia, who had already lifted her head searching for him in the direction Faye had pointed. She found the ultra-tan and blond local celebrity in the middle pews and scurried to snag a spot in the row right behind him, motioning for Beth to come sit with her. Chanel, Audrey, Faye, and Grace slid into a bench on the other side of the aisle and waited for the family, who arrived right on the hour in a procession behind the casket laden with peach roses.

The minister opened with welcomes and prayers. The organist played a solo of *For the Beauty of the Earth*. Then the congregation sang and more prayers were offered. The minister announced that in lieu of a formal eulogy read by one family member, the family had invited several family members and friends to share remembrances of Trenna's life.

Ryan spoke first, then an aunt, and then Grace.

"I haven't known Trenna very long," she said, apologetically, to the audience gathered in this immense space. Out of the body of people, she found one face, a woman she didn't know but who looked back with interest at her, to focus on while she talked. "But I have come to know her power to love and how it transformed those around her.

"When I hired Trenna last year, I actually thought I was the one mentoring her, like others have mentored me. I encouraged her to be independent and find her own path. Over the last eighteen months, she developed in her job, in her art, and in her family—adding her unique personality and skills to each. But in reality, she was the one who was showing me and all around her about the real approach to life—one that builds true friendships and bonds of love.

"Trenna interacted naturally with customers, showing a genuine interest in them. She dove into art as a seemingly individual respite but ultimately used it as a means of powerful expression. And then there was her family. She was fiercely independent—almost stubborn—in becoming a mother. When I saw her and Max and Jillian together, I could see why. In a very short time she created this circle of love that surrounded them, protected them, and nurtured them. Trenna's life shows us that relationships happen in the everyday events, conversations, and decisions. These are the days that make a life. "

Grace read a verse from the Bible and then fished a tissue out of her pocket before she walked back to her seat. The organ played a prelude and a soloist began to sing, *How Great Thou Art.* Afterward the minister prayed, yet again, and then he raised his head and thanked those who spoke.

"Consider the words which Trenna's friend, Grace, spoke about our day-to-day interactions. 'These are the days that make a life.' Trenna's life, while short and interrupted unexpectedly, filled our days and lives, with her beauty and reminds us that we are each His creation.

"In days of sorrow, today, and in the past with the parting of Samuel, and in the struggles that will come tomorrow, we will do well to remember that if we are His creation, He will also prop us up in His strength when we falter. Just as a sparrow cannot fall without the Father knowing, He knows us. He knows 'every hair of our head.'

"In St. John 15:5, Jesus states, 'I am the vine, ye are the branches, He that abideth in me, and I in Him, the same bringeth forth much fruit: for without me, ye can do nothing.' Those of us who've been left behind know what it means for life to be stripped away. In this low place, we comprehend our nothingness. His grace enables us to live on, not only unto eternal salvation, but fully live each day with faith for the future.

"With His grace, we extend grace. Let us reach out, despite our own grief, as a branch. Let us feed the hungry, clothe the naked, and visit the sick—remembering always that those with the most food and the best clothes may be the ones who are the hungriest and sickest amongst us. This active faith will soothe the sting of death. In St. Matthew, it says, 'He that findeth his life shall lose it: and he that loseth his life for my sake shall find it.' May the fruit of His love flower in us and around us."

Grace slipped out of the bench and down the aisle. Faye found her bent over the stair railing with her head hanging in the bushes, gagging. Faye reached in her bag for tissues and handed them to Grace when she stood upright. She waved them away.

"Just dry heaves." Grace sat down on the stairs of the church with her head on her knees, wanting Faye to say something encouraging. "I want to feel positive, like they do, about all of this. But my whole body is reverberating with sadness."

"Who are *they*? No one feels positive about what happened. But you spoke, too, and you weren't bleak. You found a sparkle in her life to highlight."

"But the sparkle is all gone."

"Only if you let it be."

A couple pushed open the door behind them and left the service. Faye could see through the door that the pallbearers surrounded the casket and were bringing it up the aisle toward the door. The door swung shut. She took Grace's elbow and coaxed her to her feet.

"Please, just remember, for now," Faye said.

The ushers propped open the church doors. Faye steered Grace to the far side of the stairs where they watched the pall bearers—Ryan, the cousins from the wedding, other young men she didn't know—descend with Trenna's casket. Max followed beside Roberta and Alan. David walked behind them with a hand resting on Michelle's shoulder. She held Jillian, whom Grace hadn't seen yet that day, upright in her arms with a protective hand across her back. Jillian twisted her head, covered in a white bonnet, and struggled away from Michelle's chest to look beyond her. As they passed, Grace saw the smiling eyes of an infant who didn't know better.

Chapter Thirteen

The days of mourning quieted into weeks of individual grief. Work called them back. Normal routines needed to continue. Sorrow seemed undetectable in most of the family, friends, and coworkers as they fit themselves back into the usual activities. Grace wondered if it still remained.

When Max didn't call to ask her to baby-sit or even to talk, Grace called Roberta to see what she could do to help.

"I'm watching Jillian during the days while Max goes to work," she said. "But when he's here, he doesn't leave her. He's with her until the minute he has to go and right there when he returns."

"Okay. It sounds like you're handling things. If you need anything . . ." Grace kept their conversation short, and Roberta didn't extend it.

The end of the call disconnected her from the relationships of a family that were really not her own but had become like that—for the good and the bad—in the circumstances of the last year.

Grace returned to work, too. The mall security guard patrolled the parking lot of The Plaza in his usual figure-eight pattern. The gray-haired couple that walked the stairs every morning for exercise nodded to her as she came inside the west entrance at her regular time. When she turned the corner at the top of the stairs, she almost tripped over the window washer who knelt in front of the glass window at Caruthers.

"Right where you always are at this time of day," she said casually to the air—more than to the man himself.

That familiarity of the store didn't welcome her, even when she lifted the gate, unlocked the doors at Honeybee, and turned on the lights. In the back room, she laid her bag aside and continued in the routines she always followed when she opened, completing most of the tasks without thought. When she came to the front counter to unlock the cabinet and turn on the computer, however, she stood for a long while, staring out the doorway of the store at the mall awakening beyond.

"Good morning," Chanel said as she came through the door and continued talking as she passed Grace to go to the back room. "Did you see Sue's email to us?"

Audrey walked into the store in a gray pantsuit, which finally awakened Grace to the changes she'd felt upon her return.

"What are you doing here this morning?" Grace asked. Audrey, who worked in the afternoons, usually wore chinos and a button-down after she got out of her school uniform.

"Faye scheduled me full-time this week," Audrey slowed at the counter and explained, but her gestures and steps toward the back room while she talked marked her eagerness. "Chanel said I could do the stock room assignments in the mornings, and then she's going to train me to work on the sales floor."

Audrey shuffled the hangers on the racks as she continued toward the back room. Then she stopped completely. "They said I would be a good fill-in until I leave in August. Hope that's all right."

Grace nodded. She hadn't really expected Faye to manage the store without her, but Audrey's appearance in this new position impressed this upon her. She had graduated, anyway, hadn't she? Besides, Faye had moved on to her regular rotation amongst the stores.

She opened the email from Sue, but before she had a chance to read it, Chanel was back at her elbow.

"Can you believe she's coming for a whole week to assess the store and 'retrain as necessary'?" Chanel said, mimicking Sue. "What do you think prompted that? Do you think they will close one of the stores when they open Wild Horse Creek?"

"What gave you that idea?"

"Sales are slow, even below this time last year. You've noticed, haven't you?" Chanel said.

"Let me read the email." Grace turned back toward it. After a few minutes she looked up. "She says, 'assess sales, management practices, and employee conduct' and 'reemphasize company policies.' I imagine she's doing it at all the stores in the region. It may even be company-wide."

"Well, at least we have a couple of weeks to get ready," Chanel said, trying to sound encouraging.

"But how? I can review the sales sheets and be familiar with what's already going on, but beyond making sure the place looks good, I don't think we can prepare much," Grace said, worried now by the concerns Chanel aired.

"I guess that's what I meant. Sue hasn't seen the store in a while—a month or more. Faye redid the front window on Friday, but she's not due back again until after the fall merchandise arrives. The merchandise, itself, looks as fresh as it can, but the store could use some help beyond the daily maintenance. The back room, the dressing rooms . . ."

Grace tuned out the list of things to do. Her passion to make it the best store in the region didn't stir in her like it used to.

"Whatever you think you need to do—go ahead and coordinate it," she said, quieting Chanel.

Later, Grace snapped at Audrey for a shipment that she sent to the wrong Chicago store. She blamed Faye in her absence for scheduling too many people during the day and not enough in the evening. She assigned Chanel to make the necessary changes and inform those it impacted.

She reviewed the sales sheets for hours at a time. But while she read the figures two and three times, her concentration waned, and she couldn't grasp what she needed to know. The fact was that sales were not only lower than the year before, they were as low as they'd ever been under her management, and she couldn't analyze the patterns like she usually did.

When she came out of the backroom to check the inventory or speak with employees, she didn't even see the customers, let alone offer to help them. During those weeks Grace neglected anything that did not directly fall into her path during the day or night.

Grace did notice that her regular customers now went directly to Chanel for advice in putting together outfits, and Beth asked Chanel for schedule changes, not Grace. She also overheard Sylvia go to Chanel with her concerns, too.

"That corner dressing room has a lock that clasps too tightly," Sylvia said quietly to Chanel. "I'll put up a sign. We don't want anyone to get stuck in there."

Chanel gestured her approval without consulting Grace.

Grace saw the exchange. She wanted to lead, to solve problems, and make decisions, but in those weeks she couldn't find the energy to do so.

****

Grace pulled on a skirt suit. Too uptight. She ripped off the jacket and substituted a print blouse with the light gray skirt. Still too dressy. She held up her black trousers from the back of her closet. Maybe if the weather wasn't too hot, she could wear these. The thermometer on her alarm clock already read 79 degrees at 8:35 a.m. Those wouldn't work.

"I have to get to work," she moaned at the clock. "What am I going to wear?"

Back to her closet, she took the dry cleaning plastic off a tan linen suit, knowing it would be wrinkled before her lunch meeting with Sue, but she had to get into the store.

The gate in front of Honeybee stood two-thirds high, and the lights were on inside the store. Grace groaned. Either Chanel switched her afternoon schedule without telling her or Sue arrived early. She lifted the gate the rest of the way, pushing open the doors. So much for the scheduled lunch.

"Good morning, Grace," Sue said, from behind the front counter, in the same gray Honeybee jacket Grace had thrown back in her closet.

"I didn't expect you so early," Grace said, noting that the computer was already fired up.

"We have lots to cover this week."

"So it seems. Where are we going to start?" Grace said.

"You've read my emails, I'm sure." Sue stepped from behind the counter, wearing black trousers with her gray jacket.

"I know what you wrote, but it feels like there's more to it."

"Yes, there is, but I don't want to get into it here," Sue said curtly. "I'll observe this morning, and we'll talk at the Landing as we planned."

At lunch Sue didn't wait for questions or discussion or even for the menus.

"I'm going to level with you," she said. "We've been reviewing the figures for The Plaza and the store in Clayton. We know what the numbers say, and we have to close one of these stores."

"Then why are you opening a brand new store in an expensive location like Wild Horse Creek when we're trying to recover from a recession?"

"It just appears expensive. Wild Horse Creek is less expensive than either here or Clayton. The square footage costs less, the maintenance costs less, and the traffic is better. Most importantly, that's where our customers have gone."

"I thought you said they've gone online."

"They have. We've grabbed that opportunity with special online deals on our own site and upped our social media marketing. There's more to it, though. Last November we thought a demographic shift was to blame for reduced sales in Clayton and Frontenac. But when sales fell again after the holiday, our analysts did more research. Too many people have traded down from the luxury stores here and moved on to those places they perceive to have a better value."

"I've been to Wild Horse Creek," Grace said. "And, honestly, I only see a modernized redo of this place."

"Grace, people like that set-up better than the mall. They can go to the discount stores on the way in or out. They perceive that they saved money in one place and can afford to spend it in another. How can this old model compete with new customers?" Sue waved her hand toward the lavish but empty mall beyond their table.

She picked up her flavored water to avoid an answer. Was this a test of her loyalty or to gauge her foresight in the future of retail? Months ago, she'd pined for a change to Wild Horse Creek, but now, with the reality that it may mean the loss of this store, she wasn't sure which to choose.

"It can't," Grace said with only a glimmer of sarcasm. "Nothing can compete with the marketing scheme of the moment. But, you're right, we'd better hurry while we can still pass on our lease before everyone else moves west."

Sue paused, perplexed, but regained control of the conversation quickly. "That's the direction I'm leaning. I'm glad you can confirm it."

"No problem," Grace said in mock cheerfulness, knowing the loss of The Plaza store was inevitable now.

"I'm glad you're in with us. Don't let the word out to your staff. I still need to observe, interview, and deliberate for the rest of the week. I'll announce my decision—and staff placement— on Friday."

Grace only agreed with Sue's direction to prompt her to verbalize her real intent. But, now, the reality provoked her. The anger swelled in her throat and stung her eyes.

"Excuse me." Grace pointed to the restrooms, rising from her seat. She dodged a couple also leaving their table but brushed against a server carrying a tray, which tipped and spilled red sauce across his front.

"I'm sorry," Grace mumbled, searching helplessly for a rag or anything to hand the server. No free napkins lay anywhere. "Excuse me."

Pressure pushed against her pores as if it were going to tear her open in front of everyone. In the ladies' room she grabbed the edge of the vanity to steady herself. Thankfully, the two stalls appeared empty.

Her store. Her staff. It was the only place she frequented, knew the people, felt valued. All of it would be gone. She couldn't imagine the future without Chanel, Faye, Beth, and Audrey—even Sylvia. Or Trenna.

But Trenna was gone. So were Jillian and Max, or they would be soon. Even Roberta hadn't come in since before the funeral. Lilly's most faithful customer—gone. Now the store, and more importantly, her job, would follow.

In this empty but very public place, her whole body released the heat of fierce anger until it only shook from the coldness of sorrow.

****

Grace dressed the way she wanted on Tuesday, without even trying to make an impression on Sue. Her quick exit to the restroom and her eventual return with splotchy makeup and red eyes ruined any possibility of that. Today's choice of green swing skirt and yellow cardigan freshened her morning, instilling calm in her emotions. The oppressive heat would certainly be upon them before noon, in more ways than one.

Sue seemed to own Honeybee by the time Grace arrived. Own it? Of course Sue didn't own it. Neither did she. So why had she invested such feelings of ownership in it, or the staff, or the customers for so long? This store wasn't her home. These people weren't her family.

Now, she could pursue a job anywhere and work with anyone, maybe another store at The Plaza or at Wild Horse Creek or even back in Minnesota. Change could happen, like she had wanted.

Grace nodded a greeting to Sue, who trailed her to the backroom. Grace set her raspberry yogurt and an apple in the refrigerator and stowed her bag in her bottom desk drawer. A stack of employee files lay on the desk.

"I need to use your desk today, if you don't mind," Sue announced behind her.

"No, not at all," Grace lied.

"Now that I'm fairly confident that we're going to close this store, I want to interview the staff and discover who we might want to transfer."

The "we" confused Grace. "Does that mean you'll want me to be part of those interviews? Or will you just want my assessment?"

"By 'we,' I meant the company, not you and I," Sue clarified. "I may have questions for you when I'm finished, though."

"Sure, whatever you need."

Grace glanced back at the stacks of files on her desk. The visual image of that very desk with Sylvia's file lying open on it flashed into her mind. The day she'd reprimanded Sylvia had been Jillian's birthday, more than three months ago. She'd left for the hospital with the file open right there, without ever returning it to the locked file cabinet.

Sylvia's file wouldn't be in that stack.

Sue would need that file in a matter of hours, and she had no idea where it was or how to explain its absence, but she knew she would have to account for it by the end of the day. Most likely, Sylvia had removed it from the desk. But Grace herself would now be responsible.

Guilt and confusion sparked irritation. She couldn't even lift it by tearing through her file cabinet one more time hoping to find the missing file. Instead, it seeped into all her interactions. She snapped at Audrey who still couldn't run a credit card properly and asked Grace for help when she was waiting to ring up another customer.

"Like this." Grace took the card from Audrey and swiped it from the other side. She gave it back to the customer and finished up both orders while Audrey stood watching. "Do you think you can do it by yourself, next time?"

Audrey nodded.

After lunch, Sue spent an hour alone with Chanel, which barred Grace from the backroom. To keep some semblance of authority she scolded Beth and Audrey from hanging around the door to eavesdrop, even though she wanted to herself.

"What do you know?" Grace asked in curiosity when Chanel exited and called Beth to go back.

"I can't say," Chanel said. "She says we'll all know by Friday."

Friday. Yes, that was still a few days out. Since Sylvia worked that evening and all day Wednesday, there would be a good likelihood that Sue wouldn't interview her until tomorrow afternoon. She could talk with Sylvia tonight after Sue left. That thought eased her anxiety.

But when Sylvia arrived, Sue wasn't close to packing up her bag and going home, even though she'd been there longer than Grace. Instead, Sue came out and worked the floor. She conversed with customers, wandered around outside in the mall, and even suggested some outfits to Sylvia that she thought might look good with her red hair.

Every action or word diminished Grace's management role. She wasn't sure if she should gather her things to leave or shadow Sue in the hopes that she was still considering her for a transfer or new position. Grace stood indecisively beside a rack of clothes, smiling and nodding at the customers, Sylvia, and another part-timer.

Sue approached and decided for her. "Will you meet me at your desk in a few minutes, please?"

Grace complied willingly with the invitation to return to her own territory. Sue sat down at the desk and motioned for Grace to sit on the chair from the break table.

"That employee. The redhead. Her name is Sylvia, right?" Sue said. Grace nodded.

"What do you think about her?"

"In what sense?" Grace asked.

"Where might you place her in a new store?"

"I wouldn't necessarily transfer her. I might just let her go."

"On what grounds?" Sue questioned. "I didn't see a file for her. Do you have it somewhere else?"

"No," Grace said. "It's complicated."

"I have time."

"This may not be the best time," Grace said, titling her head toward the door.

"It closes, doesn't it?" Sue stood up, moving the big carton of spare hangers that had held the door open for every minute Grace had worked there. "There."

Grace was now sitting in the same place where Sylvia had stood that day. But now she was the one answering for her actions while Sue sat in her desk. She swallowed, wetting her throat so that her tone wouldn't sound as resentful as she feared it might.

"I don't have her file. I met with her at the end of April, the same day another employee—Trenna—delivered her baby. I left the file on my desk to go to the hospital. It was gone when I returned."

"Are you implying that someone took it while you were gone?"

Grace nodded.

"Why did you meet with her that day?"

Grace contemplated her words carefully. "A personal item, a gift, had been stolen from my desk. She gave that item, the gift, to another employee in my full view, as if it were her own. I asked her to explain it."

Her accusation sounded ridiculous to her now when she said it, but she continued to explain. "I made a probation report of her actions that I showed her. I intended to file it, but her file and paper weren't here when I returned. There were two other incidents on the report, as well."

Sue studied Grace while she spoke. With those eyes upon her, she had to remain unemotional as she related the other incidents, if they were to be viewed as plausible reasons, not just personal attacks. Sue sighed.

"Not to mention, Sylvia continues to pick at me personally, whenever she gets a chance."

Sue sighed even deeper, as if she was intentionally exaggerating the silence. She picked up another file from the desk.

"Grace, you're the manager, and I trust that you acted in the best way. But I believe these mysteries with Sylvia are just mysteries. Just coincidences, probably."

The same frustration and humiliation Grace felt the day before in the restaurant rose in her throat and pulsed against her neck.

"But, the remarks," Grace reminded her.

"The offensive language about the customer, for sure,

was inappropriate. But she was fairly new as an associate when that happened, wasn't she?" Sue raised her eyebrows with a questioning look. "She learned, didn't she?"

Were those rhetorical questions? Grace didn't trust her voice to answer if they weren't. Inside, she was standing outside her junior high teacher's door being chastised for reading a book in class, and she was either going to fling the book at the teacher's face or burst into tears. Neither would be pretty since she wasn't thirteen anymore. She dropped her eyes to her thumb and prodded the edge of a slightly infected hangnail with the index finger of her right hand.

"Since you played a part in the disappearance of her file and that report, we can't lay it all at her feet. Can we, Grace?"

Grace looked up at her for some indication that this was indeed a conversation between adults and this was not her condescending science teacher all over again.

Sue smiled. "But, just to be sure, I'll ask her about it in my interview with her tonight." She stood and gestured for Grace to also stand. Most women were not as tall as Grace, but Sue reached a few inches above her and always wore heels. She took Grace by the elbow and leaned in close to her. "Why don't you go home, now? You don't look like you've been sleeping well."

Grace kept the scream inside her gut until she left the store, then it crept into her throat, and rattled against her tongue. She wanted to run as fast as she did when her science teacher finally stopped belittling her and sent her to wash her face in the restroom before she returned to class. But she didn't want to just wash up and return; she wanted to leave altogether.

She clasped her hand to her mouth and walked as fast as she could through the mall. She made it safely to the doors at the southeast entrance without encountering anyone. Just as she released her hand from her mouth and pressed on the first set of doors, Colleen walked in from the outside. She had no time to mask her expression.

"Grace, what's wrong? I heard you guys might be pulling out? Is that true?"

"I'm sorry. Not a great day. Needed some air." Grace stepped outside and motioned toward the parking lot.

Colleen followed her into the humid evening. "I have chocolate." She fished in her take-out bag before producing a chocolate brownie.

Grace came back to the door. "That would be great."

The entire 900-calorie double fudge nut brownie disappeared in five minutes. She wiped her fingers on the white pastry paper, but they still felt too sticky to touch the steering wheel. The glove box always held the leftover napkins from drive-thru meals, and she found several brown ones right in the front, in between a bottle of hand sanitizer and . . . the black velvet box. That black velvet box never seemed to get mailed back to Jeff like she intended. Did that very fact—having never returned it—give *him* hope that she would return?

"Keep it; if you ever change your mind," he had told her, leaving the door open for her to come back if she would compromise her desires. All this time she'd held on to the hope that he would change his mind. But now, maybe she finally would change hers.

Chapter Fourteen

The parking lot looked the same fifteen hours later, but the price of spending the majority of it crying off and on was that she couldn't identify if the car she parked beside was really Roberta's familiar black luxury sedan or just a look-a-like.

She checked her puffy eyes once again in the rearview mirror. They still scratched like she'd caught several eyelashes underneath her lids. Her cloudy vision didn't clear with just a few blinks. Her feet followed their usual quick pace up the stairs and toward the second level shops, but she deliberately slowed them and changed direction. A detour downstairs to the shops on the first level would increase the probability of a chance meeting with Roberta, if she was there. A surprise contact, even with this woman she dreaded to see, would be easier than a planned attempt to reach out for information that might bring comfort.

Grace passed the jeweler and the bookseller where a stray employee or two came and went in the window and the department store where the women dressed in white coats behind the cosmetic counters prepared to advise clients on color enhancements. She passed the luggage and gift store where she'd retrieved the wedding book more than a year ago and the few customers who roamed about this early. She passed all of this without seeing Roberta.

Grace rode the escalator to the top, in full view of Honeybee's front entrance. At the top, she stood still, incapable of moving from the metal escalator pad, looking through the open store doors. Sue stood in Grace's place at the front counter. Chanel popped into sight behind her and left again. Grace glanced at her watch. Chanel never arrived until the minute Honeybee opened.

"Excuse me." Grace stepped out of the way for a customer coming up the escalator. A woman passed her on her right. Now she could clearly see all the way inside the front of the store. Sylvia, of all people, stood by the front table, arranging a new bouquet of flowers on the front table. The flowers appeared too fresh and new for a store that would darken its lights in a matter of weeks, if not days.

Sue came toward Sylvia, still plumping the flowers, and Chanel joined them on the other side of the table in a band of smiles awaiting the day's first customers. From her center place, Sue flattered them with words Grace couldn't hear but with an expression that Sue had given her when she was a new management trainee. This scene looked too familiar to be as distant as it felt when viewed from her now isolated position.

The gestures of nurturing. The genuine words of praise. Where were these flowers? What had become of her work? Her effort and contribution? Even her reward from the beautiful blooms of Lilly's plant had disappeared.

No. Lilly's plant hadn't disappeared. She'd just neglected it.

Grace rushed to the front window, searching for the plant in Faye's new display. Where had Faye hid the hibiscus among the early fall ensembles? The hand-knit multi-colored sweaters piled in a wooden trunk? The false staircase layered with dark denims?

She craned to see the hidden places in the background, but no plant emerged, even among the accessories.

The confusion of thoughts she'd carried around for the past month eclipsed her memory. What had they done with Lilly's plant? She mentally tracked past events, as she would search for a set of lost keys. She couldn't pinpoint a place—in the display or in her head. The greater the confusion, the more anxious she became to resolve this new loss. In this frantic state, she entered the store.

"Good morning." The chorus of women rang too self-satisfied. Grace grunted something—she didn't know what—and dashed to the back room to begin her search.

Grace sifted through the boxes by the shipping table, looking for the pot. She retreated to the bathroom when she heard Sue's heels hit the hard surface. Three shelves lined the wall above the toilet; odds and ends were stacked behind the door. The shelves obviously couldn't hold a heavy planter, but she climbed up on the toilet seat, anyway and teetered with a foot on either edge as she sorted through the extra toilet paper, cleaning chemicals, and scrub brushes, looking for an answer to where the plant had gone.

Sue stepped into the doorway. Grace fell off the toilet trying to get down, stabilized her right foot, and hobbled to the door.

"You told them, didn't you?" Grace demanded of Sue.

"It was only fair to give them an idea of what to expect," Sue said calmly. "They're both going to receive a transfer. I know that. And certainly a managerial position is in line for Chanel, maybe even Sylvia."

Grace closed the door to check behind it. In the corner were several planters, including one that even held a fake plant whose leaves had turned gray with a covering of dust—not Lilly's plant. She reopened the door. Sue stood passively in the doorway, unconcerned.

"You told me not to say anything. That you would announce it on Friday," Grace said. "Can't you sense—isn't it clear—the awkward position you set up for me?"

"Your position is still undecided."

"That's obvious to everyone. Can't you see the feeding trough right at your feet? They've already begun to treat you as the manager, not me."

"I honestly think that's you projecting your own feelings on the situation. Maybe you should consider that before you come back to the front."

As Sue returned to the front Grace slowed her breathing, renewing her energy. She jammed her key into the back door lock, turned the handle, and wiggled it open. Boxes stacked behind the door obstructed her entry into the well-lit but eerily empty back hall. They often piled trash behind the door instead of taking it to the trash room where it would fall multiple stories down a chute into the compactor in the basement. She never liked to go there alone—or send anyone else.

Sifting through the mounting pile of neglected trash gave Grace time to vent. She yelled at Sue, hoping she would secretly hear her, though she knew when the door was closed the walls were soundproof—another reason she feared this place. No matter what you said or how loud you yelled, no one would respond, unless they were in the hallway with you. But today, she was alone.

People didn't typically empty trash in the morning, but she would. For the next thirty minutes, she pushed the rolling trash can filled with packing peanuts, plastic coverings, and bent hangers to the trash. She dumped it into the chute and yelled down inside, releasing trash and emotion.

With the first few loads, she vented to herself about the company's plans to chase the market to Chesterfield. She hauled the boxes that had delivered new merchandise and blasted Sylvia's missteps that no one believed. By the time she cleared the hallway for the last loads—and hadn't found any planters or a dying plant—she even began to tell Roberta all the things she'd wanted to say to her.

Between the trips up and down the hallway and the passionate expressions, her heart rate pumped faster than the runs she used to make with Trenna in Tilles Park. She clamped the back door shut and dropped into her office chair exhausted. She consciously slowed her breathing as if this was her cool down. She didn't find the plant, but she felt better. After a quick retouch of her makeup and hair and straightening of her clothes, Grace appeared ready to meet the public again.

Focus on the customers. That's what she'd do. It's the part of her job she liked best; they were why she stayed in retail—interacting with them, working with them, getting to know them, and helping them. She turned the knob of the backroom door, pushed the box of hangers in front of it, again, to prop it open like it'd been since the day she'd started, and stepped out to meet whoever walked in the door next.

Grace heard her before she saw her. Roberta Foster's throaty laugh carried over the clothes. Between racks she could only see Sue and Sylvia, not Roberta.

"Our most important—and my favorite—customer," Sylvia said to Sue.

"Not any more, I think. I haven't been in for weeks," Roberta admitted. Grace craned to see her face. Was she flustered? Or was she serious? Could she really belittle her daughter's death with the suggestion that her shopping had been neglected for grief?

"I know. Let me say, again, how sorry we are for your loss," Sylvia said. "Trenna meant the world to me."

She did not. Grace left the shadows of the dressing room and joined the group gathered around Roberta. She struggled behind Sue and Sylvia to reach Roberta. With a turn of her shoulders, Grace moved between them and hugged her. Roberta embraced her with gentle but honest affection.

Roberta pulled back and smiled at Grace.

"It is good to see you, again," Grace said first. "We have much to talk about, but can I help you find something first?"

"No," she pointed to Sylvia. "Sylvia's already suggested a few things, and Sue has an eye for what works on us larger figures."

Grace nodded. "They've got you taken care of, don't they? Let me know if I can help."

Sylvia led Roberta back to the alcove of dressing rooms and rattled the handle on the right corner dressing room loud enough that Grace could hear it where she'd stayed.

"Oh, I don't know what's wrong with this handle. I thought we had it fixed, but it doesn't seem so now." Sylvia jiggled the knob again, and the door flew open. She held it wide for Roberta to step inside with her clothes.

"Oh yuck," Roberta screeched and immediately retreated.

"Oh, I'm sorry. I'm so sorry you had to see that mess. Let's try this one." Sylvia settled Roberta in another dressing room on the opposite side.

Sue rushed to their aid. "What happened?"

Sylvia pushed open the door of the dressing room, and Sue looked around. "What is this mess? Why is it here?" she demanded.

Sylvia shrugged.

"Grace?" Sue called loudly.

Grace felt faint at the swinging door of the back dressing room. Her face heated. Her stomach curled. She knew what she would see. But still, she lurched forward at Sue's command and saw something worse than what she feared.

The missing planter lay on its side on the corner bench of the dressing room. Half the soil had spilled atop the cream plush carpet. The other half clung to the exposed roots of the hibiscus plant. But no leaves defined it as a living plant any more, just one brown stalk with several thinner stems protruded from the sideways angle. Any leaves that had filled those stems were now scattered about the floor as crispy brown and gray shriveled paper.

Grace fell against the door. "I didn't do it," she screeched with pain. "I didn't kill it."

She didn't wait for a response, couldn't stay to defend herself. She pushed her way out of the tight alcove into the open store. Chanel's frown conveyed a sorrowful placing of blame.

"Excuse me." Grace calmed her stride, attempting to return an air of civility. She paused at the store entrance, wanting to escape. She ducked into Kitchen Gourmet and slipped into the utensil aisle.

The death of Lilly's plant cut into her. One more loss. Accusations felt loose on her tongue, but who could she blame? She'd cut the plant. Over trimmed it. She'd left it there to die. She'd neglected it.

The display of expensive knives mocked her. She'd killed Lilly's plant.

Maybe she could salvage a branch. Maybe she could bring it back from the roots.

She rushed back to Honeybee where Roberta stood at the front counter waiting on her purchase that Sylvia was ringing. Roberta handed over her credit card and turned toward Grace.

"What's happened here? I've never seen such an uproar."

Grace rocked forward on her left foot, poised to rescue the plant from the dressing room and repair her mistake. She shifted her weight onto her right foot, wanting to justify herself to Roberta and in some way remove her guilt.

Sylvia wrapped the new clothes in tissue paper, placed them in a Honeybee bag, and handed them to Roberta.

"Let me walk you to your car." Grace held out her hand to carry the bag.

"I've got it." Roberta clung to her new purchase. When they were almost to the escalator under the atrium windows and a safe distance to be out of earshot of the store, Grace paused, leaning forward against the balcony railing.

"I need to be honest with you, Roberta, and I need you to be honest with me," she began. "First, it is falling apart, isn't it? The mess in the back—that's just a symptom, not the cause of the 'uproar' as you call. Honeybee is closing at The Plaza."

"Really?" Roberta leaned her back heavily against the balcony banister, looking between Grace and the Honeybee sign in front of her. She set down her shopping bag and leaned forward, "Can we stop it? Can I call someone? Do something? Say something?"

"I doubt it," Grace's voice caught. "I've done everything I can to turn it around, but circumstances—the economy, new technology, a different generation—change everything."

Tears wet her face. They were not violent tears of anger like before, but slow tears of realization. Roberta grasped her hand.

"It will all be okay, Grace." Roberta rescued a crumbled tissue from a packet in her purse, and Grace blew her nose in it. She reached out to Grace. Even though Roberta only came to Grace's chest, Roberta lifted her arms around Grace's neck in an awkward embrace.

"It will be okay," Roberta repeated. In a more muffled voice she said, "Maybe not for me, but you'll find something else."

"No, I don't suppose it will be okay for you for a long time. But at least you have Jillian. I don't even see her anymore."

"No, I won't. Max put in a transfer back to Kansas City. He's taking her away as soon as he can."

Grace pulled back. Max wasn't "taking" Jillian away. He needed his own mother's support. Of course, this was Roberta's typical mindset—thinking she needed to dominate everyone's life. Anger churned in her chest as the list of grievances Grace had flung toward the trash chute this morning flew back into her mind and out of her mouth.

"You controlled Trenna," Grace snapped. "Now you think you can control her husband and child, too."

Roberta backed away from the assault. "That's absurd."

"Is it really?" Grace shot back. "Think about it. You kept her so close—trapped beside you—that it was inevitable that she would suffocate, sooner or later."

"Are you saying I'm responsible for her death?" Roberta screeched, trying to understand.

"No," Grace burst out, pulling her hands to her cheeks and wanting to cover her ears. Grace didn't mean those words literally, but Roberta's accusation turned them around into such a cruel suggestion. She covered her eyes in frustration. Roberta didn't understand her point, which was the real crux of what had happened in her relationship with her daughter. She needed to explain it, to help her see. Grace pulled down her hands with force. "But did you let her live? Really live?"

Roberta looked stunned, flattened against the balcony railing without anywhere else to retreat from Grace's emotional attack. But still, Grace continued.

"What about her choices? They were yours. What about her feelings? You pressed yours on her. What about her desires? She could only follow your direction. You smothered her."

"Is that how you see my actions? Is that how Trenna saw them?"

"Yes."

The searing pain on Robert's face crumpled the fire in her eye.

"You try it, Grace. You try motherhood and show me how you'll do. How you do think you'll be?"

Grace couldn't hope to answer. She wouldn't have that chance.

"I lost a child—just like that," Roberta said. "He was alive, and then he was gone. No warning. No apparent cause. Now another. The same way. You wouldn't have been able to save them either." Roberta picked up her bag calmly from the floor without even raising her eyes. At the top of the escalator, she stopped. "But I also did everything—all I could—because I loved them. I certainly won't stop trying with those I have left."

Roberta stepped on to the escalator, which carried her to the first floor. She limped past the concierge booth and toward the exit, until she'd disappeared from Grace's view.

Exhausted, Grace reentered the store. She ignored Sylvia and Chanel competing for a better angle beside Sue and walked through the maze of costly apparel. In the now-quiet alcove her mess still lay on the corner dressing room floor. She righted the plant on the bench, brushed away the spilled dirt, reached her hand in the soil, and cupped the root end of the plant in her right hand. The soil clumped like a dry rock in some places and fell away in others. She bent a stem at the top with her left hand, but it snapped away, revealing no green plant beneath. There was nothing left for her to do. She couldn't revive it. She had nothing left to give. But even more, she had no one left to receive what little love remained.

Chapter Fifteen

Honeybee at Wild Horse Creek opened on the first of September, which was also the day that Honeybee at The Plaza closed its door to customers. Their lease hadn't ended, but the company didn't want to hire extra staff for the overlap period.

Faye was chosen to manage the new store and retained almost everyone from The Plaza store except Chanel, who was promoted to manage the Clayton store. Sue insisted that Faye hire Sylvia for a trial training period as the assistant manager at Wild Horse Creek, and Faye complied. She had asked for Grace, Faye told her later, but Grace received her new assignment the morning after the plant incident—pack the remaining inventory at The Plaza for shipment to other stores and close out the space in two weeks time. Sue did not offer her a position at Wild Horse Creek or anywhere else in the company.

The time before everyone moved to the other store followed by time alone at The Plaza store humiliated her. Customers rushing in with mock sentiments at the store-closing sale asked about her plans.

"I'm pursuing other opportunities," she said three or four times a day.

Grace didn't attend the grand opening at the new store, and they all moved on without her. She traded fashion-conscious career clothes for faded jeans and old button-down shirts for the work she did in the near empty store, hoping her counterparts in the mall wouldn't see her coming and going.

After her last day in September, she half-heartedly sent resumes to a dozen department stores in St. Louis and Minneapolis. The job loss contributed to the real loss she still felt from Trenna's death, and depression took over while she waited for responses.

She moped around her house until Halloween. Five neighborhood kids came to trick-or-treat, and she couldn't even find an apple to give them. She scavenged in her car and found two tootsie rolls, three quarters, and the black velvet box that lay perpetually in an undecided state in her glove box.

She wasn't sure if Jeff's number was still the same, but after she turned out the porch lights, she dialed it anyway. The phone rang three times before a woman's voice answered. A party of voices filled the background.

"Hello?" the woman said. "Hello?"

Grace hung up. New girlfriend? Changed number? Wife? It *had* been more than three years now. She hoped he had a new calling plan and his old number had already been recycled.

On the way to the jewelers the next morning, she backed over a pumpkin and squished its moldy innards beneath her tire.

"We don't buy used diamonds." The jeweler peered over his glasses.

"But it's brand new. Almost."

He shook his head and directed her to some pawnshops downtown on Jefferson Avenue. She returned home with enough money for another month's rent, bills, and groceries and the residue of pumpkin mush left in the grooves of her back tire. Trenna's yellow Volkswagen sat in front of her house with a "For Sale" in its window.

Was Max here? No one was in the car or on her front porch. Interested, she parked her car in the driveway and peered into the windows of the car.

"Are you looking for a car to buy?"

The sun coming through the falling maple leaves spotlighted Max pushing a stroller up the block with Mr. Reynolds beside him. Grace walked toward them and stopped awkwardly, not sure what kind of affectionate greeting to give.

"You're looking good," she said, immediately regretting it.

"Thanks." Notably, he didn't return the compliment. Grace quickly came around the front of the stroller to look in on Jillian.

"She's all settled, now," Mr. Reynolds said. "I heard her crying—screaming—in your front yard and told him that a walk up to the stores and back was the only thing that could calm our crying children. Helen and I walked up and down these blocks hundreds of times with all four of them."

"I usually drive to quiet her, but I wanted to wait to see if you would be back," Max said.

"I'm glad you did. She's grown so much since July."

All three of them crowded the narrow sidewalk. At the side of the yellow car, Max pointed to the sign. "Are you interested?"

"I could never afford it, not on my non-existent income."

"I went by The Plaza. But I wasn't sure if you'd moved to Wild Horse Creek."

"I'm out of work."

"Tasty Pastry is hiring," Mr. Reynolds offered.

"Thanks," Grace said, wanting time to speak alone with Max. Other than a couple of brief conversations, they hadn't spoken since the funeral.

"Thanks, Mr. Reynolds. I appreciate your baby advice," Max said to him and then turned to Grace. "May I come in for a few minutes?"

"I'll take Jillian while you stow her stroller," Grace offered. She lifted the half sleepy baby out of her blanket and melted at her beautiful eyes as they fluttered open and closed again.

Once inside, though, Jillian simply whined. Max handed Grace a bottle, but that didn't help much so he checked her diaper and even changed it. Their busy movements felt impersonal, not like they had the night when he held her at the carriage house. Even the friendly banter they used to share was now strained.

"You've learned a lot," she told him, hoping to bring some of that connection back.

"About her and myself," he acknowledged, setting Jillian on his lap to slip her little feet back into her leggings. "Grace, I came to tell you that we're leaving tomorrow for Kansas City. I wanted to say goodbye."

"Goodbye?" She wanted to pull back the conversation to the beginning of all this so that the end wouldn't come. Grace held her arms out for Jillian, lifting her up and turning her face out so that she could still her daddy. Max handed Jillian a small, colorful toy. "I should have reached out earlier. I could have been helping."

"We've managed, but I do wish I'd included you more," Max confirmed. "So many have surrounded us to help. Right now Jillian and I need some space for us to be a family on our own."

"I can believe that. I saw Roberta in August . . ." Grace started.

"No, Grace. It's not what you think." He paused, but continued more gently, "They were worried. The autopsy results were still being evaluated, and they didn't have any answers. They still don't have them all."

"What *do* you know?" Her emotion rose with the lack of information. Jillian fussed in her arms. Grace rattled the soft, fuzzy toy. "I feel so shut out, so disconnected from what happened. I haven't understood any of this, although I guess it's not really my business to know."

"No, it is your business. You were close—even if Trenna didn't feel like she could share all of this with you."

"What else was there to share? I don't mean to be crass, but it's not like Trenna could explain her own death, and no one else has." As soon as she said this, she cringed. Here was her accusing tone, again, the one she used on Roberta.

He sat rigidly on the edge the chair—the same chair Trenna sat in the first time she came and the one she chose every time thereafter Jillian began to really cry. Although Grace wanted to keep holding onto her as a protection against the pain, she handed her to Max, knowing he would need her physical warmth and comfort more.

"Hand me her pacifier, from the front pocket." Max bundled Jillian close to his chest.

She rummaged in the diaper backpack, found the pink rubber Nuk and crouched beside the chair, rubbing Jillian's back while Max tried to quiet her.

"I'm sorry," she apologized for what felt like yet another mistake on her part for months of misunderstandings. "I really have no idea what her being gone must mean to you."

Max tipped his head down, pressing his check against Jillian's soft head. Grace backed up from his chair and resettled herself cross-legged on the couch.

After a few minutes of whimpering, Jillian's back rose and fell in waves of even breathing. Max lifted his head. "I think you know bits of information, but all together it makes more sense not just for what I feel but for what the Fosters—especially Roberta—feel. Trenna's older brother, Sam, died suddenly a little more than three years ago, right after we met but before we were seriously dating. They did an autopsy but didn't know—or didn't understand themselves—right away what the cause was. Like you feel now."

Max shifted Jillian's little body into the crook of his arm. She slurped on the pacifier in her mouth.

"About the time we began dating, they identified that Sam had a disease that causes a heart arrhythmia or irregular heart beat. Arrhythmias aren't uncommon, but this type is rare. It's called arrhythmogenic right ventricular dysplasia or ARVD. The heart muscle in the right ventricle is replaced by fat—unknown to anyone. His first symptom was sudden cardiac death."

"Is it hereditary? Is this what Trenna had, too?" Grace leaned forward, wanting more.

"It can be, yes. The family—Trenna, Ryan, Roberta, David—were all screened within that first year after his death, but there's not one single test to assure a diagnosis. There are six tests in a screening that have to be analyzed. No one test showed a positive diagnosis, but they were encouraged to repeat the screening again every few years. When Trenna found out she was pregnant, Roberta became even more hyper-protective and demanded Trenna go back to be screened again."

"She chose to wait, didn't she?" Grace guessed out loud.

The regret of that choice clear on his face, he closed his eyes, dropped his head into Jillian's neck, and cradled the blessing of Trenna's decision in his arms. After a few minutes, he lifted his head and continued.

"When Trenna died, they assumed ARVD. They just went on with the same plans they'd carried out with Sam. As if it were almost automatic for them."

"It wasn't for you, was it?" Grace guessed. "Even though you knew her when he died, it wasn't the same for you, was it? This was your wife, now, not only their daughter, not only their second child."

Max nodded and stood up. He paced around the floor, rocking Jillian, even though she was already asleep.

"The Fosters met with those same doctors a few weeks after her death, but they didn't invite me. In many ways, I was shut out, too."

He leaned against the fireplace. Of course he knew what she felt. She saw the burden of that crushing him inside. Grace began to stand up, to go to him, to relieve that. But he started speaking again, and she dropped back on the couch.

"A few weeks ago, they had another meeting—to review the autopsy—and invited me. The doctors confirmed the cause of death as ARVD based on the autopsy and family history and proposed a new course of family screenings. The Fosters are looking for something—anything—they can do to protect Ryan."

Jillian slept loudly under her blankets, and Max walked to her car seat and bent down to carefully place her into it. "Of course, they've implied that as soon as Jillian is old enough, she will need the same screenings."

He pulled up her blankets to her chin and kissed his fingers and then pressed them gently to Jillian's cheek. Grace stood next to him, handing him the backpack.

"You'll know what to do," Grace said. "I know Trenna gave her best to both of you. You know yourself how much she . . ."

She hadn't wanted to speak it, to leave it this way, but she couldn't let Max go with empty words. He walked to the door with the weight of the car seat unevenly balanced on the right side. But Grace needed him to hear it.

" . . . How much she sacrificed for you both. Now that's even clearer."

****

Grace tied on her white apron at the start of her shift on Memorial Day. The apron was a prop; she didn't really bake anything in the kitchen. She tied the apron a little looser than she had when she first started; even if she didn't bake, she ate from the trays that came out of the Tasty Pastry kitchen. She worked up front in the shop and handled the supplies, the part-time employees and a few other sundry tasks for an hourly rate of a few dollars over minimum wage. She worked more than full-time—on weekends, nearly every evening, and all holidays, like today—to earn closer to the amount of money she made at Honeybee.

The owner worked weekday mornings and managed the two pastry chefs who handled the kitchen and the catering orders. She often worked alone because the pastry staff came in at 4 a.m. and left before noon when she arrived. Then, one of a few part-time high school students holding down his or her first job would work with her during the dinner hour, and she'd be alone again until close.

The shop didn't receive many customers in the evenings, but weekends brought out the regulars who stayed and lingered longer than the five minutes people needed for her to wrap up their éclairs, cookies, or sweet breads. Even the regulars, though, didn't stop and visit with her. They talked over treats and coffee with their own friends around the tables. She stayed behind the counter, divided from them. Some smiled at her. Many thanked her for the service, but she didn't know them or their lives. Her acquaintances and friends had dwindled to very few in the last nine months, after she left Honeybee around Labor Day.

Grace waited patiently while the family of four finished their chocolate-glazed doughnuts. The whole family had finished except for the young boy who sat docilely in his swivel chair, twisting back and forth between every sprinkled bite. The mother encouraged him to hurry up but contributed to the delay.

"Want some more milk?" she asked repeatedly.

The father let the toddler down from her high chair without washing her hands, and she roamed along the edge of the chairs, leaving sticky fingerprints on the side and backs of the chairs. She cruised along the chairs until she reached a gap in the table and lunged bravely to the next one. Her dad crouched a few steps in front of her, holding out his arms.

"Come here. You can do it. Just a little further," he said.

The curly-haired girl grinned hugely but held back. From above the table, the mom continued to coax, "Just a few more bites. Eat it up so we can go to the park."

Near the floor the toddler wobbled over to her dad, and he scooped her up in a hug, dirty fingers and all. Probably the same age as Jillian. Maybe she was walking, now, too. Max had sent one email after he moved that looked like a generic Christmas greeting to everyone with his new phone number and address, but she hadn't heard anything else from him. She imagined that he might come back to visit Trenna's gravesite, but he never called if he did. Maybe he was even there today, laying flowers for Memorial Day. Or maybe he would wait until the fifth of July.

After the family left, Grace wiped the chocolate frosting off the seats and backs of the chairs. She stood at the door, watching the few pedestrians on the overcast afternoon duck into the pet store across the street. The bank was closed for the holiday, as well as the post office, and this cut down on the usual traffic. She could run out now to empty the trash can on the street—her least favorite job—before the evening rush.

Grace tossed the rag into the bleach water and pulled a new black garbage bag from behind the counter, rubbed the ends between her fingers to get the opening to part and pulled it open. Outside, the wind whipped the bag back and forth in front of her. She set it on the ground, stepping on it to keep it in place while she took the other bag out of the garbage bin. She grasped the edges of the industrial bag and pulled them over the lip of the bin, and then hefted it out of the can, balancing its weight while still trying to keep her foot planted on the new bag. As she tried to twist the top of the trash bag and avoid the mess on top, the door of The Floral Shop opened in front of her, and Roberta Foster walked out with two giant flowering pots.

They both stopped. Grace set the trash bag on the ground and wiped her hands on her already filthy apron. Roberta had her own awkward load. She edged to the curb, setting one pot on the trunk of her black sedan, and fumbled in her purse while holding the other one. Embarrassment paralyzed Grace.

Roberta moved in slow motion to take out her keys to unlock the door. A fire truck siren bleated from the firehouse down the street and awakened her. Grace lunged forward toward the plant just as it slipped off the trunk. The potting soil shifted and flew all over Grace's hands and some of it tumbled onto the pavement, but the flowers were still intact. She held it up for Roberta, expecting a terse and caustic remark like the ones she'd delivered to this woman when they last left each other.

"What a mess that would have been, and we would have lost the flowers," Roberta said. The warmth of her words surprised Grace. Grace kept the flowers until Roberta opened the trunk and lowered both of the pots into some short cardboard flats in the back. Garden tools, a spray bottle of water, and a roll of paper towels lay next to the flats.

"Hold out your hands," Roberta said to Grace. Grace held her hands over the gutter and Roberta sprayed them until the potting soil mixed with ice cream scum from the trash was moistened, and then she tore off a paper towel and handed it to Grace.

"Are you going to the cemetery?" Grace asked tentatively while she wiped her hands and Roberta put everything back in her trunk.

Roberta nodded. "Do you want to come?"

Surprised, Grace wasn't sure what to say. "I'm working until eight," she stammered, not wanting to admit where, but her apron and the task she'd been doing made that obvious.

Roberta closed the trunk of her car. "Maybe another time. Have you been there?"

"A couple of times."

"They are side by side. Sam and Trenna. Well, they're not really there. I know that, but their graves are side by side. I think of them—my kids—that way, beside each other now." She said it without emotion, but Grace could feel it in her. Roberta moved toward the driver's side door.

Grace stepped back on the sidewalk and paused beside the front of the car. Roberta lowered the passenger's side window, and Grace leaned in the window.

"Thank you for being by her side in life—always right there to lift her. Your friendship meant so much to her."

Grace could only nod as she watched Roberta wave and drive away. She stood on the sidewalk as long as she could, but two women coming around the corner of the building stopped in front of the trash that blocked the entrance to Tasty Pastry.

"Pardon me. I'll take that out of your way." With the garbage bag in one hand, Grace held the door for them with the other. They wandered in front of the counter while she deposited the trash bag on the floor of the pantry.

When she returned, she turned on the water in the sink behind the counter so that it rushed full and hot before she stretched her hands underneath the soap dispenser and rubbed furiously in an obvious attempt to show that the germs from the trash would not transfer to the customer's order.

"What can I get for you?" she asked after rinsing and drying.

"Two apple turnovers, please," one of them said.

After they left, a teenage boy came in to pick up a cake order for his mother, and the late afternoon lull turned into the spring holiday evening that she expected. The customers kept her busy, but the image of those two graves pierced her thoughts. The amounts on the cash register blurred as she envisioned Roberta bending over them in the wind. Side by side, she'd said. Double the sorrow.

Grace grieved for her own losses over the last few years—lost opportunity for a family with Jeff, lost wisdom from Lilly's departure, lost friendship with Trenna, and lost confidence in her career. But she'd become so consumed, so self-absorbed, that she hadn't even recognized the real losses Roberta felt. That grief began years ago, for both Trenna and Roberta. Their suffering—and their misunderstanding about how to handle their grief—shaped their relationship all this time. How could Grace have thought or spoken as if Roberta was the one hurting Trenna?

She counted out change to three little girls who came to share a giant cookie. They laughed and giggled as they divided it at the table. While she saw their zest for life, she thought of Roberta with her shovel, dividing the plants and putting each flower into the ground, still nurturing her children—or at least her love for them—even in death, in the only way she knows.

Roberta had just been afraid, afraid of loss, like herself. Roberta and Trenna hadn't known how to help each other anymore, how to lift each other out of that fear.

A well-dressed couple pulled up in front in their luxury SUV. The adults got out, and the two teenagers in back called to them through the window. The bell rang as they entered. Grace knew them. They came in frequently, and this time they chose a raspberry tart from the refrigerator case. Probably on their way to a party, but she didn't really know. Her observations were only imaginations.

She had imagined Trenna had everything—money, a husband, a baby, and a life of promise. Grace had envied her at points in their friendship. In reality, Trenna had carried more pain and loss than Grace had ever experienced. At the same time, Grace had assumed Roberta was the enemy of Trenna's happiness. She misread her manner of love, when Roberta only intended to protect and preserve her grown child.

The store cleared of customers with a little less than an hour until closing time. She wished she could wipe away the crumbs of her false assumptions as easy as the bleach rag gathered the cookie bits. Things were not as she observed. She swept the torn napkins bits from under the table but wanted to crumple into a chair at the thoughts of the cruelty she had displayed toward this mother grieving for such a loss.

Not able to rest, she recalled the trash she'd dropped carelessly on the pantry floor and the pastry chefs who would not be happy to find it there in the early morning. Through the swinging door she rushed, hoping she'd at least twisted it so the contents had been contained. Instead, the goo coated the dusty floor where the trash had fallen.

Overwhelmed, she slumped to her knees and dropped her head onto the palms of her hands. Roberta said that her friendship lifted Trenna, but what about the barrier she encouraged between mother and daughter?

"I was so consumed with what I hadn't received that I couldn't see what they had lost," she cried. "I misjudged her. I treated her as if she was something she wasn't. I didn't know how it was. I'm so sorry. Please help me; please help us. Dear God, please forgive me."

She sobbed openly there into her apron and poured out her heart because now she knew she'd let self-centeredness, not circumstance, keep her from the kind of love she not only wanted to give but to also receive.

****

With more confidence than she'd ever possessed going to the Foster's, Grace pulled her car into their driveway, between the carriage house and the kitchen entrance. She wanted to slip into the carriage house, not from fear or avoidance, but to take one last look around the place to see if it was just as they left it or if it was empty.

Ryan emerged from the kitchen door with a large box and almost ran into her front bumper.

"Do you need help?" Grace called, quickly shutting the car door.

"Not yet," he yelled back and leaned against the carriage house door with his back, which fell open behind him. He disappeared. She glanced inside the familiar apartment as she rounded the front of her car, curious but not wanting to be nosy. A mound of boxes cluttered the entry so she tapped at the side door.

"No one will hear," Ryan said behind her. "Just go in."

Grace hesitated, remembering the day of the rehearsal dinner when she had let herself in the front door and received the surprising introduction to Max. Ryan pulled the screen door open for her, and she followed him into the wide kitchen where he stopped to pull a glass out of one of the tall see-through cabinets overhead.

"Want something to drink?" he offered. He reached into the fridge for a jug, but she shook her head.

"I just came to talk to your mom. Is she home?"

"Yeah. She's working upstairs in the bedrooms. Helping me move."

"Oh, that's right; you graduated this year, right? Are you storing your stuff in the carriage house?"

"Nope, I'm moving into it, at least for the summer. Then we'll see where I go."

He drank his orange juice in four big swallows and bounded up the back stairs. "Aren't you coming?"

Grace hadn't been in this part of the house since Trenna's wedding day, and it felt almost like an intrusion on the family's private spaces. She left her shoes at the bottom and trotted behind him up the winding stairs.

"Mom, you have a visitor."

Grace reached the top just as Roberta peeked out from a doorway down the carpeted hall.

"Roberta, can we talk?"

"Sure." Roberta approached slowly, and Ryan bounded back down the stairs. She was dressed casually in olive kakis with an obviously borrowed university T-shirt that hugged her chest where the logo was written. Past four rooms and the main staircase, she padded toward Grace in her bare feet until she reached the door ahead of Grace—not Trenna's bedroom, but the door to her lounge—or Trenna's childhood shrine.

The trophies, awards, and diplomas were gone. Only the oak bookcase and matching desk broke up the empty walls. But the two loveseats still faced each other in the middle of the room. Roberta held her hand out to the seat opposite her, sitting on the other loveseat. Grace, wanting to close the physical distance between them, sat next to Roberta.

"Roberta, I need to tell you . . ." Once she began, her confidence dissipated. She pushed down her cuticle on her thumb with the opposite nail. Eye contact would be important for her apology to be sincere, but right then, her hands brought far more comfort than Roberta's face. "I never understood. What

I mean is, when I listened to Trenna, her pain sounded to me like something else. I assumed you were her enemy and so, in a way, subconsciously I guess you became mine."

Grace gripped her hands to keep from playing with the cuticles on the other hand, but then tucked them between the cushions on either side of her. With the distraction of her hands tucked away, she wanted to raise her eyes to see Roberta, really see her as a woman, but that act of humility meant letting go of those assumptions in her heart, not just her head.

"I misunderstood you and the good you intended for Trenna. I only saw weaknesses because that is what I was looking for." Grace's words reverberated in her own head louder than she spoke them. More than just affirmation that she'd said the right thing, the words amplified that this truth applied to her as well.

Remembering the feelings Roberta extended outside Tasty Pastry encouraged her. She lifted her face for that eye contact she knew would be important for what she had left to say. Roberta sat still, pressed against the corner of the loveseat, her eyes focused on the window, not Grace.

"Roberta, I pulled you apart instead of helping you heal."

Roberta turned her head, not with a haughty expression Grace still anticipated. Rather, the lines of her forehead that once appeared condescending now showed the anguish of grief.

"Roberta," Grace leaned toward her searching those eyes that continued to flutter around but not rest directly on her. "I gave you anger and hostility when you needed love."

Roberta looked at her with intent as if she were waiting for what Grace knew she needed to say next.

"Please forgive me."

Roberta didn't react. She closed her eyes, but didn't speak.

"I just . . ." Grace started, again, not knowing if she should fill the silence.

"Grace. Hush up. I'll talk when I'm ready."

There was that Roberta spirit. Grace pulled her hands back into her lap and picked at the nail polish that had peeled when she pushed her cuticles. Nail polish didn't last long in bleach water, anyway, and she wondered why she even bothered anymore. She looked at Roberta's nails. They were long, strong, and chip-free.

As if this observation were an opening, Roberta raised those very hands. "I know you're not perfect, Grace, so I can accept the mistakes you made and will continue to make. But, just because Trenna died young didn't make her perfect, either. Death immortalized her youth and beauty in our minds, but she wasn't a saint. And neither am I. I *am* controlling and Trenna *was* independent. But we were like that even before Sam died."

Roberta wiped her nose, but she wasn't crying.

"Our personalities were exaggerated in our circumstance. Sam died, and I feared she would, too. I kept her safe and protected here at home. But then she wanted to be a mother and give birth in the carriage house, of all places! Oh—when Sylvia told me that, I had a panic attack right there in Honeybee. I never felt so close to dying myself."

Her hands came down, and her tone relaxed. "But Grace, with all our love and all our effort to prepare, and plan, and act, we are not God, even to our own children. We still need Him. He knows them, and us, much better than even *we* think we do."

"And even though He knows we are going to mess up, He still lets us help?" Grace said, now understanding.

"Absolutely. How else would we learn?" Roberta scooted

toward her on the couch and took her by the shoulders, but softly, and now eye to eye. "I do forgive you. You have more courage than I do, coming here today. As painful as this is to say, the one I need to ask for forgiveness is no longer here. But maybe I can do something else."

Roberta pushed herself up off the loveseat and motioned for Grace to follow her through the connecting bathroom. She turned the handle to Trenna's bedroom and the sunlight released from behind the door danced off the mirror and the bathroom fixtures right into their eyes.

In a woven basket directly in front of the window, a hibiscus plant bloomed. Grace touched the single large flower, amazed at how familiar the red blossom looked. She rubbed the soil. The right level of dampness. Someone had certainly cared for it well.

"Whose is this?" Grace asked.

"What do you mean? It's Trenna's, from the cutting you gave her."

"But it's grown so much in such a short time," Grace said, confused.

Roberta cradled the sides of the plant and lifted it out of the basket, revealing the glass pot underneath.

"It's for you, Grace."

"Don't you want it? For the room?"

"No, we're in the process of taking all this down." Roberta glanced at the boxes open on the floor—the treasured trophies, ribbons, and books from the other room. "Besides, she would want you to have it."

"Thank . . ." Grace started. She could hear Lilly's words, "Never say thank you for a plant." Instead, she said, "Remember Lilly, at Honeybee?"

"Of course," Roberta nodded.

"She gave me the original. When I told her I would kill it, she said, 'You won't kill anything unless you let it die,'" Grace stopped, glancing nervously for Roberta's reaction, but her face seemed untouched by the talk of death. "But *you* kept this legacy alive."

"I only moved it in here and watered it," Roberta said, shaking her head. "Maybe I talked to it once or twice."

"Trenna said you did that." They laughed together.

"I kept this plant alive. But as far as the rest, the history, the legacy, I can't take credit for that. I didn't know any of it," Roberta said. "I'd like to think I would have brought it to you, if you hadn't come, but I probably wouldn't have."

She handed her the plant. "Grace," she said, "It wasn't me."

****

Grace set Trenna's plant on the front seat of her car. She didn't know what Roberta meant when she said, "It wasn't me," just as Lilly hadn't known what her neighbor had meant when she said, "Never say thank you for a plant."

This drive to her house resembled the one she'd made two years ago when Lilly gave her the plant in the first place. Then, she'd worried about her capacity to nurture it in a way that would not only keep it alive but allow it to grow and bloom. She'd thought that taking it to Honeybee and sharing the responsibility with those other women was the answer, but she even neglected it there. This time, she would bring the plant home and keep it close.

But that same question came again, "Where should I put the plant?"

As Roberta walked with her to the car, she told her that she'd never owned a hibiscus, but a friend of hers here in St. Louis kept hers outside in the summer and brought it into the house as a houseplant in the winter. The idea to put this hibiscus in her garden grew on her throughout the rest of the day, leading her to research outdoor care.

If it were in a pot, rather than planted in the ground, she could transport it back and forth, depending on the season. The glass seemed too small and fragile, though, for outdoor use. The website said that the roots shouldn't have too much room, so an overly large pot wouldn't work either. But before she even decided about a pot, she would need to choose where it would fit best in her yard.

Her current job never afforded her the luxury of a full day off to garden. So, in the few minutes before she left for Tasty Pastry, she tripped down the back steps to scope out the possibilities. Weeds and old vines took over the garden spot she'd cleared the first year. Under the matted growth lay discarded and decaying remnants from the forgotten vegetables planted and then neglected to harvest after Trenna's death.

This spot next to the driveway provided a lot of sun, but it wasn't visible from the house. Across the yard, the stump of the tree she'd lost last spring protruded awkwardly from the grass. What an eyesore. She turned away from her backyard and began to walk up the sidewalk to work. If only she hadn't lost that tree. Not only did it look bad but she also missed the shade the tree provided, with the sun glaring in her kitchen and bedroom.

Grace stopped in the morning sun on the sidewalk. Sun! Light now shone in places that used to be shade. Her yard now received the gold any gardener would prize. Sunlight changed everything—where she could plant *and* what she could plant.

She checked her watch. Grace would be late if she turned around, but she had to see something. She sprinted back to her driveway and into the backyard, stopping in front of the tree stump. Could she create a new garden bed here, with annuals and perennials? Could she plant flowers and fruit, herbs and vegetables together? If she planned it right, the tree stump could stand in the middle as a focal point to display Trenna's plant.

Every day for the next week Grace stole the extra morning light from her sleep. With a borrowed flat-edged shovel from Mr. Reynolds, she cut several feet of sod all the way around the trunk, which challenged her strength and her idea. But the Esplins, her neighbors on the other side, made it easier on her. Ron asked if he could have the sod to fill some bare spots in their lawn and offered to pull up the sod after she cut it. So, she worked in the early mornings, and then in the evening Ron came over with a wheelbarrow to lift these pieces of sod and take them away.

After sod removal, her tasks of edging the border with rubber, filling it with additional topsoil, and planning what to plant took whatever time she had. If she could complete it before the end of June, she could still enjoy it this year, but she soon realized that was an unrealistic goal. She purchased and planted annuals, chose several perennials, left space for a berry patch, found some ground cover to fill in the empty spots and waited on the rest. Trenna's plant, though, couldn't wait.

The medium-sized yellow pot from Lilly's plant was the exact one she wanted. Grace wasn't sure where that pot had gone after the store closed. It hadn't been in the cleanup that she'd done herself. Maybe Faye would know. Should she call her or just go out to Wild Horse Creek?

Both would open her heart and mind to further introspection that might or might not end as well as her experience with Roberta. But, she wanted that pot. It was the right size and shape. It was durable enough for the outside but polished and painted to still be attractive when brought inside. The only drawback was its heft, but that would keep it stable in the wind. Plus, when the plant grew too big, she could always find someone to help her move it back and forth.

Grace took Sunday off work at Tasty Pastry to go to Wild Horse Creek. She purposely chose Sunday since she knew that Sylvia, as assistant manager, would work that day. Grace's aim, even more than picking up that pot, was to reconcile—if only in her own heart—what had happened with her. She'd also decided that she needed to set up some new boundaries for her employment to allow her to move forward in her personal life. So, she asked to have this Sunday off, and every other Sunday as well.

Grace started her day early at a church service, a habit she wanted to begin again. The familiarity of the music and the worship relaxed her, making the drive out to Chesterfield less anxious than she expected. Approaching Roberta had prepared her a bit for what to expect. But the main difference was that she'd been seeking Roberta's forgiveness. What was her aim with Sylvia? Her actions had been an outright personal attack. How did she make amends with someone who deliberately did that?

When she sold Jeff's ring she received cash for it, but in reality, what she received was a conclusion. She could still hold on to the hope that Jeff would change someday, but she, herself, had to move forward in her own goals, the plans for a family he didn't—and might never—want. That was why she couldn't hold on to the ring. In giving it up, peace had filled in the pain of loss.

In the same way, she needed that reconciliation with her time at Honeybee. The separation of physical space and time from her job and those relationships had been necessary. Now, she returned without the anger from Sylvia's torment or the resentment toward Sue for not seeing who and what Sylvia really was. Most importantly, the bitterness toward her coworkers who had once been her friends but moved on without her had disappeared.

Honeybee anchored the right corner of the cross streets of its block at Wild Horse Creek. Its big red awning over the entrance flowed toward the sidewalk like the waterfalls at the entrance to the center. People traipsed in and out of the art gallery beside it and the Tucanos Brazilian Grill across the street. Grace slowed to park in a spot where a woman carrying updated, but still recognizable, Honeybee signature shopping bags was leaving.

Grace was neither a customer nor an employee when she opened the right side of the double doors and let herself into the bright and sunny shop. The store was quiet during this lunchtime lull, so she could stand beside the entrance table decked with flowers and observe the whole place. It was Honeybee, only better. The new furnishings, updated paint colors, and windows toward the sidewalk on both sides opened the whole store into a new generation of retail that The Plaza store could never have achieved.

"Grace!" a woman called.

Faye bounded toward her, as chic as ever in a black leather skirt and button-down blouse. She pulled on the corner of her own striped blouse from Honeybee's sale rack last spring.

"You look great," Faye said, almost sensing her need to be set at ease here.

"Likewise. Now show me around your place," Grace said. "Tell me what everyone's doing."

"Well, it's just me today with one of my part-timers. I'll show you the place, but you're not really here for the place, are you?" Faye guessed.

"I am looking for something . . ." Grace started. Faye's directness and these new but familiar surroundings, though, pulled the shutters off her heart. Positive memories of her time at Honeybee—not the bad ones—came into her mind. Most of them included Trenna or Lilly. Grace's eyes filled, and she wiped them, but the tears poured down her face faster than she could catch them. Faye led her to a chair in a private dressing room and left for a box of tissue. They sat there in silence as Grace quietly allowed her tears to continue, tears she'd not realized were still with her. These tears were not wrapped up with her own lost opportunities but these tears were now just for Trenna, her friend.

"I did come for something else," Grace finally said. "I thought I could wrap up all those complicated relationships I faced in my time as manager." She blew her nose on the last tissue and piled all of them in the trash can Faye passed to her; she stood at the door and looked out over the store.

"But the place itself—even though it isn't the same Honeybee—reminded me of all the good that happened, too. I think that's helping me to finally accept Trenna's death."

Faye stood up beside Grace, and they walked together around the store. Faye introduced her to the part-time saleswoman helping another customer, but she didn't mean much to her.

They'd moved on, just like her. But she had to ask.

"How's Sylvia working out?" Grace tried to speak as casually as she could.

"Oh, Sylvia!" Faye rubbed her forehead dramatically. "You called that one."

"What?" Grace looked more than confused.

"She didn't last the six months Sue asked me to give her as a training period. At first, she made up stories about why she couldn't work certain shifts or why she had to work with certain people. Then I saw that she courted the customers who she perceived to have influence and ignored the others."

Grace nodded her head knowing the pattern. "I hope you wrote it up."

"I did Grace, and I was glad that I did. Sylvia made some critical errors that she couldn't explain. She's no longer with the company."

"That vindicates me a little with Sue, doesn't it?"

"After it all happened, Sue said she wanted to believe you, wanted to side with you, but there wasn't any documentation, so she couldn't."

"I needed to know that," Grace said. Even though she couldn't change Sylvia or her behavior, knowing this helped. "I wasn't wrong, and she knew it after all. Can I ask you something else? Do you know where that pot is that you used for Lilly's plant?"

"I do, actually." Faye laughed, leading her into the back room. On a shelf at Grace's eye level was the familiar pot. She took it down, expecting it to be filled with dirt, but it was clean and piled to the top with cast-off belts rolled up with rubber bands.

"May I buy it from you?" Grace asked.

"You can have it," Faye said. "I donated it at the start . . ."

"And kept it through the very end," Grace finished.

"No, that was Sylvia. I think she kept it there to remind her of her sin."

"Her sin?" Grace said.

"Killing Lilly's plant," Faye said matter-of-factly.

"She didn't kill it. I did. Don't you remember?"

"What I remember is her boasting about it to Beth. She locked the door from the inside, she said, so that no one could find it—until it was too late."

Grace fell back against the wall of this foreign backroom with its own hub of activity, with people whose lives she didn't know, and laughed. "I didn't kill the plant?" she said gleefully. "I didn't kill the plant. I may have neglected it, but I didn't kill it."

Grace took the pot home and transplanted Trenna's plant that very day. Throughout the week she set it outside for a few hours every day so it could acclimate to its new location on top of the tree stump in the center of her garden.

She awoke early in the morning at the end of the week. With temperatures already close to 80 degrees, it was time to move Trenna's plant into the garden to stay. She dressed in shorts and a T-shirt, ate a bagel, and moved the hibiscus outside to the tree stump. Once an eyesore, the stump now anchored the garden and provided a foundation for the plant, lifting it above the other flowers.

"Thank you for being by her side in life—always right there to lift her." When Roberta spoke these words on Memorial Day, Grace only remembered all that she'd done wrong.

She pulled on her gloves and harrowed up the soil around

the stump to loosen the weeds and residual grass that had already begun to come back.

She often struggled to love instead of envy or speak words of encouragement instead of words of irritation. Beyond the obvious problems Grace had with Roberta, Sylvia, or Sue, she worried more about these smaller, more significant moments—like those with Trenna—when Grace fought within herself to be who she wanted to be. To put aside her own fears. To speak with the right tone. To focus on someone else. Her inability to win these internal battles had become like her own personal eyesore that blocked her capacity to love.

She gathered the weeds she tossed aside and took them to the yard waste can in the shed. Beside the shed door were some creeping phlox that Mrs. Esplin had thinned out of her perennial garden and given to her.

Receiving Trenna's plant showed her that that despite her weaknesses, despite her lack—Lilly's plant had flowered and bloomed.

She divided the phlox into six sections and knelt in the dirt to dig holes that surrounded the base of the tree stump. After she set a section of phlox in each one, she patted the ground around them. With that work finished, she sat back to admire the hibiscus plant now in its elevated place in her garden. Since that morning, a bud had started to open. Now it appeared to unfold, as if she could discern its every movement. Roberta was right; she hadn't kept the legacy of the plant alive. These were God's flowers of grace.

Chapter Sixteen

A Few Years Later

Mr. Reynolds walked by the window of Tasty Pastry reading a book, but still slowly inching forward. Grace rapped on the glass.

"Be careful," she said loudly. He looked confused. Grace leaned out the door. "Put your book down before you turn the corner. The sidewalk is terrible."

Mr. Reynolds closed his book. "You're right. But Darlene was even more right when she recommended this book." He tucked it under his arm, waved, and disappeared around the corner.

Grace still loved to walk to work and home again, even in the dark and the winter, but now she had the security of a little flashlight in her pocket to keep her from tripping on the uneven sidewalks.

Yes, she'd had her missteps. Now, she noted the good steps, too, like the little evidences of love, reassurance, and comfort that she'd always sought but never seemed to be able to find. God's love didn't just come in the form of a person or even a plant, but it filled her nonetheless.

While her job supported her, it had become a means to the end, not the end itself. Still, she liked working close to home and in her own neighborhood. After Grace's first year as a cashier and assistant manager, Fred moved to Florida and left her in charge. He continued to own Tasty Pastry and the pastry chefs ran the kitchen and pantry, but she managed the business, which meant a real stake in the success of Webster's main street.

People frequented the stores on Lockwood; they always would. But what if they could grow the retail section to bring customers from beyond Webster and the small communities that surrounded it? Grace, Darlene from the bookstore, and Liz from The Floral Shop, traded ideas several mornings a month. They'd gather before Tasty Pastry opened to discuss what they could do to bring customers away from the quasi main streets of places like Wild Horse Creek into the heart of a real community.

Liz thought it was that people were going after a sense of style, and they should make their shops more style-driven, more current. More pretentious, Grace thought.

Darlene thought it was that people didn't care about community anymore and suggested hosting more events like volunteer cleanup days or parades to draw people back to their hometown roots. More work with little return, Grace thought.

She knew it was just that the housing was cheaper out in the outer suburbs and the development inevitably followed. People could afford more home for less money. But since they couldn't lower the cost of real estate, she didn't propose a solution.

Her view, the one she did offer, was that they were making a difference, just by being there, day in and day out, consistently offering their services.

What she didn't say was that if they were in the black, which she knew the pastry shop was and she assumed was true for the other two, then they could just keep diligently doing what they were doing. But, that didn't translate well into a growth plan for business.

"I'm not in debt," Darlene said. "But I wish business was better. I own my shop. I just have the overhead of a few sales people, and I've made a good living over these twenty years. John's left me more than enough. I want to stay and do this, even if I'm not making huge profits, but people aren't browsing and buying books in the same way as they used to. You guys have the customers, but they're just not coming my way."

"I wish I could switch places with you," Liz said.

"You mean you'd like to have fewer customers, too?" Darlene asked.

"No, I mean literally switch places with you," Liz said. "You're a browsing place. The Floral Shop is a destination. If your building was in between Tasty Pastry and The Floral Shop, you'd get more of our destination customers filtering in."

A few days later, Darlene showed up one morning while Grace was still opening the doors.

"What if I buy all three stores and combine them into one?"

"How is that any different than the big bookstore on Lindberg?"

"We'll sell flowers, too."

"I don't think it would save costs much."

But Darlene was back the next day.

"I could buy the stores, and you could manage them. That would cut the costs of three mangers down to one."

"What about Liz? What would you do?"

"Liz is just a florist; she doesn't run the business. In my case, I would be the owner, not the manager."

"Keep thinking," Grace said.

When Darlene returned at the end of the week, she had a new idea. "I won't buy them up and make one big store, but keep them as three little stores. I can have a doorway put between each of them so people can wander in and out."

"Then they would be like three stores in one," Grace said, enthusiastically.

"Yeah," Darlene looked quizzically at her epiphany. "You just got that?"

"No, but I just got the concept and why you would want to do it. You would be better suited to compete with all the bigger retail outlets because you're drawing customers from each of the businesses. But you retain the intimate quality, the small-scale personal character of each store."

"You do get it," Darlene said. "So you think I should I pursue it?"

"It's an idea," Grace said positively, nodding her head.

Darlene dropped hints that she was working on it, but she didn't give away any of the details until a few days before Thanksgiving when she stopped in to order a pumpkin pie. Her bookstore had just closed for the night so she was eager to chat, but Grace knew the small talk about their Thanksgiving plans was not what she had on her mind. When the last customer left the store, Grace took off her apron.

"Now what is it?"

"I signed the papers today to buy The Floral Shop."

"You're serious?" Grace said. Darlene nodded. "You *are* serious."

"Annnd . . ." Darlene drew out the suspense. "It will involve you, too. Sit down and listen to my proposal."

Grace held up her hand to stop her for a minute, turned

off the lights out front, and hung the closed sign over the door. After locking the door, she tossed her apron over the top of the counter.

"Ready?" Darlene said. Grace nodded and pulled up a chair. Darlene sat down next to her.

"When Fred comes back for Christmas, I'm signing papers with him to buy Tasty Pastry, too. Before the first of January, I will own these three stores, all in a row." She gestured toward the other stores.

"You're really doing this," Grace said.

"*We're* doing it," Darlene said. "I'd like you to manage them."

Grace paused, the seeds of doubt springing up again. "Do you think I'm qualified? I don't know anything about the floral or book business."

"You're more than qualified. Your business and retail experience at Honeybee crossed over nicely here." Darlene gestured around the front of the pastry store. "It will even more when you're looking at the big picture of all three together."

Darlene's validation didn't sound like flattery or false assurance.

"Tell me your plans," Grace said, excited with the thoughts of contributing to a new endeavor.

Darlene spoke quickly, as if she was designing a new home. "Well, Liz's idea about switching places started this whole thing. If we did move the bookstore to the middle, then we could remodel them all to look unified inside, not like one big store crushed together, but also not just a door to walk between them either. Then, on the outside I would still want them to resemble three intimate unique businesses."

"We'll need an architect," Grace said.

"I know. I've been browsing some websites for ideas, but you're right, an architect can bring this together in the right way," Darlene said. "Wait a minute, you said 'we,' didn't you? Does that mean you will accept?"

"We'll have to work out the details of what we're both committing to, but yes, I'd love to be in on this."

"We can do that. In the meantime, I know most of this is going to be a discussion about the structure. But I want you to think how we're going to pull this all together with a marketing plan that intertwines the three together for our target demographic."

"Who would that be?" Grace asked.

"People like you and me and most other women twenty-five to sixty—similar to your Honeybee demographic, but a lot less uppity."

"Not the men?" Grace said. "My pastry chefs are both men, and some of my best regulars, too."

"Mine, too. We're not going to ignore them, but look at the concept from a women's perspective and start brainstorming."

The idea rooted itself a little at a time and sent shoots of inspiration to her mind in the oddest ways and at the oddest times. She bounced ideas off Mr. Reynolds when he came for Thanksgiving dinner. She knew it wasn't too smart to involve him before the final deal was complete, especially since he lived so close, knew so many people, and frequented most of the businesses on Lockwood. But she couldn't let it keep. Besides, she wanted to glean his wisdom; his age—and the fact that he was a man who still understood women—complemented her creative thinking.

"I swear I won't talk," he said gruffly over the pecan pie when she hinted at the need for confidentiality.

"To others, I hope you mean. Because I want to hear your thoughts about what I've already got in mind. But wait. I need to get something first." Grace jumped from the couch and scooted to the second bedroom where she grabbed the pink stool and brought it back to set beside Mr. Reynolds. "Now I can listen properly."

"You're like every woman, Grace. You want to talk, not listen."

"No, I really do," she protested.

"I understand that, and neither one of us is hurt by admitting that. Verbalizing it is as important to your thought process as stewing is to mine. Go on. Finish telling me about the concept."

He was right. Grace could only stay on the stool for so long before she had to talk it out. "Well, it's not that they're going to be geared totally to women, but the more I think about it, these three stores have a sense of femininity to them, in a way. They each nurture a part of us—any of us, men and women."

She was up and down and all over the room gesturing as she struggled to tie her thoughts and the businesses together.

"But the hard part is that the growth that each provides isn't something tangible or measurable," she said with a look of concentration set in her features. "It's like what you said about Trenna's painting of me. You said . . ."

She screwed up her eyebrows, confused without the words at hand. She held up a finger and darted back to the second bedroom again, plucking the painting off the dresser and then bringing it back. But still, even as she looked, the words didn't come to her.

"The flower of femininity, I said," Mr. Reynolds helped her.

"Right. You said it was more than physical, more than just a form. That's what I want to capture in these stores and offer to anyone—woman or man, young or old—when they enter."

"Flowers are obvious. But translate it for me—what's feminine about books? Or pastries?"

"Isn't it obvious? Doesn't your mind expand when you read?"

"And my gut when I eat," Mr. Reynolds played along.

"Well, I was going to say that good food cultivates our taste for things that fill," Grace said, "But can't you see? There's so much more, and not just on one level. Each store, each product grows the mind, body or spirit in some way."

He chuckled.

"Don't laugh," she blushed, knowing she needed more.

"I'm not laughing at you. Just a reminder of something Helen did many years ago. I finally understand what she meant. Why she did it."

"I know it's not a marketing plan. But that's the place I want to start."

That flow materialized into some concrete ideas over the busy Christmas baking and selling season and in a hurried trip up to Minnesota for the holiday. Fred came into town and let her go off for a few days while he "took care of some business at the store."

He broke the news to the Tasty Pastry staff the day she returned, right before New Year's. He introduced Darlene as the new owner, who then announced Grace's job as manager of all three stores. Fred returned to Florida, satisfied with the deal.

"We're meeting next Monday with the architect," Darlene breathed hurriedly on her way over to the bookstore to share the news around there. Everyone already knew she'd bought The Floral Shop, but now she could share the rest of the plan.

"Where? When?" Grace said.

"Here. Before you open. 7 a.m." Darlene left Grace with a list of unanswered questions that now she was going to be responsible for answering.

On Monday Grace jerked awake in confusion. Was it morning? Did she need to go to the bathroom? She couldn't see the alarm clock, but from the window, it looked like dusky dawn. What time was it, anyway? She turned over on her pillow. She peeked at the clock. 6:28.

Oh no. It didn't go off. Hadn't she reset it from the weekend?

She ran to the shower, but stopped midway in undressing. No time to dry her hair; the wind would crisp it on her walk. Instead, Grace tied her long hair back, washed her face, brushed her teeth, and gargled away the morning sore throat that seemed to be creeping higher and higher.

Clothes were easy. She threw on a pair of jeans and a slimming knit sweater, grateful that even though she liked to look professional, she didn't have to agonize over the details of her appearance like she had at Honeybee, even in this meeting with Darlene and the architect. She pulled on boots and zipped up her coat. The flow of ideas that she would now need to communicate weren't just her own. Despite her rush, Grace paused to pray and acknowledge gratefully what she'd received.

Ready and out the door with only five minutes for the walk. Should she drive? There wasn't decent parking closer than home anyway. That would be a challenge they would have to consider. Since no snow covered the frosty ground in her front yard, she set off walking toward the store.

The dark, cold air in her Webster neighborhood felt more like a Minnesota morning, and she half forgot that she'd come home. Yes, home. This felt like home now. She reached in her coat pocket for gloves and her flashlight. But she grabbed only the slick lining of her coat pockets and nothing else. Her steps slowed to avoid the uneven sidewalk and searched for the little light being cast from the rising sun. She'd be late.

The street traffic picked up ahead of her as she neared the corner and gave more light to the street. Darlene's green car was at the traffic light. Grace stopped at the corner and waved. Two cars drove by after Darlene's, and then the street quieted again in the early winter hour. Darlene would park behind the bookstore, giving Grace time to open. She fit the cold key into the lock on the front door of Tasty Pastry.

"Good morning," a deep voice said to her right.

Grace pulled back with a startle. A male figure moved away from the shadow of the column on the other side of the storefront window, and when he was just a few feet from her, she could see his face.

"What are you doing here?" Grace said, bewildered.

"I'm your architect," Max said.

"Here in St. Louis? Working here?"

"Yes, working for Darlene—I hope—after our meeting this morning. We have a meeting, don't we?"

"Yes," Grace said with a little more lightness to her tone. "Except you appear at the oddest moments."

"Have those moments been *that* bad?"

"No, just unforeseen." Grace finished unlocking the door and flipped the switch inside the door that lit the entryway and the café tables. He held the door for her, and she stepped up the half step ahead of him.

"I'm coming," Darlene yelled from the front of The Floral Shop.

Max paused at the door and waited for Darlene before the three of them settled into the warmth of the room. The sweet smell of baked goods filtered from the busy kitchen and pantry in the back. The trays behind the counter were already filled and waiting for customers. The cashier, who had arrived from the back door, was slipping an apron over her head to help.

Apparently Darlene's son knew the man who had hired Max as a new associate in his office, a smaller firm that restored and remodeled older buildings and neighborhoods.

"Historic preservation?" Darlene asked as she gestured toward a table while Grace brought coffee, muffins, and pastries.

"There is someone who will do that, if that's what you want. But I like to give life to old buildings according to how we use them now."

"That's a big switch from a huge firm, isn't it? Why this sudden change of focus? Why here?" Grace asked.

"I'm confused. Do you know each other?" Darlene asked, trying to discern the relationship from their background conversation.

"Yeah," Max and Grace both said at once and then took turns explaining their connection. "Are you living close by?" Grace picked the nuts off her caramel roll.

"In a duplex in Demun, by the firm's offices. Near Sadie's, if you remember that restaurant we went to."

"I do. What about Jillian? How's she?"

"She's the reason I'm here," he said, resolutely. "My dad's retiring, and they wanted to go to Florida for the winters but didn't want to leave us. But I told them—and I really believe this—I needed to evaluate my direction, too, and what I want for Jillian and for me. I had the option to transfer back to the St. Louis office, but I want more—in life and work than that. So here we are."

The meaning behind his answer held more questions for Grace, but most of them she knew were far too personal to ask here and probably still had answers that were yet to come.

Max set his portfolio on the table and took out a pen. "So, tell me, what are you looking for?"

Darlene began to describe the project in response to his question, but to Grace the question sounded like Max was asking her personally "What are you looking for?" Did he mean it to sound that way?

Grace tried to focus on Darlene's words rather than looking at him, but Max's hand on his fountain pen, writing in a controlled script continued to distract her. The line of his hand when he rested it on the paper subtly accentuated his arm and his shoulder. Grace dared herself to study his face while he wrote, nodding to Darlene as she spoke. He glanced up, right into her eyes, and smiled. The bell above the door jingled and awakened her to the place where she sat. She drew in her breath, rubbed her hand across her mouth and excused herself from the table.

"So that's what I want on the outside," Darlene was saying. Grace turned away to grab a few napkins out of the dispenser and wipe her sticky hands. Her cheeks tingled with heat, and her sweater clung to her like August had come again.

"We want to move The Floral Shop to the space with

the bookstore," Darlene said to him. "That would bring the bookstore to the center . . ."

"No," Grace said. She spun to face them, not with the fire of contention in her countenance but with a display of energy sparked from creative passion.

"Grace?" Darlene said with a dull confusion.

"I've being thinking on this from a marketing standpoint, but now it makes sense from a structural one," Grace said. She stood at the edge of their table, gesturing with her hands toward the building itself. "Yes, we want to put the books out front, in view of the customers. That was the purpose of this in the first place—to bring more customers from here and The Floral Shop into the bookstore. But this isn't a bookstore with treats and flowers on the side, is it? That's not why they're going to come, and if that's what we turn it into, we're no different than that big bookstore with a coffee shop on Lindberg Boulevard, and they'll stop coming here."

"Not if we make it more intimate, more personal," Darlene said.

"You're right, but that's only a part of it," Grace said. She knew she was taking a risk shooting out ideas over Darlene's head, but she had to know if they could brainstorm openly like this, before they even started. "We have to identify why they do come here, so we can enhance that in the structure, not change it, and lose them in the process. Let's be honest—we provide wants not needs."

"But people need books," Darlene said.

"You're right, they do, but at some internal level. They need a good story or what tastes good or what's beautiful. But we sell products that nourish our emotions, don't we?"

"So what are you saying, Grace? That we should leave it like it is and just put a doorway in between?" Darlene said.

"Not really. No, that's not it, either. There is still more," Grace answered. "I wish I could put this into words. Max, I want you to visualize this for me to see if you can identify the structure that goes with what I'm saying."

"I'm right with you," Max said. "Tell me about that picture you see. Talk about each piece and bring them into one whole."

"The bookstore cultivates our minds, organizes our thoughts, and stimulates our new projects or ways of thinking." Grace gestured around her. "And here, the smells, the way these pastries and cakes look—all of it builds anticipation and excitement for how it will taste."

Max listened without asking questions, but his eyes danced while his fingers gripped his pen, whipping lines, arrows, and words across his page.

"At the core of this—is the The Floral Shop," Grace said. "Flowers inspire us to surround ourselves with beauty. But even more, they inspire us to see beauty in each other and in our lives. Can't you see why it has to be at the center? The Floral Shop nurtures the spirit."

A woman paused by the door, not sure whether she should walk any further, afraid she might tread on the speech. In front of her, Darlene's mouth had parted, as if she were going to add something, but she simply held her one finger in midair and stayed silent, not sure what to say.

Grace smiled at the customer. "Come in, you're not interrupting anything."

The woman moved to the counter where she chose a dozen sugar cookies and a coffee to go. Grace pulled out her chair again and settled into it.

"When these customers walk through these stores, they may just be here for cookies or books or flowers. But, what if the positive energy of the store design *and* the products feed off of each other to nourish that emotional response?"

Max stopped scribbling and drawing to lift the left side of his mouth in a half grin. "We're going to work well together."

****

Grace suggested they meet in Tilles Park by the pond. A part of her, maybe, secretly hoped she would sense Trenna's endorsement of her reconnecting with Max. Or, at least Grace hoped she wasn't dishonoring their friendship if she met Max and Jillian at "their" running spot to throw bread to the ducks.

Grace arrived early and sat on the trunk of her car in a nearly empty parking lot. The teenagers were in school, and the children who were too young to go were on the playground down the hill, yelling and running against the occasional breezes that reminded them it was not quite spring.

Since she'd been nervous to meet Jillian, this girl she didn't really know but who meant so much to her, she put off Max's invitations. But with the final drawings near completion and plans going out to bid soon, she knew her opportunity to see him so often would diminish. She may not be prepared for what their out-of-work visit would bring, but she had to go ahead anyway.

A navy blue compact car looped around the corner with a signal to turn in the parking lot. Max drove in, parking in a spot across from her. His car door opened. He waved but then immediately ducked back behind his seat. Undoing her booster seat, Grace guessed.

A curly brown head of hair emerged, then a purple tennis shoe. Another shoe attached to yellow leggings planted itself on the pavement, and then she emerged.

"I want my rain boots, case it's muddy," she said dictatorially.

She couldn't be Jillian. The two people, the baby and this girl, were disconnected by the gap of time. Grace waited as an observer for them to come to her. Max handed Jillian the red rain boots, and she grasped both of them under her left arm. He held out his left hand, and they walked toward Grace.

Jillian's hair fell in dark locks around her shoulders with bangs across her forehead pointing to her bright eyes. Her features were a minimalist's drawing of Roberta's face. When they were nearly to her bumper, Grace slipped down to the pavement in front of them.

"Hi," Grace said, trying to sound casual.

"Hi," Jillian volunteered, precociously. "I'm going to wear my boots."

She handed them to Grace, who looked to Max for a sign of permission. He shrugged.

"Do you need some help?" Grace asked.

But Jillian was already plopped down on the gritty asphalt pulling off her sneakers down to her white socks. She held up her shoes with both hands, but they stretched only a short distance in front of her. Grace bent down and kneeled, taking the shoes and handing her one of the boots. The dexterous little fingers gripped the sides and pulled each up onto her leg.

"Now I'm ready." Jillian bopped back to a standing position, leaving Grace at eye level with her.

"But you don't know me, yet. I'm Grace."

"Dad says you're my mom's friend," Jillian said.

Surprised by Jillian's candor to speak as if she knew her mom well, Grace simply said, "Yes."

"Okay." Jillian held out her hand to pull Grace up from the

ground. Max and Grace walked on either side of Jillian through the picnic shelter, down the wooden stairs of the deck that jutted into the pond, and toward the bench.

"I forgot the bread," Max said.

"At home?" Jillian asked. "We have to have bread. Or they won't come."

"No, in the car; I'll get it."

As Max returned to the car, Jillian and Grace called to the ducks and geese that were swimming on the other side of the pond and gathering along the outer fence. When they didn't come, Jillian scampered across the matted gray grass, flipping her feet along the edge of the pond, waving her arms, and calling to the ducks. When she tired of that, she picked up whatever interested her on the ground, sometimes setting it down or bringing it back for Grace to observe. Grace treasured the softness of Jillian's hand when she pressed an acorn into her palm or the sight of her little ears when the wind blew back her hair.

Jillian didn't find any puddles, but she stepped into the mud swells along the sides of several big rocks. She tried to pull her feet out but her boots clung to the mud, sticking her in place just as Max returned with a half loaf of bread. They both went to her at once. Dropping the bread, Max pulled her up by the arms, but the boots stuck in the mud. With Jillian in his arms, Grace knew she would get the dirty job.

Grace lifted the boots out, but the goo stuck. Should she rinse it in the pond with all the muck that was there? Max pointed her to a water faucet while he carried Jillian under one arm to sit on a picnic bench. Grace pumped the faucet, but it didn't come on. Probably not yet opened for the season. So she carried them down to the dock, laid down on her stomach, and leaned over with one hand tucked into the ends of each little boot and rinsed them in the pond. The waves and splashes carried, alerting the ducks and geese. Grace pulled up quickly.

"Get the bread, Daddy," Jillian flew off the table before Max could catch her, but Grace did.

"Patience, Jillian," Grace called, heading toward this girl who was no longer a baby, no longer a toddler. She lifted her off the ground, setting Jillian on the bench. Together, she and Max brushed the gravel off her socks and pushed her boots back on her feet.

"You're pretty," Jillian said.

"Yes, she is," Max turned toward Grace.

"Thank you." She blushed.

"Was my mom pretty?" Jillian asked. Grace could feel him watching her, maybe waiting and wondering what she would say.

"Yes," Grace said, losing her smile as she thought of Trenna's beauty that was so much more than what anyone saw on the outside.

"Was she smart?"

"Yes," Grace said, thinking of her hard work at the store and all the effort she took to learn how to take care of Jillian.

"Did she smile?"

"She smiled all the time. I could never keep a smile as long as she could," she answered honestly in a way that was probably more than a four-year-old could understand.

"Was she happy?" Jillian continued to prod.

"You made her happy."

"Are you happy? You're not smiling," Jillian observed. "Dad, make her smile. Help me make her smile."

Jillian jumped up from the bench and tickled Grace's stomach.

"Don't tickle me," Grace warned both of them as they came toward her together. This unleashed Jillian's giggles and fingers even more. Max laughed cynically and lunged toward Grace. Grace jumped up from the dock, running toward the picnic shelter. He tossed Jillian up and over his shoulders, holding on to her rain boots. Together they chased Grace across the parking lot, down the hill, and toward the playground, leaving the bag of white bread lying forgotten on the dock while the ducks yapped and the geese fluttered on the bank.

Acknowledgements

Thank you for reading *Flowers of Grace*. Thank you to all who inspire, support, and receive my writing and publishing efforts—including, and most importantly, my readers. If you enjoyed this book, please consider posting a review of it online so that others may discover it.

Flowers of Grace is a novel inspired by a true story—well, actually, a real plant and a true story. Many years ago, I received a beautiful hibiscus from a friend. Over time it did not thrive and eventually died, but I knew its legacy could live on in my writing. Almost twenty years ago my dear friend Holly Blackwell Jacobson, who unknowingly suffered from arrhythmogenic right ventricular dysplasia, passed away suddenly. She was survived by many who love her including a young husband, a precocious toddler daughter, mother, father, and siblings. Her legacy of nurturing inspired me to love more freely and give more fully, ultimately leading me to write this novel. Although both of these stories inspired *Flowers of Grace*, this is a work of fiction, and the characters, setting, and plot are not intended to portray or resemble real people, a real business, or actual circumstances.

I appreciate all those who helped me write and publish *Flowers of Grace*. My editors—Camille Kerr, Rachel Corbett, and Tracy Perry—worked for many long hours to improve the content and correct my errors. I truly appreciate their feedback and corrections. I express heartfelt gratitude to Carrie Christiansen for being one of my most faithful beta readers and daily cheerleaders. I especially want to recognize and thank Kirsten Hirst for designing the cover and offering her graphic design consulting on the interior. She has an artistic eye and mastery of fonts that I covet. Finally, I owe much to Paul Hirst, who freely gives his constant encouragement and technical skills to this book and all my projects. Specifically, he formatted this book and designs and administers my blog and website. I respect his abilities and can never express enough love and gratitude to him.

About the Author

Teresa Hirst observes and tells insightful stories—both nonfiction and fiction—that characterize our emotional experience with life. *Flowers of Grace* is her first novel. She is also the author of the inspirational nonfiction book *Twelve Stones to Remember Him: Building Memorials of Faith from Financial Crisis.* Teresa lives in Minnesota with her husband and teenage children. She enjoys gardening, sentimental movies, Sunday afternoon walks, and great conversations. To learn more about Teresa and her books, please visit www.teresahirst.com or her personal blog, Illuminate Everyday at www.tjhirst.com.

www.ingramcontent.com/pod-product-compliance
Lightning Source LLC
Chambersburg PA
CBHW061932170626
46813CB00006B/2376